Praise for Anita Rau Badami and *Tamarind Mem*

"Badami weaves a tale of bittersweet nostalgia in her first novel, imbuing her descriptions of Indian domestic life with achingly palpable details as she explores all the small ceremonies that make family life so simultaneously rich and infuriating.... A DELECTABLE BOOK, filled with pungent sights and sounds and poignant memories. It proves, yet again, that each person in a family experiences that microcosm differently. Only by synthesizing these disparate views do we grasp the full flavour of events."

Quill & Quire (starred review)

"...AN EXCITING ADDITION to the burgeoning tradition of Indo-Canadian writing that includes Rohinton Mistry, M.G. Vassanji and Shyam Selvadurai."   *Maclean's*

"A BEAUTIFULLY CRAFTED BOOK with meaning delicately woven through the text, meaning that is evoked more through absence than presence...Badami has a gift for understatement and subtlety, something first-time novelists seldom possess."   *Hour* (Montreal)

"A POWERFUL STORY ... it allows daughter and mother to each speak for herself, and the resulting ironies and differing perspectives make for a richly textured work."

Books in Canada

"WITH PASSAGES THAT READ LIKE POETRY, Badami mixes mystery and domesticity into a story about the life of a young girl growing up in India ...Badami is wonderful at evoking mood. Her dialogue is so natural you can hear the voices and accents in your head."   *FFWD*

PENGUIN BOOKS

TAMARIND MEM

Anita Rau Badami's short fiction has been published in *The Malahat Review, Event, The Toronto Review of Contemporary Writing*, and the anthology *Boundless Alberta*. She lives in Vancouver.

Tamarind Mem

Anita Rau Badami

Penguin Books

PENGUIN BOOKS
Published by the Penguin Group
Penguin Books Canada Ltd, 10 Alcorn Avenue, Toronto, Ontario,
Canada M4V 3B2
Penguin Books Ltd, 27 Wrights Lane, London W8 5TZ, England
Penguin Books USA Inc., 375 Hudson Street, New York, New York
10014, U.S.A.
Penguin Books Australia Ltd, Ringwood, Victoria, Australia
Penguin Books (NZ) Ltd, cnr Rosedale and Airborne Roads, Albany,
Auckland 1310, New Zealand

Penguin Books Ltd, Registered Offices: Harmondsworth,
Middlesex, England

First published in Viking by Penguin Books Canada Limited, 1996
Published in Penguin Books, 1998

1 3 5 7 9 10 8 6 4 2

Copyright © Anita Rau Badami, 1996

Publisher's note: This book is a work of fiction. Names, characters, places and incidents either are the product of the author's imagination or are used fictitiously, and any resemblance to actual persons living or dead, events, or locales is entirely coincidental.

Manufactured in Canada.

Canadian Cataloguing in Publication Data

Badami, Anita Rau, 1961–
Tamarind mem
ISBN 0-14-025714-4
I. Title.

PR9499.3.B33T3 1997   823   C95-933334-7

Visit Penguin Canada's web site at **www.penguin.ca**

For my parents
Nalini
&
Rama Krishna Rau

Acknowledgments

I would like to thank the people who helped to bring this book to life: Aritha van Herk whose constant friendship, guidance and advice I will always cherish; The University of Calgary for its financial support and encouragement; my mother Nalini for giving me the strength to dream; my husband Madhav and son Aditya for their love and tolerance; Fred Wah for teaching me that prose too can be poetic; Ven Begamudré and Shelley Sopher for believing in me; Jackie Kaiser at Penguin Books for her perceptive edits; and all the wonderful friends in Calgary who helped in ways too numerous to list.

Tamarindus Indica

Tamar-i-Hind, or Date
of India. Folklore has it that the
tamarind tree is the home of spirits
that do not let anything under the tree
survive. Accordingly, travellers are advised
not to sleep in its shade. The tamarind tree
is never used for auspicious ceremonies, as
its fruit being sour, it is believed that the
ceremony will turn sour and thus
become fruitless and lose all
meaning.

Tamarind Mem

Kamini

I called my mother every Sunday from the silence of my base-ment apartment, reluctant to tell her how I yearned to get away from this freezing cold city where even the traffic sounds were muffled by the snow.

"Well, who asked you to go?" Ma would have demanded. "Did somebody tie your hands behind your back and say 'Go-go to that Calgary North Pole place?'"

So instead I said, "Ma, there are mountains in the distance, all covered with snow. I can see them gleaming like silver cones in the sunlight when I go outside my apartment."

"You sound like a travel brochure," said Ma. "I hope you wear that sweater your Aunty Lalli knit for you, you catch cold so easily."

"These mountains are almost as tall as the Eastern Ghats. Do you remember that trip with Dadda in his inspection saloon?"

"The Western Ghats."

"We never went up the Western Ghats, Ma. You are talking about the Eastern Ghats."

"Don't tell me what I am talking about," snapped Ma. "We went up Bhore Ghat and you started crying when the engine had to reverse downhill because you thought we were going to crash off the cliffs. Roopa had an asthmatic attack—your father left us nothing but a legacy of sickness—and that foolish office peon we had then, what was his name?"

"Bhurey Lal," I said. "But Ma, that was not on Bhore Ghat. You are inventing your memories."

"Yes, Bhurey Lal, he was loyal though, do you remember, he stayed up all night leaning against the fridge door because every time the train jerked the door flew open and all the food fell out? Do you remember now?"

"Ma, I remember perfectly, but it was on the Araku Valley section. Where we stopped in the middle of the Dandakaranya forest and Dadda told us that this was the same forest in the Ramayana where Sita was kidnapped by the demon Ravana. And we got fresh honey from the tribals in the forest."

"Kamini, what tribals? You are making up stories."

"Why do you always believe that I am making up stories? I don't, I never have."

"There you go again," said Ma, triumphant. "What did I tell you? Hanh?"

I sighed and changed the subject. Ma still wanted to win every argument, she would never-ever change.

⁂

The year that I turned six, I began to sense a strange movement deep inside Ma's body, a pulsing beneath the skin. Yes, certainly there was a difference. I, who was so sensitive to every nuance in my mother, could feel it every time I climbed into her lap. Ma sat motionless in the verandah, and her hands, normally busy with knitting or hemming, darning or cutting, lay quiet on the folds of her sari. She barely spoke, and I felt that if I had missed my mother before, when she disappeared into one of her moody silences, now I had lost her completely.

She wouldn't allow me on her lap, pushed me gently away, pleading in a distant voice, "Baby, I am tired, go and play."

I was suffused with a helpless jealousy against this thing that had stolen Ma. Not even my father's hug, his stories about the man-eater of Kantabhanji, the elephant who fell in love with a steam engine, the beehives hanging like upside-down palaces beneath a forest bridge, none of these stories diminished my hurt.

"*Noni,*" said Dadda, "come, I will tell you about the Lakshman-jhoola bridge. That bridge is hundreds of years old, it is said, made of rope and wood and prayers. It swings thin as a dream over the River Ganga thundering down a rocky gorge, and on the underside of the bridge is a city of bees. You can hear their buzzing over the sound of rushing water, and you have to walk across the Lakshman-jhoola without shaking it even a bit, for then the queen bee wakes up from her sleep and sends her armies after you. *Noni,* are you listening?"

I closed my ears to my father's tale and asked instead, "Dadda, why is Ma so quiet?"

Perhaps I would run away, then Ma would rise from her silence and wail after me, "My darling, come back." I packed my Meenu doll, a toothbrush and the chocolate bar Dadda had bought from Billimoria Uncle's petrol bunk.

"Where are you going, my *kishmish?*" asked Linda Ayah absently.

Even Linda had no time for me, so busy was she fussing over Ma, who was now beginning to look like a taut and lustrous mango.

"Nowhere," I said, shifting my bag to the other hand.

Linda Ayah looked up sharply. "Uh-huh, what mischief are you up to, monkey-child?" she asked.

I burst into tears and immediately Linda Ayah became all attentive and sweet. "My *kanmani,* my baby, Linda will hoof-hoof everything away," she said, wiping my face with the end of her sari, stroking my hair. "Now what is happening, tell me?"

It all tumbled out. Ma had gone away somewhere, only a ghost lived in her body. When Dadda went out of town on line duty I was allowed to sleep in Ma's room, and when I woke in the night for water or peepee, she was not there. The verandah door was open, and when I thought I was going to dry up from thirst, the ghost wandered in pretending to be my mother.

"You dream too much," said Linda Ayah, her veined arms tight about my body. "Your Ma is not a ghost. She loves you still but you are too heavy for her. She has a baby inside her tummy now, my sugar bit."

I had three months to get used to the idea of having another child in the house.

When it came time for the baby to be born, Ma went back to her mother's home in Mandya. My grandmother's house was full of people, some of whom lived there and others who visited for a couple of days, caught up on all the family gossip and left. I liked the house, for unlike the Railway colony house we lived in, there seemed to be no secrets lurking in the corners of rooms, and best of all, none of the ghosts and goblins about which Linda Ayah told me. Ma was a different person here, giggling with her sisters, allowing her aunts and cousins to pamper her. I wished we could live in that house forever.

When my sister was born, all the relatives were surprised at how dark she was.

"Where did this one come from?" remarked Chinna, Ma's widowed aunt, who was a permanent member of my grandmother's household. She cupped the baby's head with one gnarled hand and cradled its tiny bottom with the other.

"No one in our family is as black as this child. Must be from your husband's side," said Ajji, my grandmother. "She looks like a sweeper-caste child."

How cruel Ajji was, I thought. I glanced at Ma, lying in bed refusing to comment, watching dreamily as the baby was oiled and massaged, bathed and rocked to sleep by Chinna or Ajji. She took my sister from them only to feed her, allowing me to watch the infant suck and snort at the plump nipple. She let me touch the baby's cheek, smiling as the creature left the breast to suck blindly in the direction of my wondering finger. "Seesee, she likes you already," she laughed. "She knows that her big sister is going to look after her."

"Meghna, that's what we will name her," suggested Ajji. "She is like a dark, rain-filled cloud."

Ma did not agree. "No," she said, "her name is Roopa."

Afterwards, people looked at the two of us and said that we looked like the sun and its shadow. Ma held Roopa against her breast and said, "No, not the sun and its shadow. You have it all wrong. Kamini and Roopa— wealth and beauty—that is what my two daughters are."

And some people raised their eyebrows as if to say, "That darkblack thing, a beauty? Only a fond mother's eyes can see beauty where it does not lie. After all, if you ask a crow who sings the best in the world, won't she point to her own chick?"

Ma and Roopa and I stayed for three months at Ajji's house. That was the amount of time a daughter stayed with her parents after the birth of a child.

"Time enough to be pampered and washed, to rest from the pain of bearing life," said Ajji firmly, making sure that Ma heard, because she wasn't willing to keep a married daughter in the house for longer than that. "After that you return to your husband."

For three months Ma went back to being a girl, sleeping when Roopa did, playing *cowrie* with me. She sat in the back verandah allowing her oiled limbs to soak up the sun, waited for Chinna to summon her for a bath, moaning with pleasure as steamy-hot water was poured over her puffy body. Later on, she stood pliant and drowsy in her blouse and petticoat while Chinna wound a soft, old sari about her belly.

"To bring your mother's waist back," she explained to me, and pulled the cloth so tight that Ma said she couldn't breathe.

Of all the people in Ajji's house, Chinna was the most interesting. She was small and quick, with the look of a darting brown bird about her. Her head was shaved clean as she was a widow and was not allowed any vanities such as long hair or pretty clothes. Fate had deprived Chinna of the joys of normal life, yet she enjoyed herself more fully than anybody else I knew. Chinna loved the latest films, clapping enthusiastically with the rowdy theatre crowds when the hero appeared on screen. She smacked her lips over the chocolates that relatives brought for her from England.

"Ah, I can taste a different land, I can taste the sweetness of the people there," she sighed, delicately unwrapping the silver paper and taking a lick at the little chocolate before popping it into her mouth and sucking noisily. Ajji watched sourly. "Who would think she is a grown woman? Look at how silly she behaves!"

I was frightened of my grandmother, a slow, silent woman who regarded me with what seemed like a complete lack of interest. She never told me stories, like Chinna, nor did she pamper me with sweets and toys. Oh yes, Ajji bought me a new silk *lehenga* and matching bangles every time we visited, but the gold on the cloth was thinner than it was on Gopal Uncle's daughter's.

"Ajji, why is mine less shiny than Aparna's?" I demanded, piqued by the unfairness.

"What a girl!" exclaimed my grandmother, her mouth stained with red *paan* juice as if she had drunk blood. "You are lucky that I even got you a nice skirt. Aparna is my *son's* child, remember?"

Nono, I did not like Ajji very much at all. Thatha, my grandfather, was all right, but he insisted on reading to me from huge philosophy books, his voice putting me to sleep. "Thus did Krishna explain the nature of the world to Arjuna," he droned, his hands waving, emphasizing every word that Lord Krishna uttered, while I looked longingly out the window or watched a large black ant march purposefully towards his twitching foot. Thatha had started twitching when he turned sixty, a couple of years before, tiny shudders that travelled in waves all over his liver-spotted body, as if a creature inside was struggling to get out. My cousins and I had made a game out of guessing when the next twitch would attack Thatha, and when the old man found out about it, he would shiver extravagantly to make us laugh. Thatha died three years after Roopa was born, a

heart attack seizing his body as he energetically chopped
the green shell off a coconut. He had performed this
task for as long as I could remember, his left hand
cradling the coconut, his right clenched on a cleaver
slicing the thin morning air and *thuck!* The pale, silver
water lay revealed like a secret lake, sweet and ready to
drink. Ajji grumbled at this ritual, complaining that
Thatha was being silly, performing young tricks with
an old body. "To show off to you little ones," she said.
"He is fond of children."

Ajji did not think there was any point in becoming
fond of people, especially children, for they grew up
and changed, disappointed their parents, filled them
with sorrow, got married and left the house, or died
before you really knew them. Chinna said that at Ma's
birth the only thing Ajji asked was whether the child
was a boy. When the *dai* said no, Ajji sighed, for now
she would have to have another one.

That year the sugar cane yield was so good that
everybody who came to see the baby said that she was
Lakshmi, the goddess of wealth, incarnate. Putti, Ma's
grandmother, wanted to name her after the goddess,
but the family priest said that Ma's name should begin
with a different letter, one that was more auspicious,
more in harmony with Ma's birth stars.

"When Saroja, your Ma, was born," said Chinna, her
old eyes squinting as if searching the past, "you could
get a whole garden of beans for a rupee. Why, you could
get three bushels of sugar cane fresh from the fields for
that princely sum of money. These days a bit of cane is

a luxury, even here in this place where the fields are full. What is the world coming to?"

I didn't want to know about the prices of things, I wanted Chinna to tell me about my mother's childhood. Did she cry till she had a choking fit, as Ma had told me I used to do? Did she like boiled peanuts better than roasted ones? Did she cry when she fell or strut around showing off her wounds, like my cousin Indu? I believed that if I knew every little thing about Ma, I would be able to understand why she was happier here in this old building with high, thin windows that let in hardly any light than in the grand Railway colony houses where my Dadda waited for us to return with the new baby.

"The month that your Ma was born," continued Chinna, trying to place Ma in history for me, "the sugar cane was being harvested and rivers of juice turned the soil to mush. If you stuck out your tongue, you could taste the wind laden with sweetness. That year, our neighbour and his son had a terrible fight. Old Thimmaya was a supporter of the British and insisted on having the Union Jack in his own compound. The British, in return for his loyalty, rewarded him handsomely with fertile sugar land. Ah! that Thimmaya was like a posh English gentleman himself, with his fine *angrezi* shoes which his servant polished with beer! But Bheema joined Gandhi in his struggle for India's independence and called his father a traitor. He built a pyre on his lawn right before the flagstaff and burned all of Old Thimmaya's fine English shirts and books, even his

watch. A foreign watch with fancy gold work on it!
Bheema was a good boy, a patriotic boy you know, and
he wanted to marry your mother."

"Then why didn't he?" I asked.

"Oh nono! He was of a different caste. Besides, their
horoscopes didn't match at all, and then his father threw
him out of the house for causing such *gad-bad*."

I could not understand this horoscope business. Your
horoscope was supposed to predict your future. The
priest would read the position of the stars at your birth
and then tell you how your life was going to be. But
then everybody I knew should have had a good life, for
their horoscopes must have told them what to watch
out for. And yet there was Ma's cousin who had lost his
leg in an accident two years ago, and an uncle whose
wife had run away from home leaving behind two little children. Take Ma herself. She could not marry
Bheema the boy next door because his horoscope did
not match hers. And yet she had married Dadda, whose
horoscope didn't exist because he was not even sure
when he was born!

Ma never failed to get intensely irritated by this story
of the missing horoscope. "Your father says he comes
from a family of priests! Probably a lie, like everything
else about him. Who ever heard of a priest's child not
having an exact record of his birth? His father must
have been the village sweeper!"

My Dadda wasn't a sweeper's son. Did a sweeper have
such an elegant nose, such a bigwide forehead, such a
way with stories? True, he did not tell me anything

about his birth, his childhood. I knew my father only
as a grown-up person who travelled in trains and sometimes told Ma to shut up when she yelled and screamed.
Ma, on the other hand, had dozens of stories surrounding her. In fact, there were so many conflicting
ones from her brothers and sisters, her mother, grandmother and Chinna, that sometimes Ma seemed as
much a puzzle as Dadda. What was I to make of her
when half her relatives claimed that my mother was
such a nice, well-behaved child and the other half
insisted that she was a stubborn fusspot?

"Saroja and her sisters used to go to school together,"
said my grandmother. "Lalli and Kusuma came back
home looking as neat as when they left. But your
mother, *Rama-Rama,* what a messy girl she was! And she
was the oldest, too!"

Ma's cousin Radha agreed, "We used to have a little
rhyme for your Ma—'Fuss-miss, fighter-cock, queen of
the mud, Sa-ro-ja.'"

The year that Ma was born, the mango tree in the
corner of the back yard bore fruit. Ajji said that it was
because she had been pouring cow-dung water around
the tree for a whole year. Chinna protested that it was
because Lakshmi incarnate had arrived in the house.
Who to believe?

Ajji spat betel juice into her silver spittoon, wiped
her mouth with her sari *pallav* and remarked, "Hunh!
Can a daughter ever be a Goddess Lakshmi in her parents' home? She carries wealth out of the door! Your
Ma climbed trees, tore all her beautiful silk *lehengas* and

lost three gold earrings. I thought she would be a sweet
Japanese doll, but things never turn out the way you
expect. Such is life, remember that and you will never
be disappointed."

"Don't believe your Ajji," whispered Chinna to me.
"*She* was happy. It was your grandfather who wanted a
son. Men are like that, they need sons to show off to!"
She dragged out a mouldy accounts ledger from the
glass-fronted cupboard in the corner of the room. In his
fine, curling hand, Thatha, my grandfather, had marked
Ma's birth in his accounts ledger as a list of expenses.
Maternity hospital—Rs. 50.00; *ayah*—Rs. 1.00;
sweets—Rs. 2.25; *jamedaar*—Rs. 1.50. (Chinna said that
he grumbled about the high sum spent on the *jamedaar,*
a mere toilet-cleaner, but he knew that it was danger-
ous to annoy her for it was she who took away the
bloody afterbirth and the umbilical cord to bury deep
in the earth, away from scavenging animals and evil spirits.) The list went on: a pink Canjeevaram sari and a
gold necklace, which cost him 200 rupees, for Ajji. If
she had borne him a son, it would have been a diamond
pendant. But there was still time for that. Ma was only
the first child, and a man must have daughters as well.

My great-grandmother, Putti, marked the arrival of
her first grandchild by inviting the entire town for the
naming ceremony. She had every doorway decorated
with mango-leaf garlands of beaten silver, and she even
bought a cradle carved by the cradle-makers of Ran-
ganathpuram. She gave silk saris to all the female relatives who came, smiling from ear to ear while her

husband sat morosely in a corner counting the rupees as they rolled out of his money-box.

"She was a wicked creature, your great-granny," sighed Chinna. "Sometimes people are driven to wickedness, who am I to say this or that? But she was very fond of your Ma, they were alike in so many ways."

I was born fifteen years after an important event called Independence. When that Independence happened, explained Chinna, all the pink people with hats packed their *pettis* and sailed for England. Then the Indian politicians said "Ho! Ho! Ho! The kingdom of Lord Rama will be restored to its glory!"

"But what difference whether the politicians were pink or brown?" remarked Chinna. "I still had three saris to wear, your grandmother chewed six *paans* a day, and your Thatha's money now bought one kilo of mangoes instead of ten!"

"And Ma," I asked, "was my Ma pleased when she saw me?"

"Of course she was, you silly child. Were you not a piece of her being?"

I was never sure about Ma's feelings for me. Her love, I felt sometimes, was like the waves in the sea, the ebb and flow left me reaching out hungrily. A love as uncertain as the year that I was born, when the Chinese had marched across the border into India, making a mockery of the slogan "Hindu-Chinee brothers-brothers." That year the price of rice shot up, a grim famine swept across the north, and nothing was the same again.

"The year you were born, the whole country collapsed," said Chinna, tweaking my nose and smiling.

Was my birth the dark moment in India's horoscope,
triggering calamity? Or was I merely one of thousands
of children whose birth that year marked the end of an
age, an age when even a rupee was worth something,
and loyalty and morality were not just words in moral
science class?

"Those days," said Chinna, her fingers working warm
coconut oil into my hair to keep it night-black, "those
days you could leave all your doors wide open at night
and go to sleep, so safe and nice. Only the *angrezi* could
not be trusted. Pink and smiling, they would walk into
your home, say hello-vello, fine day, howdoyoudo, and
take away your table-chair-cupboard!"

⚬⚬⚬

Some mornings I woke to find frost on my window pane. If I
peered at the window I could see the perfection of each icy crys-
tal. And when I leaned away, there was a glittering filigree of
ferns, silver fronds, tree branches as delicate as the ones in those
fairy tale books my Ma used to buy for me.

My mother, who had seemed unchanging as the Dhruva star
through my childhood, looked so different in my memory now
when viewed from the distance that separated us. Her hair,
once abundant, was a pathetic clump of white, her thin fingers
no longer smooth and sure in their myriad tasks. She wore
glasses to read although her eyes retained their sharp vitality.
As children, Roopa and I were transfixed with fear when Ma

glared at us with those large eyes. The same eyes had softened
and glowed when she was pleased or proud of us.

But the image of my mother as a fading old woman disappeared as soon as I heard her sharp voice over the phone.

"Why you are wasting your money calling me every week?
Will your hand drop off if you write instead?" she demanded.

I gave her glowing accounts of my research supervisor, my
colleagues Greta and Bob, who turned pink with embarrass-
ment when they tried to pronounce my name, apologizing pro-
fusely each time they transformed it into something different:
Kemani, Kimani.

"Why you don't tell them it is Kaa-mee-nee? What use
telling me?" asked Ma.

I waited for her to interpret the silences between my words,
to sense my loneliness, to say, "Why don't you just come back
home, I need you, I am getting old." I would drop my work
and catch the next flight back.

But Ma only said, "Do you remember Mr. Kumar, your
father's colleague? He and his wife live two blocks away from
my apartment. Can you imagine? I met Mrs. Kumar at the
shopping centre and thought that she was a ghost! I hadn't
seen a Railway face for so long. Their son is leaving for Toronto
in a week or so. I will send some cobri-mitthai for you with
him, and some clothes. I don't want to send too much, it is not
good to take advantage of a friend's kindness. Besides, he might
not want to take it at all. I knew the boy as a child in short
pants, but who knows, people change!"

⊰⊱

My father was a civil engineer in the Indian railways, and as a girl I imagined that he was a very important man indeed, for every time a new railway line was being planned, he had to visit the site, check if the terrain was all right, and decide if it was worth spending money on bridges and tunnels or whether there was a less expensive route that could be taken. Dadda was always being transferred to new sites. In fact, we moved so frequently that my memories have blurred and melded together, a bit like the landscape viewed through the windows of a speeding train. Then, occasionally, the picture becomes sharp and focused. For instance, I can recall in exquisite detail the summer months when Dadda's sisters visited us, for those months were always filled with the drama of unexpected events. I remember my mother's constant unhappiness, which ran like a dark thread right through our lives. And I remember Ratnapura Junction, where we were transferred when I was about nine years old.

It was a large, busy station, and when we alighted with our suitcases and bags, I was overwhelmed by the solid wave of sound and smell that hit my senses. Coolies in bright red uniforms gathered around us and fought over the luggage, striding away with boxes and suitcases piled on their heads and slung across their shoulders. Dadda disappeared behind them, shouting directions, and Ma was left holding Roopa and me tightly by the hand. I stared in amazement at the number of *angrezis*, with skin ranging from dark pink to dead white, and hair, oh their hair, so many shades of

yellow, brown and red. Ma said that they were only pretend English people—they were the Anglo-Indians of
Ratnapura, half Indian and half English. There was even
an old lady with blue hair. I stared so hard that Ma
noticed and pinched my underarm.

"Stop that, your face looks like an open pot," she
hissed.

She picked up Roopa, took my hand in hers and,
with her nose in the air, swept past the ticket-collector
at the entrance to the railway station. In Bhusaval, where
everyone knew that she was a Railway officer's wife, she
didn't need to show anyone her ticket. She just said
"Pass!" and walked through the gates. At Ratnapura
Junction it was different. The ticket collector wanted to
see Ma's pass. There were so many people here that he
could not be expected to remember who was an officer
and who was not. He took a long time staring at the
pass and then at Ma, as if he suspected that she had
stolen it, and Roopa started screaming that Ma was
holding her too tight, and there was so much fuss and
noise by the time we were out of the crowded platform
that Ma was hot and furious.

I knew that she was wishing that Linda Ayah or
Ganesh Peon had travelled with us instead of going on
ahead with the brake-van carrying all the furniture, the
fridge and other big things that had been packed up in
gunny sacks and newspaper and wooden crates. They
would be waiting at our new bungalow with pots of hot
tea and biscuits. Ganesh would have stocked up on provisions and got the kitchen going, and Linda Ayah

would sweep out the house, find out about new maid-servants, washermen and toilet-cleaners. For now, Ma had to manage the two of us herself, and she pursed her lips grimly when Dadda asked what took us so long. I was worried she would say something nasty and that they would start an argument in front of everybody, but Ma's attention was distracted by a beggar, painted blue all over, who touched her arm and sang mournfully, "Ma-ma-ma-ma, pity me mother, pity me." Ma shook her hand off but it came back like a big insect, touching and touching. Finally Ma said, "*Tchuk,* what a nuisance!" and gave the girl a ten-paise coin. Immediately we were surrounded by a crowd of children, all of them patting Ma's hands, my face, Roopa's legs and crying, "Pity us, mother, pity us!"

"Come on, come on. Why did you have to give them anything?" urged Dadda from inside the car, and Ma bundled us in, looking more and more angry.

Just as I was getting in, one of the beggars said to me, "May you die of too much food," and pushing a hand up my frock twisted the tender flesh hard.

I squealed with agony and Ma looked alarmed. "What happened, baby?" she asked, thinking that my hand or foot had caught in the door.

"Nothing," I said, slowly lifting my frock to see if that vicious pinch had left a mark on the thigh, and I felt the hot tears start in my eyes when I saw the blueing skin. I was starting to hate this city already.

The car entered the Railway colony via Noonmaati Road, a long, narrow stretch of tarmac, which curved around the walls of the colony. But it was so crowded, it took us forever to reach the North Gate, the entrance closest to our house. The driver casually announced that every day an accident took place on this road.

"Yesterday, a *padri,* Father Joseph, from that boys' school across the road, was smashed like a fly against the side of Number 21 bus," said the driver. "Total chutney, the poor man."

I imagined the priest, one moment hanging outside the gaping maw of the bus, the tail of a fat caterpillar of people tenaciously clinging to the window bars, each other's shirts, anything, his right foot barely touching the footboard, the left waving free under his priestly robes, and in the next moment brushed to death by a passing lorry.

"They'll have to bury the bus with the father. Couldn't scrape him off, that's what I heard," added the driver laconically.

Noonmaati Road was narrow, pressed in on both sides by the pavement people. There were fruit-sellers and hawkers with stands full of jewellery, shoes, lurid yellow water in Chanel No. 5 perfume bottles. Almost all the vendors looked as though they were arguing ferociously with their customers, waving and gesticulating, scowling and nodding. I had never seen so many people in one place. It frightened me, this big town with no trees, just lots and lots of angry people. There were foreigners on this road, real ones this time, with little swarms of beggar children following them, touching their pink and white arms, dancing around in front and at the back. Some of them looked confused by the children, but others just walked on and on, stopping to take pictures or watch some of the people on the pavement.

"Look at those poor *angrezi* people," said Ma. "Can't the police do something about beggars?"

She called all white people *angrezi*. For her there were only two countries in the world, no matter what anyone else said. This side of the seven seas it was India and across it was *Angrez*-land, home of the Queen-Who-Never-Shat. Ma had told me, a little sheepishly, that when she was little, she had believed that the Queen of England was so royal that human failings such as the desire to visit the toilet did not bother her. Even as an adult, her devotion to all things British never wavered. Ma regularly subscribed to *Women At Home* magazine, which cost fifteen rupees per issue.

"Why can't you buy an Indian magazine instead?" Dadda asked her when the bill arrived. "With fifteen rupees we can buy provisions for a whole week."

Ma didn't bother to reply, just told the paper man to bring the magazine. She made pretty dresses for me and Roopa out of it and even cut my hair to match one of the models. I had to read the children's section out loud to her each month, making sure that I remembered to round my mouth over the "w"s and bite my lip on the "v"s like the British radio news-readers on the BBC.. There were always two stories for children. I preferred the one about Nora and Tilly, two little girls who went for picnics all the time and ate lots of food. Their mother, unlike mine, let them wander around without an *ayah* at their heels. I always felt very hungry when I read about their picnic baskets loaded with chocolate cakes and sandwiches, pies, fruit and ginger beer. However, I didn't like the taste of ginger and could not imagine drinking something made of it. I liked Nora and Tilly but wished that they had different names—Gauri and Geetha, perhaps, or Mini and Bani.

When we received our transfer orders, Ma had to write all the way to England to give the magazine our change of address: Type Five, Number Two on Gulmohur Avenue.

I knew our address by heart. Ma said that it was important for me to keep it in my head, just in case. "Just-in-case" scared me—it included kidnapping, theft, losing my way, an accident, all sorts of horrible things that lurked around the corner waiting to happen. But if I remembered my address, all would be well. I had even memorized the route back home from my new school: straight down Pilkington Road, left on to Tiller's Lane, through the South Gate into the colony, past the Railway Club and Chopra's dispensary, left again on Gulmohur Avenue and up the red gravel path to Bungalow Number Two.

It was easy to spot our new house, with its arched, brick entrance like the mouth of a yawning lion. The verandahs had bougainvillaea and morning-glory all twined up and around the pillars, and Ma was sure that there were snakes hiding in them. A shaggy rain tree on one side of the house had dropped thousands of pink flowers on the garage the day we arrived, and a tamarind tree leaned almost into the back verandah. On the other side was the transit house where people who were visiting the Railway colony stayed. Right now there was a man from Nigeria. Linda Ayah called him a *hubshi* but Ma got angry with her for saying such rude things. "As though you are the snow queen," she said to Linda, who screwed up her mouth and refused to talk to Ma all morning.

Our back-door neighbour was Mrs. Ahluwalia, who sent us a tray full of *pakodas* the day we arrived and after that came over every afternoon for tea. Mrs. Simoes, Ma's old friend from Bhusaval, lived across the colony and she said that Mrs. Ahluwalia was a big gossip. "Don't listen to anything she says, she has only a bird's nest for brains!" Mrs. Simoes told Ma that the best rice was to be bought from Kali Charan's Grocery Bhandaar, the iron-man should not be paid more than fifty paise per sari and four annas for a shirt, and the best way to get to the vegetable market was by the Number 16 bus and then a rickshaw. No use taking the car, because by the time you did your shopping and came back, some *goonda* would have stripped it of everything worth stealing.

"And if there is something wrong with your car, a kut-kut sound under the bonnet, a whine instead of the roar of a healthy engine, you just get hold of Paul da Costa. He is an *Anglo*." Mrs. Simoes wrinkled her nose slightly. "Acts too smart sometimes, I tell you, but the best mechanic in Ratnapura. Once he puts his charmed fingers into the belly of your car, god-promise it will purr like a *billee!*"

She said that I would positively have to join Loretto Convent for Girls. "Irish nuns," said Mrs. Simoes, her thin, curved eyebrows rising sharply, as they always did when she wanted to emphasize a point. "Excellent discipline, *sooparb* manners. My Lily loves it there. She will take care of Kamini, our daughters will be best friends, eh?" Mrs. Simoes pinched my cheek.

There were six apartments in the transit house and the third one was occupied by the Nigerian visitor. I could see him vaguely through the thin besharam hedge with its yellow flowers. Ma told us that *besharam* meant shameless, and the plant was called that because it was parasitic and grew anywhere you threw it. Ma knew a lot about plants. She had studied biology and zoology when she was at the university. "I could have been a doctor," she used to say, her voice sharp and rancorous, after an especially bad quarrel with Dadda.

The Nigerian man was doing a technical course and was out every morning. In the afternoons, he relaxed in an easy chair on the verandah, staring out across the garden, occasionally looking down at the book on his lap. Some days he had visitors, but he was alone most of the time. I was curious about the man. In spite of Ma's scolding, Linda Ayah insisted that he was a *hubshi,* perhaps even a genie from my Arabian Nights storybook.

"His eyes are actually ears and his mouth is his magic eye," she warned. "You better stay inside the house when your mother sleeps in the afternoon. Otherwise he might stuff you inside a bottle and take you back with him to Afreeka!"

I was almost certain that Linda Ayah was only trying to get me out of her hair while she gossiped with her cronies. But what if the man next door was really a *hub-shi*? I wouldn't know till I saw his palms, for *hubshis* had green palms.

One afternoon, while Ma napped, I sat in our shady verandah and played with my toys, clattering the minia-ture stainless-steel vessels of my cooking set to assure her that I was not getting into any trouble. As soon as she and Roopa were asleep, I slipped out of the veran-dah and crept through the hole in the green rustling hedge on to the cement path running around the tran-sit house, my bare feet scorched by the baking surface. One-two-three, I counted in my head as I crossed the door of each apartment. I hoped the man would be in his usual chair in the verandah.

Three bamboo screens marked the end of an apart-ment, and when I reached the third one, I held my breath and stood shivering with fear. There were so many things to be afraid of. But I had my excuses ready. If Ma woke up suddenly and found me gone, I could say, "Ma, I was looking for Linda Ayah." And if Linda Ayah saw me sneaking around, I could threaten to tell Ma that she had left me alone. However, if the man glanced this way and saw me peering through the slats of the screen, he would transform me into a moth and cork me inside a bottle. I gazed at him, noting every little crease in his sleeping face, his tight curls of hair and the backs of his hands as they rested on the arms of the easy chair. Why didn't he turn his hands so that I could see the colour of his palms?

He stood up suddenly and stretched, yawned widely, then moved towards the screen and tugged on the cord that rolled it up. I stood there like a petrified squirrel. Saw his feet in blue rubber slippers, the kind you got from the pavement vendor for a couple of rupees. Then the soft cuffs of his white trousers, higher and higher, past the blue-and-white-checked shirt up to his face. He was still looking up at the *chik* as it piled in a roll near the high ceiling of the verandah. I could have run away and he might not even have noticed, but my feet were stuck to the ground: he had cast a magic spell, just as Linda Ayah had warned. I could feel myself turning into a moth. He glanced down at me and his face fell open, astonished.

"Ooo!" he said, and I turned and ran then, before he could sing the rest of his spells, before he could make my feet become dark furry wings. I squeezed through the hedge and ran into my room. Perhaps he wouldn't realize that I lived in this house. He hadn't actually seen me going *into* the house. Perhaps he had not seen me at all, for the sun was in his eyes.

I didn't go out of the house the next day. I was so quiet that Ma noticed and asked what was the matter with me.

"Nothing," I said quickly. "I just feel like playing inside today."

"Must be bored, poor child," said Ma. "Maybe we'll visit Simoes Aunty, you can play with Lily."

Ma thought that Lily was a sweet child and a good influence on me. She was actually a sneaky pie-face who cried when she lost a game. Lily had pinched Roopa the last time she'd visited. I'd seen her pinch my sister and make her cry and I'd said so.

Mrs. Simoes had raised her eyebrows, pulled my cheek and said, "What a little story-teller you are! My Lily loves babies. She keeps asking me when I am going to get her one." She laughed in a silly way.

Ma smiled as well but she was annoyed. She knew that there were some things about which I would never make up stories. And even if I did, nobody was allowed to comment but her.

"I think I have a headache," I lied, not looking at Ma. If you looked your mother in the eye and told a fib she would turn to stone.

Ma touched my forehead and gave me lots of water to drink.

"We have to go and meet the Loretto School principal tomorrow," she said anxiously. "You can't fall ill, it's so difficult to get an appointment with those people."

"Lily Simoes is a liar and she makes me sick," I confessed. "I don't want to play with her."

Ma sighed. "All right, don't go out in the sun, then. And don't tease Linda Ayah."

Two afternoons later, when Ma took her nap, I crawled through the hedge again. I couldn't see anyone in the verandah; the screens were rolled up and rattled slightly in the breeze. So I was startled when the Nigerian's apartment door banged open and he appeared suddenly. He glanced down the length of the verandah, spotted me and smiled. "Hey, little girl," he called. "What you doing there, eh?"

He knew that I was the nosy-parker girl and now he was going to yell at me. I edged back towards the safety of the besharam hedge. Would he catch me before I could squeeze through the hole to my own garden? Did it hurt to be turned into a moth and put in a bottle? My mouth was dry, my ponytail stuck to my neck.

"Hey, hey!" said the man, his voice so loud in the still afternoon. "Visiting your neighbour? I met your Daddy at work today."

Don't *shout* so, I thought, Ma might wake up. Linda Ayah might come running to see what's going on.

He knew my Dadda, so he couldn't be bad. He also had pink palms, I could see that now. He was not a *hubshi*.

"I am sorry I was peeping at you," I said.

"Ah, a curious girl aren't you? Not as curious as my little girl, though."

"You have a little girl?"

"Yes, yes, and two boys, but my little girl is the smart one, eh?"

"What does she do?"

"She reads books better than her Daddy and Mam, that's what," said the man. "Can you read?"

"Of course I can!" I replied. "Does your little girl read about Nora and Tilly?"

"I don't know about Noratilly, but she knows Tongua the jackal and Nubi the Mighty King," said the man. "Do you want to hear those stories? Better than your Noratilly."

He stared out at the garden. "In a river lived a wicked crocodile and across the river lived Nubi the Mighty Who Ruled the Land," he began, and I was instantly entranced. The story ended quickly, however, and the man said in a soft, sad voice, "That happened long-long ago when the land was green and the river heavy with water."

"And now, isn't the land green now?" I was puzzled by the change in his voice, for when he told the story it became singsong, swinging up and down, assuming different pitches for the various characters: the crocodile, the king, the jackals and the little princess who could balance ten pots of water on her head without dropping a single one.

"No, now it is as brown as these little sparrows," he said pointing at the tiny chattering birds hopping on the dusty grass growing through the cracks in the cement paving outside the verandah.

"My Linda Ayah can catch the sparrows in her sari," I said.

"Why you want to catch those little fellows, eh?"

"I don't keep them," I said, a little frightened. I had remained standing through the story, poised to run down the verandah if the man showed any sign of anger. "I just look at them and let them fly away."

"I'll show you something," said the man. "Wait here."

He went into his apartment and returned a few minutes later with a few grains of rice in his hand. "Now keep very still and watch," he said, squatting on the edge of the verandah and stretching his hand out slowly to where the sparrows pecked and hopped. The grains of rice sat invitingly on his pink palm. The sparrows hopped closer to the palm, pecking ceaselessly at the dry ground. Then a daring one fluttered on to his hand, picked up a grain and flew away. Another sparrow did the same thing. The man sat motionless as a third sparrow landed on the outstretched palm. It did not fly away; instead it stayed there as the man gently closed his fingers around the tiny body and stroked its head.

"See," he said, "not afraid of me. It says to itself, this man, he is kind, he won't hurt any living thing."

He opened his hand and the bird flew down to the ground again, throwing up little pinwheels of dust as it scrabbled for grains of rice. Outside the sun was low in the sky, ready to drop beneath the horizon. A *peon* was making his way down the verandah, rolling up the rest of the screens and letting in cool evening air. I heard my mother calling me in for tea and got up reluctantly.

"Do you know any more stories?"

"Maybe," he said, grinning. "Question number two?"

"Why are you black?" It was a question that had been

nagging me ever since I saw the multicoloured Anglo-Indians at the railway station. Where did all these people get their colour from?

The man smiled and asked quizzically, "Why are you brown, little girl?"

I shrugged. "I don't know."

He shrugged too and said, "And I don't know either."

Ma's insistent "Mini, Kamini, come and get your tiffin" echoed down the verandah.

"What were you doing, talking to unknown people?" she demanded, shaking me hard. She had been waiting to catch me as I crawled back through the hedge. "How many times do I have to tell you, don't talk to anybody-everybody!"

"But Ma, he was telling me stories about Africa!"

"Stories, stories, stories!" said Ma, shaking me again. "Some person on the road says 'Come child, I will tell you stories,' and this idiot girl will go behind him, no problem! Do you ever listen to me?"

"Never listens, whattodo?" sighed Linda Ayah, materializing from somewhere.

"And where were you?" asked Ma. "You are supposed to make sure that she doesn't get into any mischief."

"Memsahib, my eyes blinked once only and this monkey had vanished. What can I do?" protested Linda Ayah.

"Liar-liar-lipstick," I chanted immediately. "You were sitting behind the building doing *khusur-phusur* with the other *ayahs.*"

⚜

"Ma, do you know where Linda Ayah is now?" I asked, hit
by a wave of nostalgia so strong that I had called my mother
at 11:00 a.m. Indian time, when the rates were at their
highest.

"I have no idea. Maybe she went back to her village. Maybe I will stop at her village on my trip," remarked Ma.

"Trip, what trip?"

"I am going on a train journey, across the country."

"With Lalli Aunty?" I was pleased that my mother was going
to do something other than sit in her apartment quarrelling with
the milkman or her latest maidservant. Ma seemed to have a
new one every few months or so. "Whattodo?" she had said, when
I remarked on it. "This is the real world. Not like our Railway
life, with faithful Linda Ayah and Ganesh Peon."

"Are you going with Lalli Aunty?" I asked again.

"Why should I go with her? Am I incapable of doing anything myself?"

"All right, all right, but where are you going?"

"Everywhere," snapped Ma irascibly. "Do I ask you all
about your coming and going? Do I ask you why you have
to live in the North Pole, hanh? Did I ask your sister why
she ran away?"

"Ma, Roopa got married. She did not run away."

"She left college in the middle of the term, came home with
a man we had never met. He might have belonged to a family of pimps for all I knew. And then she married him in less
than a month—so suspicious it looked—and left for USA!
Of course she ran away."

"Roopa's husband is a perfectly nice man, Ma," I protested feebly.

"And now," continued my mother, "it is my turn to go away."

"At least give us an address to write to," I said. I could feel a tension headache coming on. It didn't matter how far away I was, all my conversations with my mother ended in an argument.

"I don't know where I am going," said Ma. "A pilgrimage, like those old people in religious stories. Packed off their daughters, washed their hands of the sons, gave away all their useless belongings and left on long journeys to see how other people lived."

"But how do we know if you are all right? How do we reach you?"

"What is the worst that can happen to me? I will die, that's all. And if I die, the apartment and all that I have in it can be shared between you and Roopa. The bank manager has a spare set of keys. If he dies also, well, use your brains, break open the door, whatever! I don't care."

I was worried about being left behind by Ma who, every now and again, threatened Dadda that one morning he would wake up and find her gone.

"Go, why should I care what you do?" my father would say sometimes, although he usually puffed at his pipe and refused to enter into an argument with Ma. "And don't forget to take your daughters with you."

"*My* daughters! Am I the Virgin Mary that I created them myself or what? When I leave, I go with no baggage but what I brought to this house."

Vir-gin. Good word or bad?

Their arguments were loud and made no pretence of secrecy. I think they assumed that my sister and I were asleep as soon as our heads touched our pillows.

They were right about Roopa, for she was one of those placid creatures who stayed completely impervious to undercurrents of anger or discontent in the house, certain that there would always be someone to look after her. She didn't care who made her breakfast, or took her to the club to play on the swings in the evening, so long as the job was done. I, on the other hand, couldn't bear the thought of becoming like our neighbour's daughter, a thin, silent wisp of a girl who played house-house with us every afternoon and who was easily cowed into being our maidservant or cook or someone as menial. Her mother had died of brain fever and she was looked after by a series of stern aunts. The thought of being brought up by Dadda's sisters, especially crazy Aunty Meera, was extremely disagreeable. So I stayed awake, listening for footsteps, my body tensed to spring out of bed. I thought that if I kept my ears open, I would know immediately if Ma was going to run away, and then I could scream, wind my arms around her legs and stop her. How would I manage on my own with a father who was away on tour most of the time? How would I battle Linda Ayah's host of demons and monsters that roamed the house every day? Besides, I might not be able to keep my word about looking after Roopa and I'd go straight to Hell. And Hell, warned Linda Ayah, was a most uncomfortable place, full of drooling creatures who craved little girls to satisfy their horrible appetites.

Although Ma had assured me that Hell existed only in a person's imagination and wasn't a place like Delhi or Bombay to which one could travel by train, I was sure it lurked there at the edges of my world waiting for me to miss my step and slide in. Not only did Linda Ayah speak about it often and with a sort of deadly certainty, it was brought up every Friday at school by Miss Manley, the moral science teacher. She was an overpowering woman whose thick arms were covered with a pelt of bright orange hair so that, no matter what the colour of her dress, it looked as though she had orange sleeves. Miss Manley flung questions at the class to test our knowledge of the Bible.

"What happened at Gethsemane?" she thundered, going down the classroom, row by row, making sure that she caught everyone with her questions. If a student dared to stutter, "I don't know, Miss," she paused in awful silence for a minute and then bellowed, "Dunce, you are a dunce! Go stand in the corner and improve your memory!"

The dunce had to stand inside an aluminum dustbin and learn up Miss Manley's favourite poem, "Daffodils", before the count of ten.

"'I wandered lonely as a cloud…'" murmured the dustbindunce.

"All right class, start counting," commanded Miss

Manley, and we chanted out loud, as slowly as possible, "One-two-three-four…" The closer we got to ten, the slower we counted to give the poor dunce a few seconds extra to memorize the lines. If the miscreant hadn't learnt up the lines before ten, the wrath of God and Miss Manley descended. She slammed the dunce's cheeks with a pair of chalkboard dusters, sending up billows of white powder, and said fiercely, "*Wicked* blight, may the Lord's spit hail down upon you."

Then she turned to the rest of the class, her tangerine hair flying out of her bun like streamers, and demanded with deep bitterness, "What do you *junglee* donkeys know of fields of golden daffodils nodding and dancing in the breeze?"

If Miss Manley found someone not paying attention, she casually picked up a piece of chalk, broke it in two and flung the bits with unerring aim at the miscreant, smiling at the yelp of pain as the chalk caught the dreamer on the face, or head, or on a tender ear.

"Very smart, think you can quietly sleep in my class and I won't notice, what? Think again, too-too smart. Not only is Miss Manley watching you, but God in his Heaven, too!"

I usually finished Miss Manley's homework first, because I couldn't bear the shame of being a dust-bindunce. One afternoon, she was in an unusually bad mood, flinging chalk like tiny missiles at various corners of the classroom. Twice Miss Manley had shouted at Devaki, my best friend, for stammering over an answer, and I hated her for it.

"She is a *vir-gin*," I whispered to Devaki.

She clapped a hand over her mouth and giggled. "Miss Manley is a *vir-gin*," she hissed to Shabnam.

The chalk sang across the room and caught Devaki on her cheek. "I didn't say it, I didn't say it. It was Kamini," she babbled, fat tears winding down her face.

"Say what?"

"That you are a *vir-gin*."

It was a bad word, I discovered, for Miss Manley made me sit under my desk. "The dustbin is too good for you," she roared. "You stay down there where the Lord cannot see your sinful face!"

I crouched under the desk, so terrified that I did not come out even after the last bell rang and Miss Manley left. She did not seem to remember that I was still waiting to be forgiven.

Linda Ayah, who had come to take me home, squatted patiently at the door of the classroom and tried to persuade me to emerge. "God is kind and generous, your teacher is a mad woman. She does not know anything, come out Baby-missy," she begged. "I will pray to Jesus and tell him that you are a good child who looks after her baby sister, shares all her toys and listens to Linda Ayah. I will tell God to fix that nut-case teacher of yours, don't worry. Let us go home now, your Ma will be waiting with milk and biscuits." When I finally crawled out, she hugged me fiercely and added, "What-for you have to be scared when Linda is here to look after you? God listens to this *ayah,* I am telling you."

Linda Ayah had been with our family for years and years. She was allowed to boss the other servants and nobody could utter a word. Ma said that she had never really hired Linda, at least not officially. When she came to this house as a bride, Dadda had left her alone and gone away to work. She would have been completely lost if it hadn't been for Linda Ayah, always there like Aladdin's genie, getting things done, making sure that Ma was settling in and everything was righty-tighty. She travelled with us every time we were transferred, insisting that if she wasn't around we would all sink in chaos.

There might have been some truth in what she said because Ma became horribly disorganized when we had to move. She hated the whole process of packing, of rolling out yards of stale gunny sacking that had been stored in the garage from the last time we moved, of sending the *peon* around to neighbours' homes for old newspaper to use for the china and the glass bottles in which Ma stored spices. Nobody wanted to part with old newspapers, for you could sell them to the *raddhi-*man, who paid by the kilo.

"So much expense, imagine having to beg other people for their rubbish, imagine having to *buy* their rubbish from them! Why do you have to keep getting transferred? Can't you say your wife is sick, you are allergic to new places, something, and stay here?" grumbled Ma every time Dadda came home with his transfer orders.

She especially disliked finding keys for all the locks, and we had a huge collection of both for the many trunks and boxes that travelled with us when we moved.

"Why she has to make a fuss about such silly things?" muttered Linda, making sure that Ma did not hear her. "How long does it take to find out which key is for what lock, henh?"

"And worst of all," said Ma, "I have to find schools for these children. Your Dadda sits there like a maharaja smoking a pipe and looking at the sky, thinking mighty thoughts no doubt, and I walk from one school to the next wearing out my slippers, saying to those nuns, 'Take my daughters, please, they will bring honour to your school.'"

Ma insisted on sending Roopa and me to convent schools, which were always booked full. It didn't matter where we were transferred or how far away the school was, Ma stood in the admission queues and got us in. In Lucknow we went to St. Agnes's School, in Calcutta it was Mount Carmel, and in Guwahati it was La Martinière's. If Ma could not get us in because we had arrived in the middle of the term and there were no seats left in the classroom, she told the Mother Superior that she would get the nuns railway reservations anytime they had a problem if they could squeeze in two extra desks for us. Then on the way home she would say, "The old crows, they'll do anything if you dangle a bribe. Even brides of the Lord have a price."

Dadda remained blissfully ignorant of Ma's machinations as the nuns never did ask for reservations. He would have been shocked by her lack of scruples. And he could never understand why she insisted on sending me and Roopa to the nuns anyway.

"What is wrong with a Central School education?" he demanded when Ma kicked up a fuss over getting transferred in the middle of the school term. Central Schools were set up for the children of government employees who had to move frequently.

"They teach in Hindi," said Ma.

"So what? That is one of the languages in this country, in case you have forgotten," argued Dadda.

"Only one of them," replied Ma. "You want them to learn a different language everywhere we move? Bengali in this place, Assamese there, Gujarati somewhere else? Poor things, as it is they are confused with first language, second language, third language and all. You want them to go crazy or what?"

"They won't go crazy," insisted Dadda. "They will be true Indians."

"Yes, yes, you are a fine one to talk, you and your smoking jacket and pipe and British ways. Did your *pujari* father send you to Corporation school? Hanh? Did he? Oh no, you could go to Francis Xavier and St. Andrew's, but it is okay for your daughters to go to any rubbish-pile place."

"Those days it was necessary," said Dadda. "Now we're an independent country, remember?"

"Yes, but without English they will be like the servants' children, what's the difference then, you tell me?" argued Ma.

As usual, Dadda got tired of the whole thing and ended up behind his screen of rustling newspapers, while Ma continued complaining to Linda Ayah, who was always ready with a sharp comment or sympathetic silence, depending on her own mood.

Roopa and I knew that Linda was really a witch, a glass-eyed one, who could see what we were going to do even before we tried it.

"Un-unh! Roopa Missy, no playing in dirty tap water otherwise I will tell Memsahib," she would call from her favourite spot in the verandah, without even raising her eyes from the platter of rice or the *soopa* of coriander seeds that she was cleaning. "Kamini baby, if you climb that jamoon tree, showing your knickers to all the loafers passing on the road, you won't be able to sit for a week, such a hard slap you will get!"

When Roopa was a baby, Linda checked the *dhobhi* basket every day to see that the diapers were washed in Dettol and ironed properly. She harangued the milk-woman into bringing her cow to the back yard so that she could watch her draw milk. "My babies get milk without water mixup," she told the milk-woman, who spat a stream of betel juice into the bushes to show Linda Ayah what she thought of her.

I remember the woman, with her fat breasts swinging naked beneath the faded sari, standing astride a drain in full view of the road, her sari hitched up to her thighs, pissing a fierce stream. I had only ever seen men doing this and wondered if she was actually one of the eunuchs who dressed up in women's clothes and roamed the streets during festivals, clapping their hands and singing obscene songs. I was scared to ask the milk-woman, and got a slap on my bottom from Linda Ayah

for my curiosity. "What for you want to watch man-
nerless people making dirty water on the main road?
Stupid child!"

Linda Ayah had coarse, bony hands with knuckles
large as tree-knots and palms criss-crossed so deeply with
lines that they looked like the railway shunting yard. Her
fingertips were stained yellow with *khaini* that she rolled
out of a little tin tucked into the waistline of her sari.

"What is that?" I asked, watching Linda Ayah pinch
a ball of *khaini* delicately between finger and thumb
and rub it against her leathered palms till it powdered.
Then she slapped at it briskly before tossing it into her
mouth. A deep sigh of contentment, her eyes gleaming
pleasure behind her glasses.

"A magic powder," said Linda. "Something to make
an old woman happy." The *khaini* box went back into
the folds of sari and petticoat to be taken out the next
time the household became too heavy for her.

"But you are not old," I said.

"I feel very old sometimes, Baby-missy," said Linda,
still absorbed in the pleasure of the *khaini* as it mingled
with saliva in her mouth, its vapours reaching her heart
and brain, a langorous stretching of her creaky muscles.

"Ma says she feels old too," I said. "Can't you give her
some *khaini?*"

It was true that Ma said she felt as if she had aged
twenty years since her marriage. "Look at this grey," she
grumbled to Dadda during one of her arguments, jab-
bing at her head. "You are responsible for this. Already
I look like my Ajji!"

I never thought of the arguments as anything other than my mother's, for Ma did all the talking and Dadda locked himself into a tight box of silence. A deep silence, only the soft *phhp-phhp* suck of his lips on the pipe stem. Smoke wreathed his head and his face was an indistinct blur.

"Can't you say something?" cried Ma, enraged by his relentless quiet, which was more deadly than angry words could ever be. "Say something, say something, say something!" she screamed once, flinging all the bone china cups and saucers Dadda had bought from England many years ago into the kitchen sink. My father sat in his armchair, a ballooning grey shadow, and said not a word, staring into the mist of smoke, refusing to listen to Ma's hysterical sobbing. I shook Roopa awake, forcing her into her slippers and a sweater, for if Ma was going to leave the house after smashing all the china, I wanted us to be dressed and ready to follow her.

The nicest thing about Ma's flat was the gulmohur tree that scattered its flaming red flowers all over her balcony. Here, in Calgary, I had no gulmohur outside my window, but a lilac bloomed in summer and filled my home with its delicate fragrance. Sometimes I wished that I could trap the beauty of those flowers to last me through the winter, as well. But as Dadda told me once, there are some things you cannot keep forever—youth and beauty and the breath in your mortal body.

Of Dadda himself, there remained so little to hold on to.

Roopa said that she remembered him as an absence. His chair at the dining table sat empty for at least fifteen days of the month. And when he was at home, she couldn't see his face, only the sheets of newspaper rustling before it. Roopa and I exchanged our own memories of him, hoarding them like a pair of misers. For if we did not, Dadda would float away like a puff of dandelion seed. I looked at our family photographs often, of us in Guwahati and Lucknow, Ratnapura and Calcutta. I had all of Dadda's childhood pictures as well. Roopa said that she wasn't interested in them.

"What will I do with these ancient pieces of paper?" she asked, dismissing the fading images of our family.

"How about your children? Don't you want them to know something of their grandfather?"

"I have pictures of Dadda as an adult. Those are enough, I think."

I tried to read the lives behind the enigmatic sepia silence, to fathom the meanings in those still eyes, the unmoving smiles. I phoned Ma in India and asked her about this picture or that, but she only wanted to know why I was wasting my time thinking about ghosts, and a useless bunch at that, who did nothing more worthwhile than produce children.

"Ma, stop being so nasty all the time, I can't stand it," I snapped.

"Oho, look at this madam, all grown up and thinks she can say whatall she wants to her mother!"

Yes, Ma, I am no longer a child, I wanted to tell her, will you ever realize that?

"When are you leaving on this trip of yours?" I asked instead.

*"Tomorrow, next week, next month. How does it matter?
I have all the time in the world and no one to question how
I spend it, no?"*

⬧⬥⬧

My father came home from his long trips with bags full
of stories. I liked to think that the stories were for me
alone. Besides, I was the only one who would listen to
them. Roopa fidgeted and yawned through Dadda's
tales and after a while ran away to play. For her, Dadda
brought dolls and kitchen toys and windmills and
bracelets, worthless things that disintegrated or were
forgotten in a few days.

"Dadda, tell me a story," I begged when he returned
from a trip to Shillong. I danced impatiently around
him, watching him light his pipe.

"Waste of time," grumbled Ma. Her fight with Dadda
had begun long before I was born, so I could not understand it at all. Was it because he refused to take her along
when he went away? Or perhaps because he smoked
so much? Maybe she wanted him to tell *her* all the stories that he told me alone.

"See this crown?" Dadda caressed imaginary Himalayan ranges, his hand conjuring them up in the air
before us. He recited the names of the peaks and
ranges like a sacred chant. "Karakoram, Kailash, Anna-
poorna, Kanchenjunga, each a jewel bearing a tale.
This is where Lord Shiva dances, this is where Parvathi
performed her wild penance, and here River Ganga

lay waiting for Bhageerathi to summon her down to the plains."

Dadda's trains had not breached the Himalayas yet, meandering instead across smiling valleys, occasionally bursting through stony, obdurate hills.

"We tried to fling a bridge across the Ganga at this point, but she is a creature of moods. She was annoyed that we mere humans had not appeased her first with flowers and song," said Dadda, narrating the flood that had swept the Howrah-Kalka Mail off the tracks during the monsoons last year. There were twenty carriages strung together and floating in the murky waters. People must have screamed as they drifted out of the choking windows and sank in dirty bubbles, suitcases floating all around, photographs, timetables, a wedding garland perhaps, lunch-boxes dispersing soaked *rotis,* a film of oily *dal.* The disaster had happened at night and the passengers must have been asleep, unaware that they were drowning till they began to breathe muddy water, felt it fill their lungs inflating them like bags, swelling through every orifice, flooding dreams and memories till there was nothing left but a floating chaos of wet, wet, wet. So the engineers and workers held a grand *pooja,* offered the milk of a hundred coconuts to Ganga, showered pink rose petals on her body, called out paeans in praise of her beauty, and finally the river was appeased, charmed out of her sulks.

When Dadda went away I could trace on a railway map the exact lines of his journey. "Between Kumda and Karonji," said Dadda, back home from yet another trip, "there was only one problem. An anthill as high as a hut which the villagers refused to destroy. A pair of king cobras lived in the hill along with the white ants. Nobody in their right senses destroys the home of a cobra."

"Why?"

"Because, *Noni,* it will bring a curse on your head, of sickness and sorrow. But my assistant said that he was protected from the curse by a boon which Vasuki, the king of serpents, gave to his ancestors. He said that manymany centuries ago, this ancestor had saved Vasuki, who was trapped in a ring of fire. He held out a staff to the mighty snake, who coiled around it and escaped certain death."

"So did you destroy the anthill?"

"No, we laid tracks around it, because the villagers did not believe my assistant's story."

And it seemed that as soon as we got used to having Dadda home again, it was time for him to leave, armed with a line-box full of provisions for a fortnight, sometimes a month. Each night before he left on a trip, I lay awake waiting for a quarrel to erupt.

"What is so special about these trips that you cannot take us with you even once?" Ma demanded just before Dadda left for Darjeeling, a hill-station that my mother had been wanting to visit.

"It is a duty trip, not a holiday, how many times do I have to tell you?"

"Other officers go on these duty trips with their wives and children and mothers and aunts and all. Last month Mr. Khanna took his whole family to Simla."

"I don't care what Mr. Khanna did, it is against railway policy and that's the end of this stupid drama."

"Sathya Harischandra!" taunted Ma, referring to the mythological king who sold his wife and sacrificed his son for the sake of his principles. "Never mind the fact that I have to stay alone in this house and bring up two children without any help, and in the summer, look after your crazy sister as well. Oh no, all that does not matter so long as you stick to your noble duty!"

"Rules are rules," said Dadda stiffly.

"Rules, rules, rules, that's all you care about." Ma started to cry, harsh, loud sobs that scared me. In the past, when Roopa was just a baby, she had argued bitterly but neverever cried. Dadda left the room abruptly, slamming the door behind him. He would sleep in the guest room and slip out early next morning.

Roopa, who usually slept through it all, stirred beside me and whispered, "Is Dadda beating Ma?" She clutched my hand under the sheets and I was glad to have her sticky fingers against mine.

"Dadda doesn't beat people," I hissed indignantly. How could she imagine such a thing about him?

"Then why does she cry? She cries every day when he is at home."

"No she does not! She cries when he goes away."

"They fight all the time and she cries all the time," insisted Roopa.

I couldn't decide on whose side I wanted to be. I adored my father for his gentleness, for his willingness to listen to me, to tell me those wonderful stories when he was home. And yet I hated him for making Ma so angry all the time. In fact, I was secretly happy when he went away on line, and I tried to hide my feelings with an elaborate show of grief. I opened my mouth and bawled, pumped out hot tears, clutched the stern crease of his trousers and begged him not to go. I could not let him see that I was actually relieved, for when he left, Ma changed. She swept through the house smiling and smiling, not even a shout when I spilt a whole bottle of milk, when Roopa wrote all over the dining-room wall with blue chalk, not a word when the *dhobhi* dropped a cinder from his iron-box on a party frock and burnt a hole. Perhaps she *did* eat some of Linda's magic powder.

When Ma was happy, I loved her so much that intensity tingled up my nostrils and bit at my eyes, pulling out tears. Linda Ayah seemed to feel the same way, for she gathered me into her hard, dry arms and rocked me, murmuring all the time, "Oh-oh-oh-oh, I know, I know." Her breath, leafy with the smell of the *neem* twigs she used to brush her teeth, feathered my face, her hands gentle on my head. Ma bustled through the house filling it with such joy that I felt like sobbing. It was the kind of feeling I got when I ate jackfruit in my grandmother's house. The garbage stink of the silky, gold fruit made me gag at the same moment as it slid down my throat, almost unbearably honeysweet.

And as she moved briskly about the house, her starched cotton sari whispering about her body, her thin gold bangles tinkling, my mother reached into her memory and

pulled out soft threads of song. They were mournful Saigal tunes, lilting Geetha Dutt lyrics, gentle songs from
oldold movies which Ma had seen when she was a girl.
Sometimes she kneeled before her carved elephant-box
made of rosewood and ivory, her treasure-box, a wedding
gift from Great-Aunt Manju, and drew out 75 rpm
records in powdery paper jackets. Ma was in such a good
mood when Dadda went away that she even let me try
out her satin petticoats from the box.

"See how thin I was!" she laughed once. *"Baap-re-
baap!* Look at your mother now." She made a circle with
her fingers and said, "My waist was as tiny as this, not
one chance that Scarlett O'Hara had next to *my* waist!"

She allowed Roopa and me to open delicate silver
tins still stained with turmeric and vermilion, *akshathey*
and sandal paste from her wedding.

"When you get married," said Ma, "I will fill these
boxes with joy, my blessings will perfume each of them."
She touched her wedding sari, a Benaras tissue of red
and gold. "For you I will buy only Canjeevaram. A tissue is beautiful when it is new, but in a few years it is a
pile of powder. Looklook how it crumbles and breaks!"

"But Ma, I want a wedding sari just like this," I
begged, in love with the frail, whispery fabric like a butterfly's wing.

"Listen to me *chinni,* your mother knows what from
what. Some things look better than they are," said Ma.

Hindi melodies from Mukesh movies streamed out of
the bathroom along with the sound of rushing water as
Ma washed her cascading black hair. She hummed in the

bedroom, patted puffs of talcum powder under her arms,
across her back, where sweat sprang and wet her Rubia
blouse. She sang as she wrapped a rustling cotton sari
around herself and then came out to dry her hair on the
verandah, where the sun roared out of a blue, blue sky.
I remember how she smiled at me upside down, through
a flying sheet of hair, and I stared in awe at my luminous
mother. Once, when she came out to the verandah, I was
eating my breakfast, my mouth opening and closing as
Linda Ayah spooned in *sooji-halwah* rich with raisins.
When I saw Ma, I kicked my legs and pursed up my
mouth, turning away from Linda's coaxing.

"Come on, Baby-missy, my *kanmani,* don't you want
to grow big-big?" wheedled Linda, her fingers hard on
my chin trying to turn my puckered face towards her.
But no, I wanted to go to my mother, so pretty and
smiling. I climbed her fresh crackling lap, buried my
face in the long neck and smelled her jasmine skin. I
pushed my head between Ma's breasts, wondering at
the tender yielding beneath my face. Her chain of gold
and black wedding beads pressed against my cheek,
leaving tiny imprints. Gold for the good and black for
the bad, Ma had explained. In a marriage you were
obliged to live with both. Through the spiky fringe of
my eyelashes, I could see the peacock eyes on Ma's sari
border, the fine brown hair on her arm, the two moles
like flecks of coal-dust. I could hear her heart *ka-thump-
a-thump,* the rumble of her stomach. I held my own
breath for a second and released it so that it matched
the rise and fall of Ma's breath. But I couldn't burrow

into her fragrant warmth for long for she had to go somewhere.

"I want to go with you, takemetakemetakeme," I wailed as Ma peeled away, ready to sing out of the house.

She spent hours chatting with her friends on the telephone, disappearing for a matinee show sometimes. When she returned, she acted out funny bits from the movie for Roopa and me, her long arms flying in the air, her eyes bright with laughter. Sometimes, on a Saturday, she might clap her hands and say, "Let's go for a picnic today!" And then Ganesh Peon would scurry around preparing baskets of food, grumbling aloud about the Memsahib's erratic moods. "She thinks I am a magician. Make *puri,* make *aloo-dum!* And all in ten minutes if you please!"

There were times when she did nothing at all. Her sewing piled up in great coloured heaps in the guest room, her knitting lay abandoned in its faded cloth bag. Even when strips of sunlight picked out dust patches under the furniture, and she knew right away that the maid Rani had not touched that place with her broom for days, Ma ignored it. And Rani swung her hips in her saucy skirts, tossed her head and breezed through the house, leaving dustballs and cobwebs where they were. Later, later, when Dadda came home and Ma went thin-lipped and mean, Rani would get a good scolding. Then my mother swallowed her smile and ordered Ganesh Peon to make hot *phulkas.* She spent hours in the spare room cutting up cloth to make dresses for Roopa and

me, her face so serious that for a long time I was certain that I had two mothers. Ma was a two-headed
pushmi-pullyu from Dr. Dolittle's zoo, or the Ramleela
drama woman with a good mask on her face and a bad
mask on the back of her head, changing her from Seetha
to Soorpanakhi in a single turn.

Linda Ayah went gloomy when Ma sang. Her face
crumpled into a frown like an irritated monkey and she
muttered beneath her breath. She fought with Ganesh
Peon, yelled at the *dhobhi* for putting so much starch in
my frocks that the cloth scratched Baby-missy's skin.
Her thin nose quivered with displeasure. She became
as huge as a cloud threatening to erupt into thunder,
and finally even Ma couldn't stand it any longer.

"What?" she demanded, glaring at Linda. "What's
wrong with you?"

"With me? I am as fine as this morning. Why should
anything be wrong with me?" said Linda. "Am *I* doing
anything I should not do? Nono."

"Then if everything is okay with you, stop giving me
those looks," snapped Ma, her fingers nervously braid-
ing her hair into a plait that flickered like dark light-
ning down her back when she walked.

When Dadda was at home, Ma wore all that hair in
a knot at the nape of her neck, secured by curly hair-
pins. Perhaps he had told her that it was undignified for
a memsahib to leave her hair flying about her face like
a wild woman. Dadda did that sometimes, made odd
comments that made Ma cry. If I found a pin lying on
the floor, let loose from the sliding brilliance of my

mother's hair, I kept it under my pillow, for it was almost like having Ma next to me, patting me to sleep as she used to when I was much, much younger.

❦

It was now four months since Ma had taken off on that absurd trip of hers, wandering around India like a gypsy with only a bed-roll, a flask of water and a small bag. She sent us post-cards after she had reached her destination, never letting us know where she was going next. She spent her journey telling stories to sweepers from Jhansi, fishwives from Sanghli, a min-ister from Guntoor who had just lost the elections.

"The man had a forest of hair growing out of his ears and nose," she remarked in one of her wretched cards. "And he didn't believe a word of what I was telling him about my life. I think he suspected that I had escaped from the Ranchi asylum."

I wished that I could write and inform Ma that the minis-ter was not alone in his suspicions. She was definitely crazy, an old woman like her who disappeared, leaving a trail of post-cards, not even decent letters, to mark her wanderings!

I called Roopa to discuss the situation. We talked to each other frequently now and compared postcards, for Ma did not always write the same things to both of us.

"What are we to do if there is an emergency?" I asked. "Suppose something happens to her? How will we know? And what if one of us has a problem? We can't even contact our own mother! Ridiculous!"

"Oh, leave her alone," said Roopa. Her voice sounded indulgent, almost as if I was one of her children. I think she

imagined that her marriage, her mortgaged home, even her motherhood gave her a certain status, a maturity that I had yet to gain. "Ma is probably having a wonderful time. And even if she was sitting at home and fell down the stairs or something, what could we do? It would take me at least three days to get there. I'd have to find somewhere to leave my children, can't afford to take the whole jing-bang lot with me."

Ma made her way from station to station, camping in waiting rooms, one of the hundreds of anonymous passengers waiting for a train. She travelled second class, sharing a compartment with six, sometimes even eight people, crammed shoulder to shoulder on the upper berths, the aisle, the floor.

"Whatfor is a railway pass if not to passage everywhere?" she demanded on a postcard with a picture of lurid pink lotus flowers. "All my life I went where your father wanted me to and now I follow my whims."

A long time ago, Dadda had pinned a map on my wall. It was to stop me crying every time he left on tour.

"This is where I will be," he had said, drawing a line of red ink on the map. Over the years, the map grew crimson with Dadda's routes, marking out stretches of land that he had helped to capture and tame, setting them firmly on maps and timetables, dots connected by iron and wood and sweat. Ma had the map now, and she was following the lines of faded ink.

Of all the rooms in the Ratnapura house, the guest bedroom was Ma's favourite. She said that she liked the view from the windows, and although I stood on a chair to see what she saw, there was nothing but the dirty old garage, the rain tree with the car parked under it some days, and Paul da Costa the car-magician leaning over the bonnet, or lying between the wheels with his big feet sticking out.

When Dadda left on line, Ma allowed me and Roopa to play in the room where she herself sat reading or sewing. At night we would all huddle under the yellow-and-black bedspread with its pattern of elephants, and Ma would tell us a story till we went to sleep. I did not mind this room during the day when sunlight streamed through the windows. At night, however, I was uneasy here, missing the familiarity of the lamp in my own bedroom, the rocking horse with its toothy grin and gay pink and gold tassels streaming down its arched neck, that Girdhari the carpenter had made. This guest room had too many doors and I hated it if they weren't firmly shut, the bathroom door especially, which led from the yellow warmth of the room into darkness. The toilet gurgled there suddenly even when nobody used it, creatures scurried in the dry drains, a translucent lizard clung to the wall above the mirror and went *tchuk-tchuk-tchuk*. Ma said that if the lizard made that noise when you were saying something, it meant that your words would come true. I tried it a few times.

"I will get a new dolly," I said once, although I never really cared for dolls the way Roopa did. Another time I said, "My Dadda will never go on line again." The lizard went *tchuk-tchuk-tchuk,* but neither of my statements came true.

Still, the bathroom door was less worrying than the one that opened to the cloying fragrance of the unused verandah. The floor there was deeply fissured, rangoon creeper and jasmine had conquered the cement pillars, and rolls of tattered *chik*-screens hung in arched apertures, disintegrating a little more every time monsoon winds smashed against the fragile bamboo. Sometimes the darkness lying like a pool of ink beyond this room seemed to speak.

I woke suddenly one night, my eyes trying to find Ma's body in the bed beside me, and felt cool, flower-filled breezes drifting through the verandah door, carrying the sound of voices. In the dim moon-radiance, I couldn't see Ma beside me, only Roopa's small shape, and my throat closed with panic. I pulled the sheet over my head and waited trembling for a *bhooth* to carry me away, out beyond the verandah where trees reared up like giants and the wild cry of night birds shattered the silence. After many hours, it seemed, in which I squeezed my eyes shut and clamped my legs together to stop the urgent pee from sliding out, the bed undulated slightly. Ma was there again, her smell filling my nostrils with crushed *darbha* grass and mango leaves washed by rain. Different from her morning smell. Was it really Ma?

In the morning, I asked her about the voices in the breeze and Ma laughed. "You were having a dream," she said, stroking my hair, her brilliant eyes mirroring my face.

"The dream took you away," I said, remembering the

crushed-grass smell, so different from the pale drift of lavender powder clouding Ma now.

Linda Ayah glanced up from the coconut that she was scraping and shook her head. "You be careful, Memsahib, careful-careful," she said, looking like an angry owl.

I had no idea what Linda Ayah meant. Was she telling Ma to be careful about the ghost? Why only Ma? There were times when I felt that every single person in the house was talking about something different. Hidden rivers of meaning flowed across the room, sliding beneath and above each other, intersecting to create a savage whirlpool. When we moved from Bhusaval to Ratnapura, our train had crossed a bridge, a huge iron skeleton hovering over a river still and molten in the afternoon sun. Beneath that stretched and shining calm lay dangerous eddies and crocodiles, said Dadda. He pressed a rupee coin in my hand. "Give that to the river. She will be pleased with you."

But in this house full of unexpected currents, I knew that a rupee coin was useless. I would have to move silently, carefully, make sure I did not wake the sleeping crocodiles. So I tiptoed around my room, unwilling to touch my stainless-steel cooking set, the Minoo doll that squeaked, anything that might make a noise. Through the verandah without my Hawaii sandals and into the kitchen, whisper to Ganesh Peon for biscuits from the green Dalda tin. Don't flush the pee-water in the toilet, don't spit too loud in the sink, don't open the black squeaky cupboard door. No noise, no noise, no noise.

"What is wrong with that child?" muttered Linda Ayah, irritated with my whispering, gliding, crazynon-senserubbish. "What she is trying to do, Jesu only knows!"

I went to school thinking of nothing but when I was going to be back. And when Linda Ayah brought me home I rushed straight to Ma, crawled into her lap and stayed there even when Ayah called me for a glass of Bournvita, frothy and sweet.

Ayah, who had been with me since the day I was born practically, was scary these days. She threw anxious glances at Ma when Dadda was in the house, as if she was also afraid that my mother would run away like she threatened. And when my father went away and Ma began to sing, Linda Ayah sat, malevolent as a toad, in the corner of the verandah.

"Why you are so pleased when Sahib leaves the house?" she demanded.

"Are you my servant or are you Lord Vishnu keeping an eye on me?" snapped Ma. "I can't be happy in my own home?"

Linda didn't dare to say anything more to Ma and instead took out her anxieties on me and Roopa, frightening us with stories of the ghosts and goblins that hovered about us. Over the years, the number of supernatural creatures grew and became more horrible and threatening. In every house we moved to, Linda Ayah pointed out solidified *bhooths* and monsters, frozen into innocent objects till midnight, when they came alive "to take care of naughty Baby-missies." The scrolled wooden banister supports in the echoing, whitewashed Bilaspur house were weird, hunchbacked imps. The grinding stone in the back verandah of the Bhusaval bungalow was a grey *shaitaan* with a hole in its stomach. A *daayin* with three rows of teeth and feet turned backwards lived up the ancient chimney in the Calcutta apartment. And in the corner of the verandah in Ratnapura, there inside the twisted bel tree, was the headless manwoman, and the bel fruit was its hundred breasts oozing sticky juice that coated small mouths with ooh painful boils.

Linda Ayah pointed into the dark recesses of the ceilings, where hook-nosed goblins swung in cobweb baskets, and threatened me: "Now you eat that egg *phata-phat*. No *wak-wak* and rubbish fuss. Otherwise you know what will come howling down to sit on your tummy tonight."

As we grew older, the size of the monsters grew as well. Now they had complicated stories attached to them. If I didn't behave myself at the club, the girl ghost with her feet twisted inward would walk into my room at night, for she was the ghost who disliked disobedient children. Make faces behind Linda's back and the wind *pretha* would twist my face forever into a grimace.

Roopa, with her closed-tin mind, had her own way of dealing with the spooks and haunts inhabiting every house we moved into. She believed unquestioningly in the monkey-god Hanuman, whose picture occupied a prominent place in Ma's prayer room. This god, with his puffy cheeks and pouting red mouth, was Roopa's talisman, her protection against Linda Ayah's *bhooths* and *rakshasas.* Roopa wrote "Hanuman" under her pillow with a finger and slept soundly while I lay awake, my imagination too large and multihued, too dense to be blown away with a single name scrawled beneath the pillow. Linda Ayah's creatures crept into my sleep and I would spring up, screaming wildly. There in the corner of my room where the moon shone straight into a mirror, lit up the red beadwork cushion on a chair, there sat a hag, her crimson eyes bleeding, her mouth, lined with rotting teeth, yawning wide.

"Yo-yo *Rama-deva,*" cursed Ma, stumbling out of bed, tripping over the faded cotton sari she wore at night. "What a nuisance girl. Who will marry her if she screeches in his face every night?"

She wrapped her arms tight around me and swayed to and fro, "Shoo-shoo-shoo-shoo." It wasn't good to wake a person from a dream, for the mind might remain in the dream and only the body would travel back to this world. So Ma just patted me on the back till I stopped quivering.

Ma was afraid that Aunty Meera's madness had infected me, nono, that one of those unfortunate lunatic genes in my father's family was waking up in my body like Linda Ayah's frozen spooks. These fears never extended to Roopa, normal, stubborn, whose personal demon was the colour of her skin, dark as a *jamoon* fruit. "You love Kamini more than me because she is prettier than I am," she would say to Ma, looking slyly out of the corner of her eye at me. She knew that Ma, in an effort to prove that she loved us both equally, would give Roopa an extra kiss, the bigger slice of cake, let her have the first choice of ribbon. Roopa would pick the colour I liked and then make a show of sweet generosity, giving it to me with a smile, so that Ma could pat her on the head and say, "See, Kami, what a good little sister you have! Make sure you take care of her."

I took Ma's instructions to heart, anything to win her approval, that warm smile. So when the boys teased Roopa, "*Kaali-kalooti,* black pepper, Coca-cola," I leapt at them, punching and biting, while Roopa went yelling for Linda Ayah.

"My Jesus-child!" yelled Linda, angry with us for dragging her away from a cosy gossip session with the other *ayahs* out in the club verandah. "What a tomboy. Come here you puppy, why you hitting all the childrens in the colony like a wild thing? You bad girl, wait you, a fish *bhooth* will breathe poison over your face at night!"

That night I dreamt of a fish with glittering, sharp scales scraping its way up to my cot, its dead eyes fixed on my helpless body. Then the dreaming screaming started, and Ma came running in. "*Shani!* Devil girl, why is she turning my hair grey like this? Is she possessed or what?"

The next morning she shouted at Linda, cursed Dadda and Aunty Vijaya. "Stuff this silly girl's brains with more idiotic stories! *Deva-deva,* there is no room left in her head for sense!"

But Linda Ayah still spun her spider webs, Dadda

crammed moreandmore stories in my head, and soon
it was summer, time for the Aunties to arrive, for Aunty
Vijaya to cover the heated months with trailing histories, rambling family sagas, all of which knotted and
looped messy as Meera Aunty's mad knitting, till I felt
that I did not exist except in somebody's story, completely fictional.

*A sunbeam shot straight through my living-room window, was
caught by the prismatic jewel hanging there and splintered into
dancing rainbows on the walls. I hoped that the rainbows
would stay till my neighbour brought her daughter over. Claire
stayed with me on Tuesdays while her mother was away at
work. She was a solemn child who perched delicately on the
edge of my sofa, nibbled at a cookie and listened to the stories with which I entertained her. Sometimes I spread out all
of Ma's brightly coloured postcards on the floor and we would
cook up wild adventures for the travelling mommy, as Claire
liked to call my mother. At other times, I would simply tell
her about my crazy Aunty Meera, Linda Ayah and Ganesh
Peon, the ghosts in the tamarind tree, or the cobra in our
Bhusaval garden.*

*Long, long ago, I would begin, there was an old witch named
Linda Ayah who had great big knuckles and four eyes. She
sat in the verandah of a house with bougainvillaea and morning-glory and jasmine and spun stories out of warm yellow
sunshine, honey-bee murmurs, the flash of a kingfisher's wing.
She reached out into thin air and drew out ghosts and imps;*

she clapped her hands and dancing girls and jugglers swirled and tumbled on the floor.

A little girl sat before her, open-mouthed, and demanded, "Is it true, is it real?"

"Everything is true, and everything is false. It is the story-teller and the listener who decide what-what is what," said Linda Ayah.

I wished that I could summon Linda Ayah up from the past and ask her, "Tell me, was Paul da Costa real or not? Tell me, if he was such a magician with cars, if he fixed them so they neverever broke, why did he come every Sunday for one whole year?"

Perhaps Linda Ayah would have asked, "Who is this Paul person you keep talking about? Why you thinking of useless mens all the time, hanh? I will tell your Ma wait and see."

Or she might have patted a warm spot beside her on the verandah and begun a new story, "Once upon a time, there was a poor fool who had no brains, only magic in his head. He fell in love with a queen as beautiful as a blue lotus blossom."

Butbut, Linda Ayah was only a shadow in a child's landscape. She was probably dead, or perhaps she had moved on to another Railway family. Did she tell her new Baby-missies that there were ghosts swinging from the rafters? Did she tell them about the clever goat-girl who stole fire from an evil sorcerer and flew away? And when the Baby-missy asked, "But Linda Ayah, how can a girl fly?" did she nod wisely and say, "That is the story way, my sugar child"?

In stories things could be made to happen. You could grow wings on heroes, or give the heroine a voice like a koyal bird,

and people never died. In real life, if you brayed like a donkey, no amount of honey could sweeten your throat; people
went away and returned only as memories. In real life, I refl-
ected, you warmed yourself on cold winter days in a foreign
land by pulling out a rag-bag collection of those memories. You
wondered which ones to keep and which to throw away, paused
over a fragment here, smiled at a scrap. You reached out to grasp
people you knew and came up with a handful of air, for they
were only chimeras, spun out of your own imagination. You
tried to pin down a picture, thought that you had it exactly
the way it smelled and looked so many years ago, and then
you noticed, out of the corner of your eye, a person who had
not been there before, a slight movement where there should
have been the stillness of empty canvas.

It was time to put away the crockery, hide the knives
and the forks, make sure the gardener and the maids
and the iron-man and the *peon* knew what to do,
because it was summertime again and the Aunties were
coming. We all liked Vijaya Aunty, but Meera was
straight from the lunatic asylum. Ma told her friends
that she had an attention problem and a hearing problem. That sounded better than to say that she was a nut-
case. The noise that Meera Aunty made was enough to
rouse dead souls from their blanket of ashes. She created a different noise every day that one, oh she was
clever at dreaming up new sounds each more irritating
than the last. Sometimes she burped continuously,

complicated belches whose sour odour poisoned the whole house and wouldn't disappear even when Ma opened out all the windows and lighted twenty sandalwood joss-sticks. At other times she clicked a pair of blunted knitting needles, trailed yards of yellow wool. She said she was knitting a blanket for Ma. Sometimes it was a shawl, a bedspread or a rug.

"To thank my sister-in-law for allowing me to visit my brother's house," she said in a precise, low voice that gave no hint of the screaming pitch it could reach. The wool wound between chair legs and tables, fluttered under doors, even lay like worms in the potted ferns lining the verandah.

"Knitonepurloneknitknitknitonepurl," murmured Aunty Meera non-stop for an entire day, a droning bee pausing only to slurp in the spit that filled her mouth. If the burps annoyed Ma, this knitting drove her into a frenzy. Meera was obviously imitating her, for Ma enjoyed knitting, her fingers busy twirling the wool around the needles as she supervised the servants or sat in the sunny verandah enjoying a gossip with Linda Ayah. What infuriated Ma was not knowing if Aunty was doing it deliberately or if it was part of her madness.

"Tell her to stop," she begged Dadda, the only person in the house who had any measure of control over Aunty Meera. I knew that Meera listened to Dadda not because she liked him better, but out of spite—to get Dadda's attention all for herself.

Once, Ma hid the wool and the knitting needles, and Meera walked out of the front gates in a petticoat and blouse, her plump, hairy belly, the colour of old flour, sagging over the waistband, right into Mrs. Goswami's bungalow, where she methodically shredded all her Persian Queen roses. Ma returned the knitting and locked herself in her room.

"Tell him," she said to Roopa and me through the door, "tell your father that I will not step out of this room till that crazy has left my house. He can leave with her for all I care."

She yelled orders to the servants through the door. "Ganesh," she called, "today we will have onion *dal* and rice. Tomato salad for Kamini baby, cucumber for Roopa and fried cauliflower for Sahib."

The Aunties were going to be with us till July, which meant that Ma would stay locked up for a whole month and Dadda would have to use the upstairs toilet and who would look after Roopa and me? Vijaya Aunty maybe, she was nice, at least when she stopped reading her magazines. In a way, despite the strain it put on the entire household, I was glad to have the Aunties around for the holidays. Everybody was so busy making sure that Aunty Meera was only knitting and not stabbing the cat, or trying to pinch Roopa to death, that there was no time for Linda Ayah to point out *bhooths* and monsters. There was no chance for Ma to disappear into the night when Dadda went away in his inspection saloon and no chance for them to quarrel when he got back. Instead, Ma stayed up all night listening for sounds from Meera's room, for who knew what that *shani* creature was up to? Even when Meera was quiet, the house resounded with people asking, "Where is that screw-loose?" "Is she cooking any fresh mischief, the *hucchi?*" "Don't leave her alone in the kitchen, she will burn the house down, then whattodo?"

Meera Aunty did not like children, especially not little girls who spied on her. If she saw me or Roopa staring at her she made a horrible gobbling sound as if she wanted to eat us up. One time, after she had spilled water all over my math notebook, I called her a bitch—I had heard the older girls at school call Sister Jesuina that. Meera Aunty rushed out of her chair. "You are a foul-tongued nuisance," she hissed, bringing her face close to mine. "I believe I'll have to wash your mouth clean."

She wrapped her thin, long fingers around my arm and dragged me to the lotus pond at the far end of the garden. Only a few months ago, the gardener had dropped a basket of kittens there and I'd been haunted by their drowning mewls for weeks. In my moral science class Sister Imelda had said that God was an angry person who punished people often. Now I was certain that God was sending me to the lotus pond to be drowned like the kittens for calling my aunt a bitch. I opened my mouth and screamed and Linda Ayah panted out of the house.

"Baap-re-baap!" she exclaimed, pulling me away from Meera Aunty. "What a house. One minute I turn my back and so much *gad-bad* happens!"

After wrecking Mrs. Goswami's roses, Aunty Meera turned her attention to Ma's garden. She pulled up all the tiger-lilies, plucked the guavas while they were still unripe and told me that the papayas were so sweet because she pissed under that tree every morning.

"Don't touch that," I whispered to Roopa, pointing to a bowl full of sliced papaya. "Meera Aunty did number-one in it."

Roopa thought that I wanted to eat it all myself and started crying when I held the bowl away. She was like that, cry-cry-cry.

"Don't tease your sister," yelled Ma.

"There is poison in the papaya," I said.

"Kamini!" Ma flashed her eyes at me. She was angry, and when her eyes went big and shiny and dangerous I knew that she was going to slap me.

I would catch Roopa later for getting me into trouble. What did I care if she ate Meera Aunty's pissy papayas? I was not going to touch them ever again.

In the Ratnapura house with the flagstaff on the saucer-shaped lawn, Aunty Meera sat in the front veran-dah in full view of the neighbours and sang the national anthem. Vijaya Aunty told me that Bankim Chandra Chatterjee made up the song when India achieved Independence.

"That was the year poor Meera lost her mind," explained Vijaya Aunty. "She was only sixteen then. The *Jana-gana-mana* was playing on the radio and she threw a plate at the neighbour's husband, stupid fellow always peeping into our windows to see us in petticoat-under-wear maybe."

I hadn't made up my mind if Meera Aunty was really

half in her head or only pretending. Or if she was possessed by a *rakshasi,* which was the story the servants
believed. Ma told me firmly that Meera was mad, mad,
mad.

"It runs in your father's family," she said. "Your father
hid it from us, though, he did not bother to let my Appa
know about this streak of lunacy. Do you think I would
have married him if I had known?"

"Rubbish!" Vijaya Aunty countered. "Your grandfather wanted to get rid of your Ma as quickly as
possible, that's all he cared about. We have never kept
our poor, unfortunate Meera a secret."

"Do you want to believe her or your mother?"
demanded Ma. I did not know if I was standing on my
head or what. Ma made up things sometimes, like when
boring Mrs. Khanna phoned and Ma told her that she
was going out and really couldn't talk just now.

"Oh, Mrs. Khanna," she would say in her sugar voice,
"I was thinking about you only yesterday. We must have
a long-long chat, but now I have to go out with my husband, he gets so annoyed if I am not ready. I will call
you tomorrow?" Then she would put down the phone
and say in her normal voice, "Boring old *bak-bak.*"

Ma was not always honest, but Dadda could not lie.
He did not know of hidden things buried in mere
words, so even the stories he came home with must be
true. In spite of his thick glasses with the stainless-steel
frames, Dadda could not see the invisible rivers rushing through the house, the chaos, the rage. Linda Ayah,
who wore glasses thicker than Dadda's, noticed every

minute thing, heard even an ant dropping to the ground from the rangoon-creeper flowers.

"Your father cannot see because he does not want to, and Memsahib is blinded by her anger," she explained. "It is true-but, that all of us can't see one thing or another. I, for instance, don't know whyfor I didn't spot that my husband was a loafer-insect first time I saw him, but that is my problem, whattodo?"

Aunty Vijaya, who was supposed to keep an eye on her sister, spent the visits lying in her bed reading *Woman's Era* and *Filmfare* magazines.

"See this rascal Rakesh Dutt, he leaves his poor wife and runs around with new actresses! No shame," she would comment, showing me pictures of the offending actor. I was only too happy to sit in the *chik*-shaded room smelling deliciously of wet *khus* mats dripping against the cooler, like the first monsoon rain on parched earth.

Here was quiet and sanity and, best of all, Aunty Vijaya's stories, not fairy stories but real-true ones. I insisted on knowing every tiny detail. Dates, names and places, smells and sights, each minute brush stroke that makes a picture whole. If my aunt started with, "Once upon a time," I immediately wanted to know, "When? Exactly when?" Vijaya told my sister and me about the tiny village on the Mangalore coast where her great-great-grandparents had lived, the old house in the centre of undulating green paddy, their ancestral home haunted by a benign female ghost, the cobra castle near a peepul tree behind the house, the temple priests, the *tong-tong* of bells as the cows wandered home in the hazy dusk.

Ma commented on the stories Aunty told us. "Stuffing your head with nonsense," she grumbled. "What a fine imagination she has! Cooking up a whole line of grandmothers and fathers, what a talent, ahaha!"

Hating my mother for destroying the carefully constructed details that recreated my father's world, I clung obstinately to their veracity. But Ma insisted that nothing in the world was a fact.

"The world itself is *maya,*" she said angrily. "What is there to believe? See that Meera out there in the verandah? Is she really crazy? Who knows? Not even those clever doctor *wallahs* with big-big books under their armpits. Oh yes, there was an Anjana Akka, Hari Ajja, a snake hole in their back yard. Every house has a snake hole, so what? And how can Vijaya describe Hari Ajja so precisely, did she ever see him? Was there such a thing as a photo so many years ago? Your Aunty is one big liar, that's all! And you, Kamini, should be doing reading-writing instead of listening to her nonsense."

"We belong to the Gokulnatha family," Aunty Vijaya told Roopa and me. "They were the best priests for miles around. One of our ancestors was even priest to the Maharaja of Mysore."

"Rubbish!" said Ma. "They are an unknown, beggaredly bunch of Brahmins. Priests to the Maharaja of Mysore indeed!"

Aunty Vijaya's stories had happy endings and plenty

of conversation—almost like watching a play or listening to the BBC. Even her accent was like the BBC announcer's. Ma said that pretending to be high class was one of Aunty Vijaya's talents.

"When Baba-ji got his letter from Mr. James Baldwin, Chief Engineer, B.N.R. Railway, Calcutta," said Vijaya when I asked, for the third summer in a row, the story of a grandfather I had never seen except in photographs, "his mother—my grandmother—made a huge pot of cashew *halwa*."

"But Vijaya Aunty," objected Roopa, "the last time you said that she made a pot of jackfruit *payasa*."

I was irritated with my sister for interrupting the story. How did it matter what sweet was made? The story was about how Grandfather left his village and became a big officer in the Railways. Roopa took everything so literally!

"I couldn't have said jackfruit *payasa*," said Vijaya Aunty with a smile. "My father hated jackfruit, said it smelled like rotting garbage. Now shall we continue with the story? Shankari Atthey's recipe was the best. She was my great-aunt, a wonderful cook, ask anybody from our village and they will have a recipe of hers in their kitchen even now. She insisted on two whole cups of pure, homemade *ghee*. Oil gave it a shop taste."

"They had never even smelled *ghee,* all they had in their begging bowls was *ganji-bhaath* and sometimes a piece of pickle," said Ma when I asked her about Great-Aunt Shankari. "That Vijaya has a ripe imagination! It is a pity she does not cook food as well as she does stories!"

"It was expensive for my grandmother, but now her son was in a job with the Birtish-sahibs, that had to be celebrated," continued Aunty Vijaya. "She fried the cashew, four heaped cups, in two tablespoons of *ghee* till delicately gold. Whole cashew cost a lot of money, the broken ones that shopkeeper Shetty sold in hundred-gram packets would do. Cashew was cashew after all, once it reached the mouth it got broken into tiny pieces. Two-three-four cups of sugar. Father liked things good and sweet. Maybe one more cup. Who knew what kind of food he would be getting at that Birtish railway place he was going to?"

At this point I always laughed and said, "Bir-tish?"

And Aunty Vijaya also smiled. "Yes, she didn't know how to say it right, she knew only a few words in English—'No,' 'Train,' 'Tomato.' But she made all her children attend the school that taught English, even though people in the village grumbled and said that it was not right for a priest's children to learn the foreign tongue and maybe foreign ways."

"Was it a big village, Aunty Vijaya?"

"Not very. There were enough families in it to give my grandfather a living. Those days people cared about going to the temple and listening to the priest narrating stories from the epics."

"Was it a nice village?"

"It was beautiful," said Aunty. "There were many coconut trees and acres of paddy. The sea was on one side and all night long the people of the village could hear the shush-shush of water licking the sands. In the morning the Muslim fishermen floated in their *katta-marans* on the waves and when the wind was good brought home boatloads of fish. Even they visited the temple, because the deity of the temple had been good to them. Everybody knew how powerful that god was."

When I told Ma that I wanted to visit this beautiful village of my ancestors, she laughed. "There is no village any more, you silly girl. Your aunt is telling you a tourist-magazine story. That village drowned years before she was even born. It is now a puddle of water."

I preferred to believe my aunt. It was nicer to imagine a green village with coconut trees as tall as the sky than a dried-up puddle that was once a village.

"When my father got a job in the Railways," said Aunty Vijaya, "my grandmother couldn't contain her pride. Now all the villagers could see how right she was in sending her son to an English school. The villagers knew that to be in the Railways was as good as being in the Delhi government offices. You were a part of the system, the Birtish system, and if you kept your head down and ears open, you could go a long way. What was the use of revolution-shevolution, fighting and killing? Wasn't it better to first learn the ways of the enemy and then kill them with their own knives? Oh yes, her son was clever, no doubt about it. After all, whose child was he, hanh?"

The only thing that disappointed me about Vijaya's stories was that there was no mention of Dadda. My aunt did not remember very much about her brother as a boy.

"He was much older than me," was virtually all she would say before veering back to her own father's exploits. "He never gave our parents any trouble, he was a good child, I believe."

I tried to make up my Dadda, build him from things he told me, or from the few things that remained from his childhood. I spent hours examining an oval cardboard box in which my father had saved pictures of cricket stars; they still smelled of talcum powder after forty-five years. And in a square Yardley Lavender Soap tin there were matchbox-sized pictures of Hollywood actresses with crimson cupid's bow lips, hair waved precisely into even corrugations, eyebrows like thin black rainbows. At the bottom of this pile of cards was a slip of paper with a childish drawing of a bird and a scribble, "My sister Viji is a duck," along with some sepia photographs. In one, a child, who must have been Dadda, wore a pair of baggy shorts, balanced on his left foot and squinted shyly up at the camera. With his left hand he clutched at the sari of a woman who was visible only from the waist down. To my disappointment, Dadda could not remember when the picture was taken or who the woman might have been. Behind them were lots of coconut trees, perhaps in his home village. But he never talked about the village or any of his relatives. Not even about his father, who had died years ago, before Dadda and Ma got married.

In all the photographs I had seen of him, Dadda's father looked like an English gentleman with a neat moustache, a solar hat, a jacket and a crisply pleated *dhothi*. There was another photograph in the box which must have been taken before my grandfather joined the Railways and came to Delhi, before he changed his name from Gokulnatha to Moorthy and turned from a priest's son into an employee of the British. In this picture there was a row of thin men in turbans—the fancy ones with gold borders. My grandfather was the tall, thin youth without a turban, right at the end of the line. He had a Brahmin's shaven head with a traditional *juttu* of uncut hair at the back. When he moved to Delhi, he shaved it off. Then, terrified that the gods would curse him for such a sacrilegious deed, he offered twenty rupees' worth of coconuts to the Krishna temple, and for five years after that, donated a pair of silver lamps as well. When his first son, my Dadda, was born, he stopped his offerings to the gods, convinced that he had been forgiven for the loss of his Brahmin *juttu*.

Aunty Vijaya did not remember if her father was married when the English-man picture was taken, or if Dadda, the oldest child, was born. All she had to say about the photograph was that Dadda exactly resembled their father.

"Same forehead, same eyes, can you see the similarity?" she asked, tracing a finger over the yellowing face in the photo. I couldn't see much of a resemblance. Of course, Dadda had a different haircut, and wore more modern clothes. He sat in the big red Burma-teak chair and smoked pipes. This was how I would always remember my father, I told Aunty Vijaya, and she remarked that memories were never the same.

"They are pictures we create in our hearts, you see," explained my aunt. "And each of us uses different sticks of chalk to colour them. I remember your father as a young man who came home for the holidays from college, and how much our mother waited for him to return and how she always said in a mournful voice, 'Oh Vishwa, you look so much like your father, and now all his burdens have moved to your shoulders.' We, the daughters, were burdens—only your father was worth loving."

Aunty Vijaya accepted everything that was handed out, expecting that her husband or her brother would take care of her always. In return, she gave Roopa and me her own memories, romantic and gently coloured, devoid of unpleasantness.

"I come from a line of Brahmins," I thought proudly, "poor in worldly goods but rich in knowledge."

I never told Ma or Roopa. They would laugh at me, I was certain of that. Especially Ma.

"For all their learning they were a pack of incompetents," Ma would say, "and unhealthy to boot. They were rotten inside—heart, lungs, liver, kidneys, even their blood was rotten."

Ma came from healthy stock. Her parents were still alive and her grandparents had died only a few years ago, Putti Ajji at a ripe eighty-seven and her husband at a hundred and two.

"We didn't spend our wealth smoking *bidis* and eating oily food in restaurants. Restaurants! What is wrong with home food, I ask you? Simple, no cutlet-mutlet and fried gobi every day."

Ma cursed all of Dadda's sahib ways. She told him that he should remember he was the ordinary son of an ordinary priest from a village in Udipi and not some pink *angrez* big shot.

"I *am* a big shot," snapped Dadda. "You wouldn't be living in this fine house with all these servants if I wasn't. Don't forget that."

❃

When I asked her if she remembered this incident or that, Roopa said, "Let the past sleep. Why should you poke here and there looking for memories? After you find them, and dust off all the cobwebs, you see that they are ugly and sad. I prefer living in today not in flashback, baba!"

Roopa did not allow stories to invade her life, turn the world into a kaleidoscope with believing and not believing, true and untrue. She was completely happy with her husband Vikram who adored her for her round, tight body and flat mind. He asked her questions, testing the flatness of that mind, delighted that it held none of the wild fears that filled his. She offered him a warm harbour, a lush cove where he could drop anchor and find refuge from the nightmares that haunted him of technology triggering a holocaust which des-troyed the planet and left us all floating in starlit space.

Roopa claimed not to remember the times that Ma had faded away from us. "She was always there, large as life and twice as noisy, too much noisy and nosy if you ask me! Why you are not studying, why you are doing this, why that? My goodness, like a mosquito in my head she was."

"Rubbish!" I said. "She left you alone, it was always me she concentrated on! You never remember things the way they were, just the way you want them to be."

"And you of course have a memory as precise as the part in your hair," laughed Roopa.

She thought that I was crazy to live in the past like this. "Come and stay with me for a while," she urged. "Come here before you go totally loony."

"Don't be silly, I am not going loony," I insisted. "It's just nostalgia really. Something to do when I am not working on stupid lab experiments."

"You are looking over your shoulder at ghosts, Kamini. Remember Linda Ayah's story about the fellow who did that?"

Yes, I did. He was dragged away into the nothing world of shadows. Linda Ayah had told us longlong ago that everybody had ghosts trailing behind. The problem started when you looked over your shoulder at them. Memories were like ghosts, shivery, uncertain, nothing guaranteed, totally not-for-sure.

And Ma's reply, "Why only memory? Nothing in the world is for certain."

⊰⧉⊱

I was sure that if I had hair so long that it swept the ground, nobody would notice the length of my nose, about which my aunts teased me every time we visited my grandmother's home. "Pinocchio," they said. "We know who's been telling stories." Or they would give it a sharp tweak and say, "Better grow to fit your nose, or we will have trouble finding a groom for you!"

I would loop my tresses up into intricate swirls with silver ornaments buried in the darkness—a swan with a long neck, a lotus, stars, moons and suns—like the ones adorning the hair of Princess Draupadi in the brightly coloured picture books Dadda brought from Delhi station. Ma said that my hair was too thin right now, but perhaps if she washed it often enough with *shikakai,* it would turn thick and luxuriant.

"You didn't get these strands of grass from my side of the family for sure," she said one Sunday, vigorously rubbing castor oil into my scalp. A friend had advised Ma that castor oil was better than coconut oil. And what was left over from applying to the hair could be drunk to cleanse out the bowels. "Dual-purpose oil, Mrs. Moorthy," she told my mother. "Inside and outside it will clean and shine."

I imagined my intestines glistening like polished silver after a dose of the thick, evil-smelling oil and told Ma that I would never-ever talk to her again if she made me drink it.

Ma laughed and said, "Now stop going baka-baka and sit there quietly till I finish getting your sister ready for a bath."

She pushed me towards the warm dry corner of the bathroom where Linda Ayah waited to massage my arms and calves.

"I don't want to be a Mr. India muscleman weight-lifter, Linda," I protested, squealing as she pulled and stretched my limbs.

"Ohho, missy," snorted Linda, "a woman needs all the

strength she can find to carry manymany weights in her life. If you don't have the strength to look after yourself, who will?"

I suffered Linda's hard hands till Ma was done oiling Roopa and both of us had to get into the ancient porcelain bath-tub which filled half the room, where Ma would wash our hair with the *shikakai* powder.

"I don't want a head bath!" yelled Roopa as Ma whipped her petticoat over her head and Linda Ayah stripped off my bloomers and we both stood naked and helpless, shimmering with oil.

Linda Ayah pulled her sari up between her thighs and tucked it into her waist at the back like a fishwife, her skinny legs smooth as mosquito net poles. Roopa and I had watched Linda on her free afternoons, sitting outside her quarters, pinching all the hair off her legs. She dipped her fingers into a bowl of cold ash, gripped the tiny hairs and ripped them out one by one.

"Oh-oh! Oh-oh!" we howled each time her fingers jerked, irritating her intensely.

"My skin is like a crocodile's, too ancient to feel anything," she said. "So whyfor you are screaming like a pair of hyenas, henh?" Then she wagged her finger warningly and said that Roopa and I were not to try it on ourselves. "All that is not for baby-dew skin. Later, when you are older and troubles have given you thick hides, then you can pinch it back to life!"

Much better, Ayah said, to use a paste of *besan* and sandal and milk, helping Ma to apply the fragrant, faintly abrasive mixture on our arms and legs, our backs and stomachs. Then came the *shikakai* for our hair, a dreadful green fire that singed our eyes and nostrils, making us scream and curse Ma. Even if I squeezed my eyes tight as Bournvita tin lids, the sour burning pierced my eyeballs, my ears, filled my mouth with its bitter taste.

"No need for shampoo-tampoo," said Ma, working the *shikakai* into a lather while Linda Ayah, damp and spattered, poured mug after mug of steaming water.

"Ma, I am burning!" I wailed, thrashing and sliding in the oily tub.

Ma slapped my buttock. "Stop that, you silly girl, you'll slip and break your head. Don't you want nice thick hair?"

"Nonono!" I howled, and Roopa, her eyesmouthnose pursed tight against the onslaught of *shikakai,* skidded blindly against me, trying to escape while I had Ma's attention.

"If you behave like a monster, your hair will fall off," threatened Ma, her relentless hand shooting out to grab Roopa, and whoosh, Linda Ayah emptied a bucket of blessed water on my head, wrapped a towel around me, and before I knew it I was out of the bathroom, the *shikakai* fading into a memory.

And as Linda Ayah towelled me dry, ran a gentle comb through the wild snarls and knots, she murmured, "Nothing in this life comes easily, child, you want long hair, you have to weep a little for it."

The *shikakai* did not work, nor did the carrot juice which I thought was how piss must taste, and neither did castor oil, almond extract or olive oil. My hair never grew beyond my shoulders. Ma would not let me grow it any longer because she said it looked like a rat's tail. So when Basheer the barber arrived to cut my father's hair, he was ordered to trim mine and Roopa's as well.

Basheer arrived every third Sunday at seven o'clock in the morning. On those days, the back yard of our house was the scene of great activity. A chair was placed in the shade of the rain tree, a sheet draped over the back and a mug of water on the ground beside it. Basheer bustled in, right on time, trim in a spotless white *choori-dar* and fitted Nehru jacket. My father was first. Basheer snapped open the sheet, draped it across Dadda's shoulders with a flourish. Then, with a flick of the wrists, he anointed Dadda's head with water, tilting it forward just so, and started to trim. Clickety-click went the scissors, and over it, the barber's voice speaking a rich blend of Hindi and Urdu. Basheer told us stories of the princely family who had once ruled Ratnapura.

The conversation usually started with Dadda asking, "So Basheer, how are you these days?"

The barber nodded his head slowly and said, "Getting along. But times have changed since Nawab Sahib, changed a lot."

"Nawab Sahib?" prompted Dadda, setting off Basheer.

"Such a life! We were lucky to have lived such a life," sighed Basheer. "We were only servants, but my grand-mother served *kheer* in silver bowls! Nothing like the bowls of gold decorated with Japani pearls used in the Nawab's kitchens, oh nono! Although there *were* some people in the Nawab's court who lived better than his highness. Lots of crookedness went on! More often than not, the poor Nawab did not know what was happening behind the silk curtains of his own bedroom!"

Basheer transported us into a world of riches and romance, of dark eyes peeping through slatted bamboo screens and vast *durbar* halls adorned with chandeliers, of dancing girls pirouetting in swirling skirts and sly intrigues within palace walls. His grandfather was the royal barber, which explained his own intimacy with the happenings in the Mor Mahal. One Sunday he told me the tale of Begum Haseena, the youngest of the Nawab's harem.

"She was more beautiful than a thousand jewels," said Basheer, tilting my head so that he could trim a little bit of hair on the side of my face.

"How do you know?" I asked.

"*Arrey* Baby-missy, it wasn't just I who knew, the whole world had heard about the *begum* whose face shone like the moon. Now don't move your head this way and that, I will cut off too much hair and then you will have a boy-cut," said Basheer.

"Oh, can you do boy-cuts?" If I couldn't have really long hair, I would keep it as short as my father's. "Can you cut my hair really short, hanh? Hanh?"

"*Baap-re-baap* this child chatters more than a pack of monkeys!" exclaimed Basheer. "Baby-missy, if I cut your hair short, your mother will chop off my head."

I giggled, and didn't tell Basheer that Ma probably wouldn't even notice if he shaved me bald. Since we'd moved to Ratnapura she seemed to have stopped caring about anything. She often lay in her room with a headache and Linda Ayah was ordered to make sure that we did not get into any mischief. On some days, she dressed up in a starched cotton sari and called for a taxi to take her out on an unknown errand. I hated these outings and always made a fuss.

"Now you be a good girl," Ma would say, gently pulling away from my clinging arms.

"Where are you going? Take me with you." I didn't want to be left alone in this great big house with only Roopa and Linda Ayah for company.

Now, sitting in the shade of the rain tree, I said imperiously to Basheer, "Cut my hair short-short. Ma won't say a thing."

"But Baby-missy, don't you want to look as beautiful as Begum Haseena?" asked Basheer.

Instantly, all thought of looking like a boy flew from my head. "What happened to her, Basheer?"

"The other queens were so jealous that they kept trying to hurt her. Oh! I cannot even describe the awful things those jealous queens tried."

"Then what happened?"

"So the Nawab had a maze built into the palace and the queens lived in separate apartments within the maze. This way they never met each other, the five begums, each with the temperament of a tigress, and the Nawab could visit his beloved Haseena without creating a typhoon of envy in the *zenana*."

Basheer sank into a little silence, his scissors stilled, his hand resting on the top of my head. I jiggled impatiently in the chair. "Then what happened, Basheer? Why have you gone to sleep?"

"*Arrey,* what a child! Can't an old man stop a moment to swallow some spit?" After a minute or two he continued, "Everybody knew that Begum Haseena was a milkman's daughter and the Nawab had met her in a little village outside the city. Rumour had it that she had been chasing a butterfly when the Nawab came upon her and ever since he had called her his *thithali.* But so possessive of her was he that she was allowed none of the finery the other queens had."

"Not even a pair of earrings? And bangles, what about bangles?"

"Nothing, not even a pretty dress," said Basheer, his scissors clicking away, creating a fine black dust of hair that danced in the sunlight before drifting down. "The Nawab Sahib was afraid that the evil eye might touch her, you see. He also insisted on her wearing heavy black robes, even in the privacy of her apartment, so that nobody would see her beauty but him. Poor butterfly, she languished in the labyrinth, yearning for the bright fields of her childhood, the gay mirrored skirts of a milkmaid, for the colour and light denied her. Then one day she disappeared. No one knew how she escaped the maze. Perhaps she turned into a butterfly and flitted out of the window."

"Where did she go?"

"Ah Baby-missy, if I knew I would tell you, but I

don't. It is believed that she still roams the streets of this city disguised as an ordinary person. She wears a veil, I have heard."

"But she must be very old, so nobody will be able to recognize her anyway."

"No, no, such beauty never grows old, she is still young and glorious as a star, the poor Thithali Rani," corrected Basheer.

I wanted desperately to believe in the charmed world he had conjured up, so different from mine of cold silences, angry voices in my parents' room and Dadda's long absences. And yet, I had to risk being disappointed, to ask, "Basheer, this story isn't true, is it?"

"Baby-missy," replied the barber solemnly, "it is as true as the hairs on my head!"

Here, in this quiet part of the town, where life moved slow as garden snails, Basheer's stories added colour to a boring summer. Roopa was a silly baby who didn't know how to play anything, Ma's strangeness frightened me, and I was tired of Linda Ayah's vigilance. It was like having a scrawny shadow dogging my footsteps. Sometimes I managed to give the old spectacle-face the slip. The corner in the dining room between the sideboard and the curving wall was my favourite hiding place. At that point, the windows that swept around half the room began their journey, and Ma, obsessed with privacy in this shameless house with its gaping apertures, had covered them with heavy green curtains. I was a ruffle in the drape, safely concealed from Linda Ayah's sharp gaze.

"Kamini baby!" she called, irritated. "I will tell your Ma, teasing Ayah all the time. Naughty, *badmaash* girl!"

I peeped out and glimpsed Linda shuffling into the verandah, Roopa slung over her hip, mumbling and cursing. Ayah was angry mostly because she wanted to be out in the back verandah with the other servants, slapping *khaini* and gossiping about the sahib in Bungalow Five. How much he drank, no control at all! His wife, it was rumoured, was so fed up that she was leaving for her mother's house. Especially after the party at the club, the day before yesterday, where the sahib had behaved like a perfect fool.

"Arrey!" remarked Ganesh Peon, leaning forward. "He went up to the General Manager memsahib—you know how she dresses!"

The servants nodded eagerly. GM memsahib was notorious for her low-cut blouses so tight that they might have been painted on to her skin. For parties she wore sleeveless *cholis* which allowed everybody else glimpses of her naked, grey underarms.

"Well," continued Ganesh, "the drunk sahib went up to her—she was sitting in a corner—and you know how she sits!"

Again the servants nodded. The GM memsahib crossed her legs when she sat, her sari gaping to reveal plump, well-shaped calves. Other memsahibs adjusted the folds of their saris so that only their feet were visible, but the GM mem had no such modesty.

"She was sitting with her sari up to her knees and the Number Five Bungalow sahib grabbed her ankle and said, 'What a fine chicken!' And then the madman bit her leg!"

"Hai-Ram!" The servants sent up a collective gasp. I giggled at the thought of a plump leg being bitten, and immediately Linda Ayah turned to catch me. I ran into the house, knowing that Linda would follow, grumbling about missing the many interesting details that could be carved out of the main story, chewed over and commented upon.

Later in the day, I played with Shabnam, who was allowed out only after three o'clock, when the sun hovered low in the sky.

"My mother says I will become dark and nobody will marry me," she explained primly.

"Then I'll come to your house and we can play inside," I suggested, eager to watch Mrs. Bano drifting about the house enveloped in her *burkha*. All that could be seen of her face were her eyes through a little panel in the veil, and her hands, tipped with bright nail-polish, emerging from the long sleeves.

"I think she is the Butterfly Begum," I told Ma, who lay in her darkened bedroom, a damp towel covering her face. She had a headache and had not left the house today. I was pleased, and instead of going out to play, I sat near the window, filling in a colouring book. I didn't say a word, even when Roopa broke one of my crayons. She had her own crayons but insisted on playing with mine, and if I made a fuss, Ma said that I was not behaving like an older sister. I didn't ask to be anybody's older sister, I wanted to say, but Ma might slap me if I did.

"Ma, do you think she is the Butterfly Queen?" I asked again.

"Oh Baby, what are you talking about?" murmured Ma fretfully. "Don't bother me now."

"The wife who ran away," I continued impatiently. I had told Ma the story a million times.

"Whose wife? Baby, don't chatter so much, you know Ma is unwell." Faint irritation tinged her voice. I knew she was beginning to get into a bad mood and I slipped out of the room.

Ma spent lots of time in bed, seemingly paralysed by the copper shimmer of the sun. Sometimes she said it was the heat that bothered her. At other times, she could not bear the constant roar of traffic outside the colony walls. And if there was nothing else the matter, Ma said that she could not stand the smell of Dadda's tobacco or the sight of his dirty shoes in the verandah. When Ma had her headache coming on, Roopa and I had to be as quiet as mice. She did not like the sound of chalk on the slate, or the whisper of our slippered feet.

I knew almost everything about my mother, even that she sometimes fibbed to Dadda about what she did all morning. But when I told her that I heard her fibbing, she pulled me on her lap and said, "My darling Baby knows everything about Ma, hanh? But it's our secret, okay? Yours and mine? And if you are a good girl and keep the secret, what do you think you will get from me?"

"A box of crayons?"

Sometimes Ma gave me only a box of Veera Sweet Mint, and at others I could persuade her to get me dolls and books. There were times, though, when Ma got mad with me and slapped me instead.

"What cheek!" she would exclaim, her slaps brisk and sharp, stinging my thighs.

I would wait for Dadda to come home, and cry, "Ma beat me, I didn't do anything, only asked her not to go out, and she beat me."

It always worked. Dadda scolded Ma, his face cold with anger, "Your place is in this house, not out there in the streets doing social work and gossip while my daughters run around like gypsy beggars."

I collected these small instances and bided my time. It all depended on how annoyed I was with Ma. Sometimes, it didn't even matter how many toys Ma got for me. I disliked being left at home with Linda Ayah. She made me eat up all the carrots and peas that I picked out of the food and arranged on the side of the plate, insisting that if I didn't eat them, the vegetable *bhooth* would sit on my stomach when I went to sleep. Or she would force me to take a nap along with Roopa so that she could watch both of us without chasing about the house.

Once when Dadda came home from a trip to Chittaranjan, he asked Ma what she had done all week and she shrugged and said, "I wasn't well, I slept most of the time."

I hated my mother for leaving me with Linda, and for not getting me the paint-box she had promised, so I told Dadda, "Ma is fibbing, she went out in a taxi."

For a few days after, Dadda came home at five in the evening only to have a quick shower before driving away to the club, where he stayed till late at night. Sometimes I woke to the sound of his keys in the front door and the low angry murmur of Ma's voice. Sometimes I thought that the angry voice was Dadda's, but in my half-sleep I was never sure. Then I felt sorry for having tale-tattled to Dadda. I wished that I was more like Roopa who kept her mouth buttoned up tight, never breathing a word people did not want to hear. I envied my sister's willingness to listen to everybody and then swallow all that she had heard. It made her seem such a *good* girl. Even Linda Ayah, with her glasses that saw right into a person's heart, could find no fault with Roopa. "Why can't you learn a few things from that sister of yours? Half your size and twice as smart, that child," she sighed.

On Saturdays, Ma took both of us for a trip to Simon's Market to buy provisions and other necessaries for the house. It was also the day she bought us a toy or a trinket. She got a little gift for herself as well, telling us with a naughty twinkle in her eyes, "Don't tell your Dadda, he will make a face and scold me. He will say don't waste money."

Once she bought herself a pair of long silver earrings with *meena*-work in blue and magenta and said that she would give them to me on my wedding day. Another time it was eight toe-rings decorated with tiny flowers, fish and peacocks. I never saw her wear any of these ornaments and often wondered why she even bought them.

Ma and Roopa and I had so many secrets, I was becoming afraid to talk to my father in case a secret slipped out, although at one time I had loved cuddling up on his lap and telling him about school and my friends, and listening to his railway stories.

"In Aunlajori, where we had to stay for the night," said Dadda, "the stationmaster warned us that the Railway rest-house was haunted. An English mem had died there, waiting for her husband who had gone boating up the Ganga. In the middle of the night, she started to play the piano."

"Then what, Dadda, then what?"

"Is this man any better than that stupid Linda?" demanded Ma, who only seemed to hear Dadda when she disagreed with his words. "Scaring the child with ghost stories!"

Simon's Market consisted of one main road with several narrow alleys branching out haphazardly. Cows blocked the traffic for hours, and dogs scavenged and fought in the piles of garbage outside restaurants. The pavements were occupied by vendors selling everything from American visas to fountain pens that stopped working as soon as you took them home. We walked in the middle of the road with cars and scooters, bicycles and trucks inching their way before and behind us, honking futilely. Shopkeepers sat like greasy maharajas on elevated platforms inside windowless stores and measured out rice and sugar, *dal* and spices. We always bought our provisions from Theli Ram's store, a dank, lightless hole of a place with several assistants dashing about in the gloom like rats. Ma found Theli Ram himself disgusting, for he had a habit of scratching vigorously at his sweaty armpit while he repeated her grocery list to the scuttering assistants, but he also had the best groceries in town. Sometimes when we arrived he would be finishing off food from a tiffin-carrier which looked like it had not been washed in years. When he saw us, he swiftly wiped the yellow oil from his fingers on to his fleshy calves and beamed a welcome. He snapped his fingers at his assistants, the movement making his loose, pouchy breasts quiver, his belly jiggle up and down, and yelled, "Railway Memsahib's order, *phata-phat!*" He always reminded me of the wooden dolls you could get at Waltair station—squat, round things that you tapped on the head to set off a chain of dancing motions.

Behind the grocer's lane ran Sabzi-wali Gully which had nothing but vegetables—glistening purple aubergines, polished tomatoes, plump gourds, piles of tender beans that snapped crisply when Ma tested them for freshness.

"Come on, sister," called the vendors. "Fresh-fresh, straight from the fields, and for you, a special early-morning rate. *Bauni* rate!"

If Ma did not buy, their tone would change, they would sulk and mutter, "Squeeze all our vegetables to death. They are for buying, not for touching only! She wants us to give it to her for free!"

Another lane was thick with the stink of ripened
fruit. Here flies and sticky black mango insects buzzed
and hung like a miasma over the baskets and pyramids
of fruit. If you did not watch your step, you could slip
on banana slime or step into a pile of rotting papaya.
My mother bought oranges here, carefully picking out
the ones with big-pored peels because they would be
the juiciest. She usually wanted the ones at the bottom
of the pyramid and the vendor would glare at her, reluctantly dismantling the tower of fruit.

I hated the fruit-and-vegetable lanes but dared not
grumble because then Ma, already puffing and irritated
by the dust and noise, might refuse to take us to Gad-
hbadh-Jhaala. This tiny street was an Aladdin's cave of
glittering jewellery, shiny ribbons, beads and baubles.

"Ma, pleaseplease, I want this and this and this," I
begged, gathering up handfuls of stringed beads, tinkling bangles. I darted in and out among the clusters of
burkha-clad women who filled the market, drifting like
shoals of dark fish, haggling with the shopkeepers. I
could see nothing of them but brightly slippered feet
flashing in and out of their heavy robes, ringed hands
and the gleam of eyes. They moved slowly through the
sunny lane, squatting before baskets heaped with
Anarkali necklaces, Hyderabad earrings, Sholapuri
bangles, nose-pins and hair-clips, their fingers sifting
through the shimmering piles. I stood as close to these
hidden women as possible, trying hard to get a glimpse
of their faces, ignoring the pungent smell of sweat oozing through coats of talcum powder which filled my

nostrils. Once I watched a tall woman in sequinned slippers drape a necklace over the black cloth of her *burkha* and turn coquettishly this way and that before a tiny mirror on the wall of the shop. She must have seen herself without the confining robes, and I too wondered how the ornament would look against her skin. Ma never understood this odd fascination.

"They look like anyone else, those women," she said, dragging Roopa and me from stall to stall, urging me to decide on a trinket or ribbon quickly and we might have time for an ice cream before we went home.

That summer, after Basheer told me the story of the Thithali Queen, I lost interest in the Saturday trips to the market. I liked to think that Shabnam's mother, Mrs. Bano, was the mysterious queen, and I spent my entire day following her, watched avidly as she climbed into her car, noting, when the robes lifted a bit, the colourful frill of a petticoat or the drift of a sari edge. I wanted to see Mrs. Bano's face. Behind her veil, was she frowning, smiling, crying? I hung about their house till I heard Linda Ayah's voice calling, "Baby-missy, *arrey*, where has the monkey disappeared? Baby-missy, aren't you going to eat anything today?"

Shabnam and I tussled constantly about where we should play each morning because she preferred my house to her own.

"I don't want to play in my house," said Shabnam. "My mother will make us sit inside and draw pictures." She made a face and whispered, "She said that she would beat me if she caught me in the sun."

It was strange watching Shabnam in her own home, for over there she was sedate and soft-voiced, playing with her collection of plump, pallid dolls and pinching her sisters into silence if they cried for one of her toys. In my house she became quite reckless, climbing right up to the top of the tamarind tree, careless of tears in her billowing bloomers, while I, amazed at her daring, yelled from below, "Shame-shame puppy-shame, naked bottoms is your name!"

"Why does your mother wear *purdah?*" I asked Shabnam.

She shrugged and said, "I don't know, maybe because my father told her to."

"But why only her, why not you?"

"Ammi says that I will get my *purdah* when I become a big girl."

"Have you seen your mother's face?"

"Of course I have," said Shabnam.

"Is she pretty?"

"She is the most beautiful person in the whole world."

When I told my mother about this conversation, Ma got thoroughly annoyed. "Why you poke your nose here and there?" she asked. "Haven't I taught you any manners? Mrs. Bano, Mrs. Bano! Nonsense!"

I did not tell her about Mrs. Bano again. It never occurred to me that if I just asked Mrs. Bano to show her face, she would very likely have done so. Or perhaps I wanted the thrill of not knowing, of never being quite sure who Mrs. Bano was. The magic of Basheer's story sustained me through those sun-charged summer days. So long as I had the story, I could ignore the tight lines of anger and frustration building within our own house. In Shabnam's home I could forget Ma's puffy face, her rages swirling up like a cyclonic storm. There was space for stories to blossom, for my imagination to wander. In my friend's home I would ask to go to the toilet and on this pretext snoop around, peering into silent rooms, hoping to see Mrs. Bano. If anyone asked me what I was doing, I could put on an innocent face and say, "I was looking for the bathroom."

Nobody ever caught me, and once I even went so far as to examine the contents of Mrs. Bano's dressing table. The top was absolutely bare except for a set of combs and a small pot of kohl. The drawers had piles of handkerchiefs and two bottles of attar that belonged to Mr. Bano, who always smelled like a bouquet of flowers. The large cupboard yielded more. In it, row upon row, hung brilliantly hued saris and *salwar-kameez* sets, each with its matching petticoat, blouse or *dupatta*. I was exhilarated, almost as if I had gotten to know Mrs. Bano a little more intimately. From that moment my imagination built on those exotic clothes. Mrs. Bano was as beautiful as her daughter claimed. She must be very rich, too, to have so many glorious clothes. Ma had only four silk saris which she wore on special occasions. Mrs. Bano was a magical queen who threw off her drab *purdah* at midnight and twirled about the house like a Kathak dancer, her arms weaving delicately, her feet tapping out the drummer's beat, her gauze skirts floating about her body like mist.

"Ma, do you think she knows Kathak dancing?" I asked.

"Who are you talking about, crazy child?" asked Ma. "Have you been poking around in Shabnam's house again? What *is* the matter with you? Do you want a couple of slaps, hanh?"

I decided that Mrs. Bano's consort was not her perfumed husband but a mysterious figure who hovered on the periphery of imagination. All my fantasies turned poor Mr. Bano into a villain who kept his wife prisoner, forcing her to wear black instead of her shimmering silks. Anything she said acquired a special significance. If she admired a frock I was wearing it was because she was filled with a heavy longing to get out of her *burkha*. When she asked me what my favourite colour was, it was because she yearned for the bright satins she was not allowed to wear.

Then, out of the blue, my myth was shattered. Mrs. Bano was expecting a baby. She was no different from Ma, who had ballooned for months before giving birth to Roopa. I heard drifts of conversation that lent different overtones to Mrs. Bano's shrouded life.

"She seems desperate, three girls in a row, and now another child on the way," said Linda Ayah to the washerwoman.

"*She* is not desperate," said the washerwoman with a loud sniff, banging the clothes on the stone platform a bit harder. "It's her *miyan*. He wants a son."

"Son, son, son," grumbled Linda, spitting a stream of betel juice straight into a bed of spinach.

"I'll tell Ma that you are spitting in our plants," I said, wagging a finger at her.

Linda ignored me and continued, "All these men are the same. If I didn't have my Matthew the first time itself, you think that drunken bastard I married would have left me alone?"

"May all the men in this world go to *jahannum*," said the washerwoman cheerfully. "But you know, Bano Memsahib is too old for another child. I might be illiterate yet even I know that."

"And she has a bilad-pressure problem," added Linda nodding her head and sending out another stream of red juice, at the tomatoes this time.

"Linda, I will most definitely tell Ma," I said loudly.

"Yes, yes, tell her, let's see what will happen," laughed Linda.

Although Shabnam was my best friend on Sundays and in the evenings, at school I preferred Devaki. We sat next to each other and whispered through Sister Julia's history class. If I broke my pencil lead, Devaki sharpened it for me, and I did the same for her. But at three in the afternoon, from the minute the home-bell rang, we went our different ways. I could never invite Devaki to my birthday parties and she would not invite me to hers because her father worked in the workshop and mine was an officer. Roopa and I played with the workshop people's children at school, but the friendship stopped at the doors. Worse than playing with workshop children, however, was playing with the snot-nosed brats from the servants' quarters.

"How many times have I told you not to go near those dirty children?" Ma had said, towering over me, her hand tight around my wrist as if she was going to snap it in two. "You will catch some dirtyfilthy disease and then who has to run around for doctors and medicines and all? Me, who else?"

When I did get a violent attack of chicken-pox, Ma applied cool *neem* paste over my inflamed, itching body, muttering all the time, "Go-go, play with every slum child you can find, what did I tell you? Never listen to me, just like your father. And where is he when a child is sick in the house? In some jungle building lines for the nation. Thinks he is Gandhi, Nehru, Kamaraj, a hero for the nation! Hunh! Sell his own home to save the country, that kind your father is."

"My Dadda is nice," I protested, my nose tingling with the crushed *neem*-juice smell.

"Yesyes, all he does is tell fantastic stories when he comes back. Are stories enough to bring up a child?" asked Ma, her voice as bitter as the *neem* paste that turned my skin so green and cool so that when I drifted to sleep it was as if I had been buried in a pile of rain-soaked leaves. I dreamed then of Dadda going away, always-always, of Ma staring out the window at the Anglo-Indian Paul da Costa who hunched over Dadda's car and hummed songs from Engelbert Humperdinck, Cliff Richards, sometimes Saigal's mournful Hindi numbers, and Linda Ayah telling Ma half angrily, as if she were a mischievous child, "Watch out Memsahib, watch out!"

Devaki knew lots of secrets. She said that she had seen her father kissing her mother.

"I have seen my father holding my Mummy's hands," said Rani Bose with-the-big-fat-nose.

"How does she cook food then?" If I made fun of Rani, I could sneak out of saying that my parents did not hold hands or kiss.

"If you kiss a man, you have a baby."

One day I had seen Paul da Costa catch Ma's hand when she paid him for repairing the car. He called my mother "Tamarind Mem" behind her back and laughed with Ganesh Peon and the iron-man about it. Then he grabbed Ma's hand. He was as wicked as the demon Ravana who dragged Queen Sita into the sky. The next time he bent over the bonnet of our car, I would throw a stone at him.

"No, you have a baby if you kiss *and* hold hands."

"My mother said that God gives you babies," said Rani.

"Stupid, you believed her?"

"You stupider stupid!" Rani pushed Devaki.

"Stupidest!"

"Your father is a servant!" sang Rani.

"And you are a *vir-gin*," I said. Nobody was allowed to make fun of my best friend.

"She lives where the Anglos live," shouted Rani. It was true that Devaki lived in the Type Three Quarters at the other end of the colony.

"So what? Does that make her an Anglo?" I shouted back.

"If you touch an Anglo you become an *acchooth!*" said Rani with absolute certainty. Rani's mother had told her that the Anglos were half-and-half people who hated Indians. She also said that Anglo women were spiders who waited to trap decent Hindu boys into marriage. They were shameless things, showing their legs in their little frocks. They might as well walk around naked and save money on clothes!

"And if an Anglo talks to you, you turn into a half-breed too," continued Rani.

"You are a *vir-gin* liar!" I said. Ma had touched Paul's hand but she was still the same, wasn't she? Wasn't she?

Mrs. Bano ripened within the dark heat of her *burkha*. Even the searing summer sun couldn't persuade her to remove those horrible garments. She moved ponderously about the house, one hand resting against the small of her back. Finally one afternoon there was unusual activity in their home. The *peons* ran in and out of the house carrying bags and baskets, piling them into the car. Mrs. Bano emerged followed by her husband and daughters. She ruffled the children's hair, kissed them and climbed into the car. She was, according to Linda Ayah, going to her mother's house, for her time was nearing. Shabnam told me that in a while she would have a baby brother.

"How do you know it will be a baby brother?" I asked jealously. Not only did she have two sisters to my one, now she was going to have a brother as well.

"Because my father said so," replied Shabnam in a voice full of confidence, "and he is always right."

"How do you know your mother will do what your father wants?"

"She always does," said Shabnam. There was something about the way she said things that prevented all argument.

Just before school reopened for the new term, her mother came back with a new baby in her arms. Once again the gleaming black car had a flutter of servants around, unloading the luggage, hampers of food, baby-bags full of diapers.

"*Arrey,* Jhunjhun," said Mrs. Bano to her *ayah,* "get some red chilies, we have to make sure that the evil eye does not touch our son."

The *ayah* beamed happily, snapped her knuckles against her forehead, waved her hands over the baby and said, "Oh-oh-oh, may two hundred blessings hover over you, little monkey, little parrot."

I stared at Mrs. Bano. In the confusion, she had forgotten to lower the veil over her face. My soul was flooded with disappointment. As long as the veil was in place, I had allowed myself to ignore the fact of Mrs. Bano's pregnancy, to believe that behind that veil was a beautiful Butterfly Queen. Shabnam's mother was a plain woman, her face pale and sharp with exhaustion. Her nose was too long, her eyes too small. Why, my own Ma was much better looking than her. I cried that night, my face buried in Ma's lap.

"Basheer Barber is a liar," I sobbed. "He said that the Thithali Queen was beautiful."

Ma stroked my hair, unable to understand why I was so upset. "Why do you have to think all stories are true? Stories are a waste of time, I have told you, no?"

When Ma was a girl, her mother told her that stories were dreams, and that dreams were a waste of time. Girls had no time for such useless activities.

"Especially," continued Ma, "when the pressure cooker is doing *chhuss,* the baby is crying, and there is so much to do. Only crazy people and men have the energy to dream!"

Once upon a time I had lived in a world where things were guaranteed. When Dadda was transferred from one town to another, I knew that there would be a house waiting for us. The house would most certainly have a garden run by a wrinkled gnome of a *maali*. We would always have Linda Ayah and Ganesh Peon with us and there would be a Railway Club with a library full of crumbling books—volumes of *Punch* cartoons bound in faded maroon cloth with gold lettering, ancient Penguin paperbacks, Cherry The Nurse romances and children's treasuries filled with virtuous tales about well-behaved children named Deirdre and Tabitha, Roger and William. When the books were opened, you found pages carved into strange shapes by white ants and silver-fish, and the powdery residue wafted into your nostrils and made you sneeze.

The librarian, tired of bloody officer brats, would say

in a waspish voice, "Get out, get out! What you are spitting and sneezing into my books for? Spreading germs
everywhere, no manners!"

It seemed to me that each Railway librarian was a
carbon copy of the previous one: tyrannical, clinging
grimly to his thin thread of authority as guardian of the
books, watching bitterly as that authority was eroded
by generation after generation of wretched railway children. The Railway hired its employees for life, and the
librarian, his good humour soured by the boredom of
the job, aged along with the books, hardly discernible
against the brown teak of the shelves, the ancient chair
with its sweat-stained leather seat, the creaky table with
the marks of manymany years stamped, scratched,
etched and rubbed into it.

In Ratnapura Junction, the librarian was Gulbachan.
My friends and I teased him as he sat stiff-necked and
annoyed in his high-backed chair. We strutted around
his table, pinched his umbrella from the back of the
chair where he hung it every day and giggled as he
searched frantically for it, cursing at us under his breath.
We annoyed him with our high-pitched chatter, our
useless entreaties to sign out more than five books.

"Oh Gul-ji," we chirped, delighted to see the way his
fingers danced and drummed agitatedly on the table, a
sure sign that we were getting on his nerves. "Ple-ease,
we'll tell our papas what a nice man you have been
today!"

We batted our eyelids at him like the older girls at
whom he smiled and simpered foolishly, but he only

yelled at us, waving his umbrella like a sword. "Getout! Getout! No books you will get, no favouritism I say. I give same treatment to each and all. Now getout, *bad-maash!*"

Ma sent Roopa and me to the Railway Club every evening with Linda Ayah. I didn't mind going, because Linda was so busy following my sister around and gossiping with the other *ayahs* that she left me alone for long stretches of time with a stern warning not to wander out onto the road. All around the Ratnapura Club was a low hedge of bleeding-heart cactus. There was no wall, not even a gate at the entrance. Whatfor you needed a wall when everybody, from Basheer the barber to Rampyari the sweeper-woman, knew that entry was restricted to the officer sahibs and their mems? A long driveway led up to the generous portico where three cars could park side by side. By unspoken order, the space under the portico roof was reserved for the General Manager, the Chief Mechanical Engineer and the Chief Civil Engineer. Lesser personages, such as the officers who lived on Fourth and Fifth Avenue, parked beside the tin-roofed badminton court or beneath the tamarind trees shading the tennis courts.

It was all extremely pleasant, out on the lawns in summer or in the cosy lounge when the weather was bad, being served *pakoras, samosas, tikkas* and tea by the bearers. The club reaffirmed the identity of the officers. They could relax here, be among peers, talk politics, while their wives, in pale chiffon or crackling organdy saris, exchanged news about children and servants.

"My son Rahul, such a naughty boy you know. His teacher says he finishes his sums in five minutes and then disturbs other children. What to do with such a *badmaash?*" one of the ladies would say with an indulgent smile.

And another would remark, "Can somebody please-please recommend a good servant-girl? I am having such problems with my present one. She wants one full month off with pay, can you imagine! What cheeky fellows these servants are becoming."

The officers discussed foreign powers who, they claimed, were creating all the chaos in India.

"Mark my words," one of the officers would say, "there's going to be a war in a few months if things go on the way they are! The foreign hand is at work again." The foreign hand was responsible for mysterious groups of terrorists from neighbouring countries who were on the prowl, raising the price of rice and wheat, driving people to drink and suicide.

At the club, the officers could call the shop-floor workers "idiot" or "silly bugger" without fear of a union fight on their hands. They could talk about that famous affair in Dhanbad in '69 or '71, when an officer nearly got himself killed. The Eastern Railways had a militant union, rough bastards who went with the territory.

The Works Manager had said to one of the fitters, or perhaps a turner, "*Abey saala,* are you going to finish this work in your next life or what?" Sometimes even officers were brainless twits, whattodo? Perhaps this one was drunk—the Dhanbad posting drove even a sanyasi to drink, with all that bloody black coal-dust everywhere.

"Who are you calling a *saala?*" growled the turner-fitter-fellow, showing red eyes at the Works Manager.

"Yes, you mother-*chooth,* who you insulting, eh?" yelled another worker.

At that point the officer should have apologized, "Sorry brother, the coal dust has affected my head," or "My wife's mother is driving me crazy," any old lie would have done. Instead, the fool said, "What-what rascal, get back to work. How dare you?" and other nitwit stuff like that. So the union jumped in, there was an almighty chaos, the officer was surrounded by hordes of ruffians, wasn't allowed to drink water, eat anything, not even go to the toilet. If he so much as moved a finger they threw cow dung and eggs at him.

I had heard versions of this story a hundred-thousand times. It was repeated to every new officer and wife and child in the club, part of the folklore passed from memory to memory, sacred as the epic *Mahabharata.*

At exactly four o'clock, the club doors were opened by Tony Braganza or his father Mathew. A flight of steps swept up from the portico into a wide corridor with polished wooden floors and walls decorated with detailed India-ink drawings of tiger hunts. There had been talk of replacing these dull prints with paintings by the General Manager's younger daughter, who was believed to be artistic.

"Hunh!" remarked Ma scornfully. She always had a remark about this or that. "The child won a prize in baby-class for painting, so her mother thinks that she has a Ravi Verma or Amrita Sher-Gill on her hands! Well, if they decide to hang that girl's paintings, then I want them to hang up my Kamini's crayon pictures, too!"

The corridor swelled out into a vast hall with a bar where, sometimes, Mathew's granddaughter Leona leaned over the counter. She helped out periodically when she was home after running away from her husband, who followed a few weeks later, apologizing abjectly, giving her vast clumsy bunches of ixora flowers that he had picked from somebody's garden. Another corridor curved around from that end, pocked with doors leading into the tiny library, the washrooms and the billiards room. There, above the rack for the cues, hung the skin of a large tiger. The inscription on a tarnished brass plate next to the lower right paw said: "For my fellow officers. In memory of the Shaitaan. John Winslow. August 8, 1935."

Winslow was the Chief Mechanical Engineer at the time, and the town was renamed for him when he shot the man-eating tiger. After Independence in 1947, however, there was another change of name, from Winslow Nagar to Ratnapura Junction.

"Confusion only!" said Ma. "Why you need to change names all the time? Does it make the rivers in this country stop flooding? Does it feed all those poor-thing beggars-veggars out there? Hanh?"

Except for old Mathew, the Anglo-Indian bearer, nobody remembered the story behind the tiger skin.

When Mathew was drunk, he told it to anybody who cared to listen. Since he was in charge of the bar he was often drunk and the story was repeated in varying versions.

"That was a great sahib," mumbled Mathew, weaving into the storeroom behind the bar for orders of Fanta or Coca-cola, beer or whisky. "You know, man, his daddy was a lord or something back in England. This Winslow sahib, he shot this great big monster tiger. That dirty dog of an animal, he was killing and eating all the peoples, man!"

Nobody bothered to listen to the entire story, since the British were irrelevant from the moment India got her independence.

Rani Bose, who seemed to know everything, said that the teenagers came to the billiards room because they wanted to kiss and hold hands. "I've seen them touching each other on their *chee-chee* parts," she giggled. They would all have babies as a result, she said, and we did not believe her until one of the girls who went often to the billiards room became pregnant. Rani said that she had peered into the billiards room more than once and seen the big boys doing bad things with their pants down.

"Those aren't boys," I argued, "they're demons, my *ayah* told me." I rarely went near the billiards room.

"By Jesu-Christo's bleeding heart, Kamini baby," Linda Ayah had informed me with terrifying solemnity, "I swear, if you go in that room, you will never come out again. You will go mad because the demon that lives under the table there will eat your brain, I tell you, listentome!"

Rani laughed. "You stupid! There aren't any demons. The boys go there to dream about that Leona Wood with her big boobies." Rani bunched her fists against her chest and swayed up and down, pretending to be Leona in her transparent black shirt through which you could see her cream-coloured breasts like two melons.

"I don't believe you," said Shabnam. "God will punish you for making up such stories."

"Come with me to the billiards room," said Rani. "Then you will see whether there are any ghosts there or not."

"Linda Ayah will tell my mother," I said nervously.

"She isn't here right now, too busy gossiping. Come on."

"You are a liar," insisted Shabnam, but she trailed along with us. I knew that she disliked Rani as much as I did and was just as scared to go near the billiards room, but like me, her curiosity was greater than her fear. We had almost reached the room when we heard quick footsteps behind us.

"Linda Ayah," I whispered, hurrying into the toilet instead.

"It's not your *ayah,*" said Rani, dragging me out again. "It's Rajiv Goswami, and he's going to the billiards room. What did I tell you? Come on, let's see what he's doing there."

The teenager had a magazine clutched against the front of his trousers and we giggled at the way he was walking.

"Like he wants to pee," suggested Shabnam, sending Rani and me into whoops of suppressed laughter.

"Let's scare him," I said, feeling very bold all of a sudden. "Let's rush in there and scream, that'll be funny."

But before we could do anything, Rajiv Goswami came running out of the billiards room, looking for all the world as though he had met one of Ayah's ghosts.

"There is something in there," he gasped, not really seeing us. He looked around wildly.

Gulbachan the librarian poked his head out to see what all the fuss was about. "What and all is going on here?" he asked sternly.

"There's somebody in the billiards room. Come and see, quick."

Gulbachan sighed, "I know, I know, there is a ghost who moans and groans. Come on, sir, you think I am a fool or what?" He winked at the boy. "Lots of oonh-aanh going on there, eh?"

"No, not that, you moron," said the boy, regaining some of his confidence now that there was an adult around, even if it was only the nitwit librarian. "Come here and see for yourself. I don't want to go in there alone."

Gulbachan emerged from the library and glared at us. "You *badmaash* girls, don't go into the library till I am back. I will know if any books are missing." He trailed after Rajiv. *"Arrey baba,"* he said nervously, "don't get me into any trouble. I promise I will keep that new book for you. Harold Robbins or something, and so much naughty stuff, oh my god, you will love it. Whatall these foreigners do! I will reserve that book for you, eh?"

"Shut up, idiot," said the Civil Engineer's son, shoving Gulbachan into the billiards room. "Switch on the bloody lights."

The lights flared dimly, concentrated over the tables.

"Ooeé ma! What a stink!" exclaimed Gulbachan. I pinched my nose between my fingers, imitating him.

"What is it?" whispered Rani.

"I don't want to see," said Shabnam, holding her hands over her eyes and peering through the gaps between her fingers.

"There's somebody hanging from the ceiling," I remarked, looking curiously at the limp legs. In the dim light, I thought that the collapsed face seemed oddly familiar.

"Hey Ram, hey Ram," moaned the librarian, backing out of the room nervously. "Who is it? One of the sahib boys or what?"

"What do we do now?" demanded Rajiv.

"How do I know? Do I see dead people every day? Phone General Manager sahib maybe?" He glanced impatiently at us, huddled near the door. "And you brats, stay out of there or I will tell your mummies."

"I'll get my father," decided the boy, looking once more at the body. "You stay here and see that nobody else goes in, I'll be back in a few minutes."

Gulbachan shooed us out into the corridor and smiled weakly. "Just like Hindi movie, no?"

"You are scared," said Rani, staring at the fidgeting librarian. "Because you know that person in there." She nudged me.

"You're going to be in trouble," I said. Gulbachan was the easiest person in the world to provoke.

"Yes, and you also left the library door wide open. All the books will be stolen, you are in double-trouble," giggled Shabnam. She had lost her fear by now and was dying to peep into the billiards room again to see the hanging body.

"Rubbish! The victim is unbeknown to myself," said Gulbachan, leaning down and pushing his face close to Shabnam's. "And I will tell your daddy that you have two rupees in fines, *then* we will see who is in trouble!" There were footsteps approaching and he straightened quickly. The boy was back with a whole horde of people, the GM in the lead like an agitated Pied Piper.

"Good evening, Sir!" said the librarian. "I regret that I had to leave my post in the library for four-five minutes. But I assure you my one eye was fixed on that door so that no mischief-maker could enter in my absence. I was engaged in work when this young gentleman begged me to accompany him to the billiards room. I don't know anything else, sir, god-promise."

The crowd surged forward, sweeping Gulbachan and his explanations aside.

"Switch on more lights," said someone.

A voice in the crowd said, "Who *is* the fellow?"

I waited for a reply and when none was forthcoming, said in my best poetry elocution voice, "That is Paul the car mechanic."

I might have added a few more details about how

Mrs. Simoes had told Ma that he was an arrogant bastard, but I could hear Linda Ayah's voice somewhere in the back of the crowd saying in a stern voice, "Kamini baby, come back here now-now!"

I had managed to give her the slip for a glorious half hour but here she was again, the tail of a woman, glass-eyed witch. Perhaps if I refused to reply Linda would think that I wasn't here and go away. I wanted to see what they did with the car mechanic's body. How were they going to bring it down? Would they have to call the ambulance? Perhaps they would cover it with one of the tablecloths that Mathew the bearer brought out on special occasions. And flowers—they needed flowers didn't they? I wanted to know everything.

"Baby, did you hear me?" called Linda again, her voice loud, with an edge of anxiety. I could hide somewhere. But then Linda would go and tell Ma and I would surely get into trouble, for Ma was stretched as tight as a clothes-line these days.

I heard her asking somebody, "You saw that Kamini child, in a green frock?" I didn't move, staring up at stinky old Paul da Costa.

Linda pushed through the pressing, murmuring crowd, spotted me and grabbed my arm. "What you doing in here, naughty? Some dead person, not good for a little girl's eyes! The spirit from the fellow might still be flying about in the dark billiards room looking for a warm body to occupy. Serves you right then!"

"I want to stay," I grumbled, fed up with Linda's constant hovering.

"Wait, I will tell your Ma. You don't listen to Linda Ayah, not one word. Wretched child, staring at a dead what-not person, *chhee!*" Linda's voice sharpened, and she pulled me along behind her, glaring at anybody who objected to our rough passage out of the room. "Your Ma will say, 'no more club, no more anything.' Then Madame Kamini baby will have to sit at home with Linda Ayah and play Ludo."

I made a face behind Linda's back but kept quiet. I didn't like playing with Linda, she won every game.

"Now open your ears and listen. Don't you tell your Ma about this dead person," continued Linda, marching through the club, nodding briskly at other *ayahs* dragging their charges home, their footsteps echoing off the worn wooden floors. Soon we were out on the gravel path, a dull, red line across wet grass. "What will she think when she hears what you saw, hanh? She will get angry, very angry. So you keep quiet and let Linda tell her everything nicely. Kamini baby will brush her teeth and go to sleep like a good girl."

I did not listen, concentrating instead on the elusive cry of a koyal bird darting from tree to tree, its voice exquisitely sweet as it hung in the warm night air. Linda Ayah said that the koyal was actually the lost voice of a princess, not a bird that could be seen by human eyes.

"Ayah, lots of people have seen the bird," I argued. "My teacher said it is a tiny, black creature, very timid."

"Ah, she said that to make you think she is clever. Just like the story of the emperor who wore no clothes and thought he did."

"Which emperor?"

"Another time, if you are good, I will tell you that story," said Linda.

Linda and her tales, I thought, keeping an eye open for the koyal. I was nine years old, almost ten, and she thought that I was still a silly baby who believed in Santa Claus and *jadoo-mantar!* True, some of her demon tales frightened me, I did not want to test if they were real or not. That did not mean I believed every single thing she ever said. But I was not going to let her know that. It was one way to dodge the old *kannadi*-face—so tiresome having her around every minute.

The billiards room suicide provided the Railway colony with a fresh source of gossip that lasted for weeks. The identity of the body did not interest most people. It was the gruesome idea of a death, an actual death, in the club of all places, that moved them. And the indignation that a mere workshop mechanic, an Anglo too, had broken the rules of membership to hang himself in the Officers' Club!

Ma had learned the unspoken rules of the Railway colony very quickly, for she had Linda Ayah and Ganesh Peon guiding her from the day she came to this life as Dadda's bride. Ma knew, for instance that although the Inspector of Works was much lower than an officer, he wielded greater power, for he was in charge of maintenance. All the electricians, plumbers, gardeners and masons were at his command. So Ma never forgot to send Diwali sweets to his house. She might have a leaky faucet or a problem with the wiring and the IOW would send his men immediately. Ma hadn't known how to make cutlets, or what to do with whisky and sherry and all that stuff in bottles, when she married Dadda. As a Railway wife, she was supposed to know, for instance, that you couldn't serve whisky with dinner and wine was never, never to be poured into a pretty glass jug and kept in the fridge. These things Ganesh Peon taught her on those long days when Dadda was out on line and he was sitting in the back yard polishing Dadda's office shoes. He had a definite order of polishing. First he would carefully wipe away all traces of dirt from the shoes with a soft rag blackened with weeks of polish.

"This is a necessary step," he told me and Roopa as we squatted close to him, watching with fascination the old hands flick deftly across the shoe. "Lots of *peons* I know miss this step and that is very, very bad for the shoe. VERY BAD. When you do something you must do it *pukka*-perfect. Otherwise what is the use, tell me? It is like plucking only half the feathers of a chicken before cooking it. You can put as much of the finest *masala* on it, but all you will hear are curses."

After wiping one shoe clean, it was time to apply dots of black polish from a tin of Cherryblossom. "Now which little girl wants to help an old man open this tin?" he would ask, glancing from one face to another.

We bounced up and down, still on our haunches, screaming, "Memememe!"

Then Peon pulled a ten-paise coin from his *kurta* pocket and tossed it in the air. "The face is for big baby

and the number for *chhoti* baby," he yelled before snapping the coin in his palms as it dropped down. Somehow he managed it so that if I opened the tin one day,
Roopa had a turn the next.

There was a special trick to opening a Cherryblossom
tin. A tiny arrow on the lid pointed down to a slight
depression. We had to press our thumbs really hard in
that shallow curve and the tin snapped open magically.

Ganesh Peon beamed with pleasure when that happened and said, "Escallent baby, escallent!" Since he was
the person I learned the word from, I could not say
"excellent" for the longest time.

❄

*I dreamed of snow climbing higher and higher against the
house, muffling the entrance to my underground dwelling. I
dreamed that there was an awful blizzard bringing down the
electric lines so that I could not even phone for help. I was
buried alive in my burrow dying slowly from the cold.*

*And into this lonely, freezing dream came Ma. "So much
drama-shama is necessary or what? If you sit on your hands
and do nothing what else will happen to you, you silly girl?"
Her voice was reassuringly strident. "Have you even tried
opening that front door, or are you simply waiting for your
imagination to kill you? Go and see if there really is snow
there or if you are dreaming only!"*

*I jerked out of uneasy sleep gasping and sweaty, relieved
that, even from thousands of miles away, my mother could
reach out and pull me away from the nebulous terrors of a*

nightmare. The rustle of paper being thrust through the slot in my front door woke me completely. From my bed, I could see the entire apartment, the tiny kitchen-cum-living-cum-dining-room, the short flight of steps leading to the front door, the scattered mail. And almost as if my dream had summoned it up, another of Ma's weekly postcards, bringing with it the warmth, the smells, the sounds of another country oceans away from Canada.

"On the train to Lucknow," wrote my mother, "I met a magician. He insisted on showing the rest of us in the compartment all his tricks. He said that the success of his tricks lay in the movement of our eyes. But we must have moved our eyes wrong or something, for the poor man made a mess of it all. Finally he gathered up his cards and flung them out of the window. Then he turned to us and said, 'Everything in this country is poor quality, whattodo?' And for the rest of the trip, he refused to speak to anybody. Such a strange person. I could not sleep all night worrying about what he might do to us, his audience who failed him. I am sure that he thought that it was all our fault!"

Except to give Ganesh Peon instructions for the day's meals, Ma refused to speak a word for a longlong time after Paul da Costa died. It was as if a terrible-horrible silence had settled over her like a shroud. I wished that I had obeyed Linda Ayah and shut up about the mechanic. But I could not stop the words from tumbling out, I could not keep quiet.

"Ma!" I screamed. "I was the one who recognized

the mechanic even though he was all funny colours! His tongue was hanging out like the goddess Kali's!" I imitated the dead man's swollen face, mimed a limp body and swayed grotesquely. "He smelled like a rat."

Linda tried to shush me. "Memsahib, you don't listen to this stupid child. I'll first take her for a bath and then tell you everything."

I missed Ma's voice, her snippy comments, and tried to coax her back to her normal state. I pinched Roopa and made her cry. Surely Ma would flare up and tell me to behave like a nine-year-old? I got zero in my math classwork, spelled stupid baby words like "there" and "here" wrong, and still Ma did not break her silence.

"Ma, tell me about Mrs. Ghosh and the painter," I begged. "You know, when the painter took a week to paint her fence and you asked him if he was done and he said, 'Yes, Ghosh Memsahib made me paint her whole house and now all that is left to paint is Ghosh Memsahib's face!' Do you remember that?"

Under normal circumstances, Ma would have had a caustic comment to add about Mrs. Ghosh and her misuse of Railway services, but now she only smiled. It was a strange state my mother was in, her body cutting through regular space, her eyes wide open, her hands directing Ganesh or knitting swiftly, purl-one-knit-one, her mind playing in another place. When she did speak, the strangest things popped out of her mouth.

"How foolish, how foolish," she remarked once as she sat in the verandah shaded from the heavy summer sun.

She stopped abruptly, her face distracted, and I waited for the end of her sentence. But Ma had already moved to a new one. "Such a waste! As if life is a handful of berries that you can nibble at and throw away if you don't like the taste." She clicked her tongue and sighed.

Why didn't Dadda do anything? He went away on line as usual, and I, angry with his indifference, refused to listen to the stories he brought back for me.

"Come child," he beckoned, his voice creaking like the floor of the Railway Club. "Do you know those tiny white ants that can be crushed to death by a falling leaf?" He was trying to distract me, but I didn't care.

"Dadda, what is wrong with Ma?" I interrupted, and Dadda's story died unheard.

Even Linda Ayah, normally so crotchety, sat close to Ma's feet in the verandah, stroked her hand and said, "*Bitiya,* my daughter, what has happened, what has happened? You want me to leave a prayer for you with Jesu-Mary? Tell only, and I will do in two minutes. Ten candles I will light."

When Ma finally crawled out of her abyss, she had become shiny sharp and more angry than ever. She ranted on about every little thing—the fact that Dadda was at home only about half the year, that his sisters still came every summer, following us around the country like a sickness, and of course his smoking. Roopa and I could hear her in their room, crying and scolding.

"Why you married and had children if you didn't care what happened to us?" she sobbed.

Dadda did not reply and I knew he was stretched out in his chair reading the newspaper.

"You think you are a bloody English sahib, posing and posturing with that wretched pipe. At least those stupids got their money's worth out of this country before they burnt their lungs out. But you, all you can think of is your own pleasure."

"What nonsense you are talking!" said Dadda finally. "The British left the country twenty-three years ago."

"They might have left the country but they took everything with them, including your brains, that's what!"

Dadda told her to shut up and that was that. But her anger grew secretly, a fire that simmered beneath the surface all the time, like an animal crouched ready to spring. She changed her tactics. Instead of scolding and nagging, she became absolutely quiet. She never asked Dadda how his trips had been, whether the food in the line-box was enough, if it had been cold or warm, raining or sunny. Dadda would touch her arm and say, "Today, will you tell Ganesh to make *aloo-parathas?*" And Ma, shaking off the touch, would march into the kitchen. Not a word would she utter, not even to agree-disagree, and Dadda retreated from her unspoken hostility into his armchair, cold and remote. They skirted around each other, never talking unless it was about Dadda's next line tour.

"I am leaving on the thirteenth," he would tell Ma in a formal voice. "Don't forget to pack a few sweaters, it might be cold."

Or, "The Palits are coming over this Sunday for dinner. And the new Personnel Officer, Janaki Ram. Tell Ganesh not to make any meat, they are vegetarian."

And Ma would reply, "Yes, I'll take care of it."

She would stop talking for days, sometimes weeks, and finally Dadda would have to apologize. For what? He had no idea. Her silence was a wall.

One day she gathered Dadda's tobacco pouches, tins and packets and threw them in the rubbish dump. "You want to waste money? Here, I will help you," she said vengefully. She was becoming a demoness, I decided, watching my mother's face collapse into a harsh, bad-tempered mask. Dadda, desperate for the soothing tobacco taste, hid packets under our mattresses, behind pots, in vases. He got Ganesh Peon to buy cigarettes from the stall just outside the colony and gave Roopa and me two rupees each to keep our mouths shut. When Ma found out she was so angry she refused to allow any cooking in the house.

"Go home and sleep," she ordered Ganesh. "Don't show your face here for a week."

"Are you mad?" demanded Dadda. "At least think of the children."

"Why should I? Are they mine alone? Does anybody think about me?"

Ma finally relented when Roopa vomited all over her bed following three days of *chholey* and *tandoori parathas* from Chowhan's Café. Roopa was the only one who knew how to get around Ma.

Dadda stopped buying tobacco, sucking at an empty pipe instead, and Ma's eyes glittered triumph.

The summer after Paul da Costa's death was also the last summer that the Aunties visited us, although Ma had nothing to do with this decision. After all these years of trying, Vijaya Aunty was expecting a baby. She would not have the time to accompany her sister to our home any more, and of course Meera could not travel alone. Her doctor had written to say that she was seriously ill. India had gone to war against Pakistan, and the sound of sirens shattering the air had affected her mind.

"What does that doctor dolt mean, 'affected her mind'?" demanded Ma. "Was it ever okay, hanh? All doctors are like that, knownothings."

Yet for all her ranting against Meera Aunty, I knew that Ma felt twinges of pity for her. Or perhaps it was guilt. She didn't say anything when Dadda sent money for her hospital bills, small parcels of Diwali sweets, a new sari for the Yugadhi festival. Ma was like that, she said one thing and meant something else. It was her way of warding off evil, I think. She used to say that no good ever came out of telling the whole truth, that there were harmful creatures listening behind every door, bad winds lurking among the trees waiting to twist everything good and beautiful into hideous deformities.

And Linda, like Ma, evaded the truth. If a friend called to compare notes before an exam, Ayah rushed to pick up the phone. "Halloo," she would say, "Kamini baby? No, she is not here."

"Linda Ayah, who was it?" I would ask.

"Some girl from your school. Cunning creature, purposely disturbing, trying to find out how much you have studied!"

"Why did you lie to her, Linda? She knows I am at home. Where would I go at ten in the night?"

"For you naughty babies," Linda declared with a martyred look, "for you only, your Ma and I are sending ourselves to Hell telling lies and all."

Ma never told me and Roopa that we were clever or pretty, since such a blatant admission would surely summon up the worst of imps and goblins. No matter how often I brought home medals for coming first in history, geography, biology, Ma neverever praised me.

"Why only one prize this time?" she asked instead. "Who got the medal for geometry? For Hindi? For English? That Reena Bukhshi, I am sure. Such a clever, hard-working angel that one is! She must have made her mother swell with pride!"

Ma scolded and pushed and criticized all the time, and yet when I came home with prizes, she arranged them in the polished glass display case that Girdhari the carpenter made. Girdhari had sat in the side verandah of the house for one month, measuring and cutting, sawing and planing. The wood dust lay in fine drifts all over the house and drove the maid-servant mad with frustration, for no matter how many times she swept and swabbed, the sawdust piled up. The showcase had five shelves and I was expected to fill them all. I started to feel that each of the subjects I studied was a demon to be vanquished. At night, I woke struggling and breathless from trying to push off the heavy *bhooth* who sat on my face, crawled into my nostrils, my ear-holes, the slit between my eyelids, smothering me so that I would not be able to finish the task Ma had set me. Fill those shelves, fill those shelves. Ma dusted the shelves herself, polishing each cup and medal, pulling the pink and yellow and orange tags forward so that visitors could see that I had won all these honours since Upper KG, nono baby-class itself! She also made *cobri-mitthai* whenever I brought home a new prize, for she knew it was my favourite sweet.

"Borrow some brains from your older sister and perhaps we can make a cupboard for you as well," she said acidly, stabbing a flat hand in Roopa's direction.

In order to deflect the evil eye from both of us, she spoke in a code language of mentioning and not mentioning that would deceive the most envious of spirits. But I wished that Ma would praise me at least once. I craved a pat on my back, a "*Shabaash,* what a clever child!" Other people were dazzled by the array of glittering trophies in the showcase and remarked, "What a brilliant daughter you have, Mrs. Moorthy, an Einstein positively, she will be a nation's pride one day!"

But Ma would frown, smile, frown in rapid succession and protest, "Ohnono, you should see how well others in her class are doing. She is only mediocre. How many times I have to tell her, work hard or you will end up an *ayah* or *jamedarni*. But does she listen?"

Ma insisted that nobody ever listened to her, only Linda Ayah.

Ma was ambitious for Roopa and me. "You have to be one step ahead of the rest of the world," she declared, "better than the best. Don't let anybody be ahead of you."

When I came second in grade one, Ma wept with frustration. Then she met the teacher and got a copy of the syllabus for the whole year. As soon as I came home, Ma gave me a glass of cold milk—good for the bones; a handful of almonds—good for the brains; and a banana—vitamins A and C. She sat with me at the dining table, teaching me to read from the books the teacher was planning to use towards the end of the year.

"Two steps ahead," she said with satisfaction when we were done.

By then we were already tackling math problems that were on the school syllabus for grade three. I longed for Sundays when Ma let me go free. All the way through baby-school, high school and pre-university, my mother pushed and scolded, her words stinging, buzzing about my head like a crazed bee.

"Why did Neetha Kamath get higher marks than you in math?"

"Why didn't you get the heroine's role in the school play?"

She embarrassed me by appearing at school to discuss my weak points with Sister Jesuina, or Sister Marie-Thérèse, or Sister Clementine.

"This silly girl," she would say, patting my head, smiling falsely, her eyes watching the nun's face, waiting for her to say, "No, Mrs. Moorthy, your daughter is doing fine." Ma was never satisfied with a mere "doing fine." She expected the sisters to tell her that I was brilliant, that I was a sure candidate for a rank in the All India School Board exams.

I studied desperately into the night, prayed that everything I had learnt would remain in my head when I confronted the exam paper. I collected bundles of *darbha* grass to place before the tiny figure of the god Ganesha in Ma's prayer room, for he was the remover of obstacles. When Ma asked, irritated, who was bringing rubbish into the room, I kept quiet, afraid to let my mother into my fears. I couldn't bear to eat breakfast on exam days, for immediately my stomach cramped and coiled, making me want to rush to the toilet.

"What is all this drama?" Ma demanded. "Making a big fuss-muss over everything. Do I give you poison in your food that you get loose motion every morning? Drink some Amruth-dhaara, you will be all right. Now eat."

I hated Amruth-dhaara. When I thought of those agonizing exam days, the anxiety of waiting for my report card, my mouth filled with the ugly taste of the shit-syrup. Roopa gave it that name—lucky Roopa who wasn't ever concerned about what Ma would say if she came last in her class.

"I don't want to do anything except get married and have babies," she said, her dark face mulish.

I wished I had the courage of her convictions. Where did that defiance grow from? Ma withered before it.

"You should be happy I am taking more interest in you than in your sister, useless monkey that she is," she said to me. "At least one child of mine should get a chance to achieve all that I wanted. It is your duty to keep your mother's head high. After you are married you do what you want, none of my business then."

Why did Ma push me so hard to studystudystudy if she was planning to get me married, decorate me with useless jewellery and *zari* saris? I would rather read Mills and Boon romances, where a tall, morose Greek tycoon clasped the heroine to his heaving chest and whispered *"Agape mou"* in her shell-like ear. I preferred discussing those torrid romances furtively with the other girls in moral science class, while Mother Superior Mary Albina whined in a high-pitched, exalted voice, "Girls, remember the three Ds—decency, *d*ignity and *d*ecorum—they are your armour in the world outside. They will help you hold your head aloft in times of *d*istress."

I wanted to swagger around the school grounds with Miranda Fernandez, who giggled through Mother Superior's sermons and said loudly, "Bloody Albino, what she means is don't let anyone get inside your sainted knickers. Keep your head aloft and your skirts down." (Miranda, the daring one, who wrote "lover" and "bitch" on the toilet walls, and sprayed herself generously with perfume, defying the Sisters' insistence that we wear no perfume, nail-polish, make-up.) Instead I was more decorous, dignified and decent than a whole convent. I plodded doggedly through algebra, geometry theorems, calculus. Ma wanted me to major in science. An engineer or a doctor made money, no need to get married then.

"You did science," I sulked, "and you got married."

"Those days things were different," Ma snapped. "My parents did not give me the encouragement I am giving you."

I had to get away from my mother. As quickly as possible. Even if it meant a hundred bottles of Amruthdhaara, dozens of eggs to make my brains work and math tutoring every evening after school. I stayed awake till two-three o'clock in the morning, my one ambition being to finish school and get out of the house, away from Ma. Maybe even get married, although if Ma was to be believed, that would be like escaping from one locked room into another, forever wandering in a maze, hitting my nose against closed doors.

When Dadda came home the earth swung around and became a warm, comforting place. I could tell him how Ma was forcing me to join the stupid dance-drama at school and after I cried a bit Dadda would rescue me from the grasping tentacles of Ma's will. But if I was my father's favourite child, then Roopa was most certainly Ma's. When I back-chatted my mother, or left my underwear on top of the laundry basket instead of burying it at the bottom as a girl with a sense of shame would, Ma would remark, "Just like your crazy aunt! You are turning out to be a Meera!" When Roopa did the same, Ma said that she was a dog's child, a dirty-dirty *shani,* but neverever used the Meera curse.

I was always alert to the rivers threading their way through every house we inhabited. I had developed a fine instinct for these unseen bodies of water, knowing which ones ran deep, where the currents were danger-ous and whirlpools lurked. I knew that a chasm gaped between my parents, a hole so deep that even Dadda with his engineer's hands could not build a bridge to span it. If I spoke of the currents and eddies to Roopa, she ran to Ma complaining that I was scaring her.

"Ma!" she cried. "Kamini says that if I don't walk carefully in the house, I will drown."

Roopa could see nothing beyond her own tilted nose, and Ma only yelled at me. "Act your age," she scolded. "You are too big to be scaring your sister with stupid nonsense stories."

As we grew older, I stopped trying to show Roopa the hidden worlds that seethed beneath the surface of the ordinary, for it seemed that she had, in her mind, closed the doors that opened into imagination. If she could not *see* a purple rose on a bush or a peacock on the front lawn, she declared, it couldn't possibly be there.

❧

"I have rubbed the peel of a ripe Nagpur orange on this card," wrote Ma. *"Right now it smells as fresh and tangy as the fruit itself. I hope the smell has not faded by the time the card reaches you. And if it has, all you have to do is imagine."*

*The postcard had the picture of a Hindi film actress with
thick, pinkish thighs and breasts that jutted aggressively under
a shimmering brassiere of sequins. Where did Ma manage to
pick up these awful cards? As usual, apart from the vague note,
there was nothing else, no information on where she was planning to go next, no return address.*

*I stared out the narrow window set high in the wall of my
basement apartment. The snow had piled up in chill swaths,
and I could barely see what lay beyond. I felt like a mole tun-
nelled into its lair of darkness, weary of the never-ending night
that had descended on the city. When I left home in the morning the stars were still scattered in the sky, the moon a pale
aureole. And at five in the evening when I trudged home laden
with coat and sweater and muffler and mitts, barely able to turn
my head for the padding around my neck, it was still night. I
held Ma's card against my face and breathed in deeply. Opened
my eyes and I could see, against the implacable white of the
snow outside my window, dark leaves and the bright colour of
fruit ripening in the sun. My mouth filled with the tart juice
of a burst orange.*

In the unkempt garden that was shared by all the apartments in our Calcutta house, there grew a lemon tree.
I loved to crush the thick, porous leaves and sniff at the
lingering spice on my fingertips. The tree never bore
fruit. Our washerwoman, pounding the life out of
clothes in the cemented courtyard behind the building,
said that it was because the tree was male. She nudged

Linda Ayah and remarked, "Like our Ganesh Peon, that lemon tree! Big-big *kottays* and no kiddies!" She cupped her hands and moved them up and down as if weighing fruit, and then shouted with laughter, her mouth wide open, revealing large, jagged teeth stained black and orange with tobacco juice.

On Sundays, after an oil-bath, Ma sent me out into the sunny courtyard where Linda Ayah waited to rub my hair dry. Our building sat at the far end of the colony, and across the high brick wall I could hear the sounds of traffic on Cunningham Road and the wail of ambulance sirens, for there was at least one accident in the city every single day. Sometimes I would catch the mournful boom of a steamer on the River Hooghly, or the siren crying out warning of the bore tide rushing in. The streets of Calcutta were so crowded that it seemed you were stuck in the same spot for hours, inching only slightly towards your destination. There was invariably a procession or a strike going on, creating tedious traffic jams, so that, one day in every week, we were late to school. Roopa and I travelled by bus now, for this was a large city and our school was too far to walk to.

"Don't talk to strangers," warned Ma. "Kamini, don't dream and stare out of the window. Hold your sister's hand, so you are together all the time. It is time you learned to be responsible for someone else."

Now that I had turned twelve, I noticed that Ma spoke to me differently, almost like a friend. Even the dreaded oil-bath day was no longer a wet battleground but a time when Ma talked to me, told me of her own childhood, gave me advice. Ayah was not allowed into the bathroom to pour water over my head any more. Now only Ma could see my body, decide that it was time I wore a brassiere. I wanted her to buy me a red one from the vendor outside our colony gates. The man claimed that it would give me a figure like that of the film actress Rekha. Then maybe Frankie Wood the club caretaker would look at me.

"Only harlots wear those things," Ma said as she pushed my head downwards, her fingers stroking oil into the base of my skull, so warm, so warm. "Be careful how you dress, be careful who you speak to. You are twelve years old and you don't know whatall can happen."

I was too grown up to be afraid of Linda Ayah's ghosts and imps, but not too old to worry over Ma's tales of girls who got into terriblehorrible trouble.

"There was a girl named Alamelu," said Ma, "who lived in a house with a garden full of shoe-flowers and travelled by bus to college."

This Alamelu loved university, her teachers, the smell of books in the high-ceilinged library, the stone buildings, even the grumpy librarian. Her favourite subject was chemistry, for the professor had the ability to turn it into something more magical than a dry profusion of formulae. Alamelu planned to do a Master's degree and perhaps a Ph.D., provided her parents did not get her married.

"It is good for a woman to be ambitious," said Ma approvingly. Her stories had several messages—study hard, reach for the best, don't be brazen—and she never failed to point them all out to me.

Alamelu wanted to spend a lifetime with sulphides, oxides, carbides, powders, ores and solutions, all those substances frothing and fuming in bell-jars and test-tubes. Which was why she was reluctant to tell her parents about the three loafers from Dominic's College across the road.

I could imagine them, with their tight pants, their loud shirts open to reveal their chests, their slick hair and bold glances. Ma said that they lounged at the bus-stand, near the tea-stalls, scribbling obscenities on walls and aiming spit at the pillars holding up the tin roof of the bus-shelter.

"They might not even have noticed Alamelu in her cotton *salwar-kameez* suits, or dull saris with long blouses that covered most of her waist," continued Ma. Alamelu's mother was strict about her clothes, insisting on getting her to hide as much skin as possible, and never mind the steaming summer heat. But unfortunately for Alamelu, the three boys caught the same bus as she, swaying along on the ride back to the colony stop. At first, they were content with comments—"Hi Miss," "Hey-hey beauty" —accompanied by leering glances that made Alamelu want to jump off the bus. Instead she sat stony-faced as near the driver as possible, staring out the window. They hung over her and pushed their crotches into her shoulder, leaned across her to peer out of the window. Sometimes they got lucky and found a seat beside her. Then they pressed against her thigh, dropped a careless arm across the back of her seat and whispered in her ear. Nobody in the bus had the courage to interfere, for these were *goondas,* violent fellows who carried knives.

One evening they followed her into the colony and one of them pulled out a knife. With a single stroke, he sliced open the back of Alamelu's *kameez,* and a little of her back as well. "She should have screamed, she should have told someone about the rogues," sighed Ma. "Listentome! A woman is never safe!"

I felt the power of my mother's fingers in my scalp, kneading the skin and bone and flesh. Knowing that this was the only time I might get a reply, I asked Ma why she loved Roopa more than me.

"You are both the same to me," said Ma.

"But Ma, you rub almond oil on her skin and mustard on mine. You never scold her when she gets her sums all wrong. You love my sister more."

"I did the same for you when you were younger. You don't remember, that's all."

Soon after, for the Diwali festival, she bought me my first sari, and pinned it in place with two dozen safety pins so that it wouldn't slide off when I walked.

"Don't rush like a wild thing," she scolded. "Take small steps, learn to walk with a little grace."

"She looks like a stick in sheets," said Roopa.

"And you are a blackie," I replied.

"Kamini!"

"She started it."

"You are older, you should know better!" remarked my mother as always.

"She is your darling baby who can say whatever she pleases. I don't want this ugly sari."

"You look beautiful in it," said Ma in a firm voice.

Dadda looked at me as if he didn't recognize me. I waited for him to say something. He smiled such a sad smile and I thought guiltily of the last time I had sat with him and listened to his stories. Was it a month ago? Six months? A year? Had he noticed that one of his daughters had moved away from childhood? Or did he exist in a changeless world, where the only things that moved were his trains? Dadda knew the trains as well as he did his own body. He knew their schedules, when they were late and why, where they had been held up by landslides, boulders, fallen trees, wandering cows. But did he remember that I had turned twelve, that I did not find Charlie Chaplin movies so funny any longer, that I wanted shoes with heels for my next birthday instead of books by Enid Blyton? On the India-map in my room, his finger moved across the criss-cross line between Siliguri and Gariahat.

"The old WG 2-8-2 engine had a roar that made the forest shake," he said. He had just returned from the site of a terriblehorrible accident. "A bull elephant as big as this house heard the engine deep inside the leaf shadow of the jungle and thought it was a mating call. *Noni*, don't you want to know what happened then? Don't you want to hear my story?"

Aunty Vijaya had told me the lore of a woman who grew fatter and fatter, pregnant with the stories that clamoured within her, till she was about to burst, hardly able to carry herself from one room to another. Finally she whispered her tales to the walls of her house and was relieved of her burden. I imagined that the stories within him had turned my father huge and grey. Sometimes I paused in my headlong flight out of childhood and noticed him in his favourite chair in the corner of the living room, his bald head glowing under the light, smoke from stolen cigarettes curling about his misty face turning him into an amorphous cloud. His buried eyes followed Ma, resigned, as she roared around the house gathering strength from his mountainous quiet. But with so many other things to do, who had time to listen to stories about trains any more?

A day after Durga Pooja my friend Nibha and I saw a naked man for the first time. In the River Hooghly, pinned against the jetty like a butterfly against the pilings, his eyes wide, his tongue bulging out, a pale fish. On his forehead near the right eye was a wound like an open mouth. He looked like crucified Jesus in the "Soldiers of God" pamphlets that Sister Angelica urged us to buy at ten paise an issue.

"God will punish you if you don't," she threatened, her face pushed close to mine, her black silk veil fluttering against my frightened cheek.

"Tell your mother it is compulsory," she said when Ma sent my copy back to school with a note refusing to buy it. Sister Angelica warned that I might fail in needlework if I didn't bring the money by Monday, which meant I would be held back for a whole year.

So I stole ten paise every week from my mother's change tin on the meat-safe in the kitchen.

The naked man was stretched out across the iron pillars holding up the jetty, his face puffy and grey. The water touched his body and he moved as if in sleep. One hand hung over a cross-beam, the other just touched the water. The bore tide often brought in pigs and stray dogs but this was the first time I had seen a human being.

"Look at his Thing," whispered Nibha.

Miss Joseph had been teaching us the reproductive system all week. She still hadn't mentioned the word penis. She sent the boys to Room 4 where Father Julius would teach them the same thing. Miss Joseph wound her sari tightly around her bee-like figure, so tightly that she hopped about in short, swift steps.

"Now all you girls will soon mature," she said, hopping from the blackboard, where she had drawn something that looked like a sack full of wires, to the desks in the front row and back to her own table.

"What will happen to us, Miss?" asked someone in the class.

"Menstruation," said Miss Joseph in a doomed voice. "Your uterus will clean itself out every month."

"What about boys, Miss, do they menstruate?"

"No," said Miss Joseph. "They masturbate."

I was in love with Frankie Wood, the club caretaker. Actually all of us were in love with him. He had eyes like Gregory Peck, a nose like Rishi Kapoor, and he had brushed my fingers when he gave me my Coca-cola. I was sure that it was deliberate. If I could summon up the courage to stay at the club till everybody else had left, he would tell me that he wanted to hold my hand.

"Hey girlie," he said instead. "Your *ayah* was looking for you. You better go home. Children not allowed in the club after seven o'clock. Go, go, your Mama will be worried."

I hated Frankie Wood.

"Where were you?" shouted Ma, slapping my legs hard. "Linda Ayah was looking all over the place for you."

"I was with my friends. I forgot to look at the time."

"She was making goo-goo eyes at the caretaker. Chochweet Frankie!" teased Roopa, rolling her eyeballs. I hated her as well.

Nobody in the world was worth talking to except my friend Nibha. She had long nails and curled her hair. She wore glasses that swooped up at the edges of her face like brown wings, and she was going to be an artist. Nibha stayed in the school as a boarder and I was the only one allowed into her dormitory because I was her current best friend. I sprawled on her bed and watched her drawing animated peas for a frozen pea advertisement. She planned to attend art college after high school and was making up a portfolio of all her art, she said. That was the first time that I had heard that word—portfolio—and the weightiness impressed me. The peas jumped all over the page and shouted in little balloons,

"I might be frozen but I am still alive!" Nibha drew the peas in mapping ink, then smudged a blob of Fevicol glue within that outline. When the glue was half dry, she painted delicately with poster colours. That way the pea looked three-dimensional. Nibha told me that her father belonged to a royal family. Or used to, till the government banned *maharajas*. Now he was the manager of a tea estate in Shillong. Which was why Nibha hated tea. The smell of tea drove her crazy. At this point she looked solemnly at me, her eyes magnified by her glasses. "Maybe I get it from my mother," she added.

"What?" I asked stupidly.

"The tea thing, and maybe the madness," said Nibha. "My mother went mad, because she couldn't stand the tea smell and the sound of panthers in the night."

If Nibha was to be believed, the railways had played as big a role in her father's life as they had in mine.

"We would have been fabulously wealthy if my grandmother had not got into the Lahore Express," Nibha told me. "She was visiting her brother in Pakistan—this was just before partition from India. Her three children and her maid Ameera were with her. She also had a casket with the royal jewels—*all* the jewels—diamonds, emeralds, pearls."

"Why did she have to take her jewels on a visit to her brother?" I asked timidly. I didn't want Nibha to think I disbelieved her. She might stop telling the story altogether.

"Who knows? Her brother was also a *chhota-mota* prince and maybe they were going to celebrate the birth of his son or something. The main point is that she had all the family heirlooms. The train stopped for some reason. You know how trains are, your father runs them."

"He decides where they should run," I corrected, not liking the thought of Dadda being reduced to an engine driver.

"Whatever," agreed Nibha. "The train stopped near a pond full of lotuses—you know those stunning magenta ones. Well my father and his younger sister started wailing to get down and pick a lotus. My grandmother got off the train with them, leaving Ameera in the compartment with the baby to guard their luggage. The jewels stayed behind in a trunk under the seat. Of course you know the rest. The train started and Grandmother, my father and his sister were left stranded in the middle of nowhere."

"Why didn't Ameera pull the emergency chain?"

"Because it wasn't working, maybe. Have you ever heard of anything in the railways actually working perfectly *thheek-thhak?*"

"So what happened to Ameera and the baby?"

"Who knows? Maybe she was murdered along with other trainloads of people crossing the border. It was Independence time, remember? Or perhaps she is living in style somewhere, having sold all those jewels, and the baby, my aunt, has been brought up by her as a servant."

Nibha's tale sounded like something out of a Hindi movie. Mother on train with children. Child lost. Mother bereft. Settles down in the village where she was stranded and takes up a job as seamstress to support the children with her. In Hindi films, helpless mothers became either seamstresses or whores. They contracted tuberculosis and spent the rest of the film coughing.

"Where did your dad meet your mother?" I asked Nibha.

"Oh, I don't know, someone's aunt's cousin's mother-in-law must have suggested the match," said Nibha. "My mother's mother was fairly well known in those days."

"Why, what did she do?" I was enthralled with Nibha's family.

"She was, still is, a herbalist, sort of village witch doctor. She was good at mixing herbs and pastes and things, she got it from her father. She used to be famous for her bone-setting paste."

"You're joking, aren't you?" I demanded.

"I never joke about my family," said Nibha. "And what's so strange about having a herbalist for a grand-mother? People in the village were uneducated, they thought she was practising magic."

"Did her cures work?"

"Of course they did! Well, they usually did, and nobody minded the occasional lapse. I mean, the big army hospital couldn't always help sick people either, so how could an old witch-doctor?"

"So, what could she guarantee cures for?"

"Malaria, cholera, broken bones, coughs and colds. Simple stuff like that."

"How about cancer?"

"Maybe. I remember there was this fellow with

cancer of the stomach. Nani Ma gave him all sorts of potions and things. Apparently one day he shat multi-coloured shit and became perfectly all right."

"That's disgusting, and not true."

Nibha shrugged. "It could have been his wife. She broke five coconuts every day at the Mangeshi temple and five at the Pir Baba grave. Maybe that cured the man."

Then Nibha lost interest and went back to painting while I stared at the ceiling thinking of maharajas and madness, tea parties and panthers. I had madness in my family, too. And tea parties and panthers. Once, in Guwahati, a panther had prowled through the lychee trees in the back garden, cracking the still night air with its sawing, rough growls.

In Guwahati, just before the monsoon broke, a thick, humid heat descended like a skin and the fans circled hopelessly, moving nothing but dusty spider webs high in the ceilings. Sometimes the power failed, plunging the house into a sticky darkness. Then Ganesh Peon and Linda Ayah moved wraith-like through the house, light-ing candles and kerosene lanterns, pools of heat shim-mering in every room, and it felt like we were inside an oven. I could hear the stealthy scuttering of cock-roaches as they came out of hiding, safe for now in the deep shadows. Ma's poisoned balls of flour and sugar no longer killed the creatures and they returned twice as numerous. They were as immune to deadly poison as the man from Madurai who had been imbibing venom for twenty years. The fibres of his body were bitter with poison, his blood as noxious as a cobra's spit. He had lived through three hundred snake bites—rattlesnakes, mambas, kraits and cobras—his skin punctured and pocked with strange discolorations, his eyes glittering maniacally. The man hoped to make it to the *Guinness Book of World Records* for being bitten by more poisonous snakes than anyone in the world. I had seen a picture of him in a magazine, along with photographs of another man who had grown his nails for twenty-five years so that they looked like knotted yellow ropes hanging from his fingertips. The snake man said in italics beneath his photograph, *"I aim to live in a cage with 200 snakes, nobody in the world has done that."*

As it was impossible to stay inside the house, we moved our chairs out onto the pitch-dark lawn and sat there draped in mosquito netting. It was the only way we could escape the swarming mosquitoes, which, like the cockroaches, were immune to Odomos repellent, Tortoise mosquito coils, *neem* paste, mustard oil, everything. They whined and swarmed, hysterical with blood lust, attacking skin, lying on arms, legs, face, bloated and inert till they were slapped dead in a crimson spatter.

"Kamini," called Ma, "tell Linda to lock the back door. Anybody can walk in and we won't even know."

"Am I a fool to leave the whole house open?" grumbled Linda from the verandah where she sat, impervious to all the mosquitoes in the world. She told Roopa and me that her useless children had sucked every last drop of blood from her veins and so the mosquitoes had no use for her. "See, something good always comes out of something bad. Don't the sweetest flowers grow out of a pile of smelly cow dung?"

In the summer the power failed for longer and longer periods of time, and along with the dark, a silence descended over the whole colony. Sometimes the quiet was shattered by the wild, rising laugh of a hyena, the soft flutter of bats over our heads. When the waiting became unbearable, Dadda pointed out star patterns in the sky—mythical birds, dancing *apsaras,* strange beasts. I couldn't make up my mind about which I hated more: the dense heat, the sly whisper of cockroaches, the saucer-sized spiders descending like acrobats from the ceiling or the demented chorus of mosquitoes in the dew-damp outside. I hated it all, the whole rotten place.

A change of season trembled at the edge of the river, just below the ice, hidden in the brown stubble of last year's grass, coursing through dormant branches. The snow outside my window seemed to shift and tiny green shoots pushed through. Almost all of them would be dandelions, which were considered weeds here in this country. But I liked their tenacious brightness. They reminded me of the besharam plants in our Ratnapura house. The next time Roopa called, I asked her if she remembered the plant, a brave plant that survived wherever it was thrown. Ma said that it had given meaning to its life by

*simply flowering. "That plant grew in Guwahati not Ratna-
pura," said Roopa. "In the front garden, where we spent the
nights swatting mosquitoes and gazing at the stars. Do you
remember doing that?"*

"Yes."

"Did you ever spot the huntress in the sky?"

"No," I confessed. "It always looked like a deer to me."

*I wondered what Ma saw those dark nights. She seemed
to have forgotten so many things, she might not even remember. Or she might remember it all differently. Sometimes it
seemed as if the past was a painting that she had dipped in
water, allowing the colours to run and drip, merge and fade
so that an entirely altered landscape remained. Perhaps she
only pretended that she did not recollect—knowing Ma, that
was far more likely than a fading mind. Ma's memory was
as sharp as the afternoon sun. She preferred to spin her own
stories.*

That summer, temperatures in Guwahati peaked at fifty
degrees Celsius. The newspapers carried stories about
people falling dead in the heat. *The Daily Chronicle* had
an item about a cow that dropped its calf on the pavement and watched it roast to death. It was impossible
to walk on the roads, which had turned to molten black
rivers, clung to tires, dragged slippers off your feet.
Winds from across the mountains howled the dust up
into whirling dervishes, and the boiling sun sliced
through cracks in the shuttered windows, entered

Dadda's body, sizzled in his veins, the hollows of his bones, and burst like a burning flower in his eye. At least that's what it looked like, the bright-red blood-spot with a frilled edge. When Dadda wore his glasses, the rose was magnified, an amoeba drifting towards his dark pupil and threatening to eclipse it. It scared Roopa.

"Nono, don't worry child, it is only this wretched heat," Linda soothed.

The violent heat dried the cold tea-juice that Ma pressed on Dadda's eye, and the eye-drops that Dr. Pathronobis recommended were useless.

"We need to see a specialist," said the doctor, alarmed by the glaring, crimson spot. "We need to run some tests."

They tested his blood, his marrow, his heart, kidneys, liver, brain, lungs. "Lose some weight," said the army of doctors at the hospital. "Take rest, eat oil-free food."

Ma broke coconuts at the Kali temple in Guwahati. But nothing helped. Poor Ma, sneaking to the temple, reluctant to believe in superstition, yet afraid not to, furious with the goddess for failing her, furious with all the gods in the pantheon, angry with Dadda for giving up so easily. Ma was always there for me and Roopa and Dadda, no matter where Dadda's trains took him, no matter where he took us in those same trains. Was it wrong for her to expect some return for her services to him? She had wanted to die first, as a *sumangali,* with her marriage beads about her neck, the vermilion bright on her forehead. Dadda wasn't playing fair by falling ill, threatening to leave before her. And so Ma argued and fought for his life with the doctors and nurses, special-ists and priests, gods and goddesses.

"You haven't finished anything," she yelled at him the first time he returned from the hospital. The doc-tors had allowed him to go home for Diwali. "You haven't finished your work, that's why they transferred you here, didn't they, to build a new railway section? You can't let the Railways down." Ma was certain that if she made enough of a noise somebody would hear her, one of the gods, perhaps.

"Don't be stupid," said Dadda wearily. "I'm not the only person who can design lines."

"What about the lines for this route?" she contin-ued, barely even hearing Dadda's voice. "Finish those, it's your duty. And what about your children? You can't just dump them on me!"

Ma even got a self-styled priest called Brother Joseph to try holy water on Dadda. Brother Joseph said he needed a new suit and a thin gold chain to be really effective. "Getout-getout, you rogue!" said Ma, and I was glad that she hadn't completely lost her senses.

"Go, go," Ma shouted at the row of silver idols in her gods room. "Why did I waste my time asking you for help? Have you ever granted any of my wishes? Hanh?"

She swept Shiva and Parvathi in their swing of silver flowers, Krishna, Ganesha, Lakshmi, all those mute figures into a bag and stuffed them into her wedding-*petti*. She did not have the courage to throw her gods into the dustbin yet.

I was sure my mother was becoming an Aunty

Meera. Why couldn't she allow Dadda release from his grey pall of pain? Why was she fighting for a life she had spent so many years cursing? I prayed for Ma to come back to normal. And I made Roopa pray to her monkey-god as well. "You said that he was very powerful," I reasoned. "Well, then ask him to *do* something. Ask him to save our Dadda, or is he just another one of your useless hoaxes?"

I drove my sister to tears, yelling at her every time Dadda had to be rushed to the hospital in the middle of the night. "Liar, liar, liar," I wept. "Your rotten god is useless, you must have made him angry or something. That's why he is punishing you and me. It's all your fault."

Roopa, silent as usual, clung to Linda Ayah, and all that Linda said to me was, "Don't be afraid, child, your mother will come back. Wait only."

I knew that Dadda was dying. It was there in the colour of his skin, the shallow whisper of his breath, the deep hollows in his face, the smell of sickness drifting through the house. I wished that I had listened to his stories more carefully. I wished that I had asked him more questions about his childhood, that I had spent more time with him. I wished.

For a year, Ma worked herself into a frenzy trying to keep Dadda alive. She harassed the hospital staff, checked every pill, swab and syringe the nurses carried in to Dadda's room.

"Bloody useless loafers only they employ in this

hospital place. See what we have to suffer after serving the Railways, giving our lives to useless train-shain? Suspicious people trying out experiments on an officer's body, that's what."

Dadda lay helpless on the hospital bed, covered in Ma's special-time green-and-white sheets.

"God knows what diseased person has used that dirtyfilthy hospital linen!" she ranted. "If I turn my head for a even few seconds, these thief *goonda* rascals in this morgue of a hospital will drain all my husband's blood for selling to rich Arabs. Kidneys, hearts, arms, legs, blood, everything those fellows will buy to stay alive forever," said Ma.

Dr. Ramesh, the Chief Medical Officer at the hospital, was not on speaking terms with Ma any more. No surprise that, considering the way Ma questioned every injection he administered.

"Are you sure you know what you are doing?" she asked, hovering over the doctor's shoulder, refusing his orders to stay outside till he was done. "We need a second opinion," she pronounced, dragging in doctors from the General, St. Vincent's Hospital, Ashwini Medical Centre. Sickness had triumphed after all, and Ma blamed Dr. Ramesh for it. "Useless bloody basket. Third-rate degree from some village college. And these are the people we trust with our lives," she told visitors to the sick-room.

Ma hated admitting defeat, even to death. She would have liked to have been a Savithri, dragging her husband back to life from the death god Yama's arms using the sheer cunning of words. When I was younger, Ma had read me the story of Savithri and Satyavan over and over again, her long, smooth index finger with its glittering vanki ring pointing at the pictures. Here was the happy couple sitting languidly under a mahua tree; there was Satyavan, face a picture of agony, clutching his chest; here came Yama on his buffalo to drag the body away. And finally, a triumphant Savithri, her arms outstretched, receiving her husband's life back from the god of death.

"You want something hard enough, you can get it. Just need persistence, that's all," Ma would say when the story ended.

For all her persistence, however, Ma could not stop the marrow in my father's bones from drying up in the heat of his illness, or his blood cells from turning a dazzling white, so that when he finally died, he was as pale as tracing paper.

❈

"I am now in Varanasi, the holiest of holy cities and the dirtiest," wrote Ma. "I don't know why people come here to die. I suppose if my heart collapses on me, I will depart a blessed soul, and some stranger will set my ashes afloat in the River Ganga."

Just like my mother to make me feel indignant, anxious and guilty all with a few lines scribbled on the back of a postcard! What was all this about her heart? Why should a stranger set her ashes in the river? Didn't she have two daughters to do that? But of course I had no way of reaching her, of finding out if she was merely being Ma or if she was really ill. Perhaps she had written to Roopa, given her a little more information than she had to me. That would be typical too, playing one daughter off against the other, teasing us by dangling that elusive bait of affection.

"Ma's written me exactly the same things," shouted Roopa over the background sounds of her children screaming, the dishwasher rattling.

"Well, aren't you worried?"

"Why should I be? It's all drama. You know Ma, she hates doing anything, even writing a postcard, without adding a bit of glycerine for the tears and chili-powder for the spice."

The sweet odour of roses and *rajni-gandha* surrounding my father had seeped through the entire house. It was a dreadful smell, reminding me that Dadda was now just a body in the middle of the drawing room. He lay on a pile of rapidly melting ice, his mouth a thin blue line, cotton wool in his nostrils. Ma's brother said it was to keep the fluids in. How disgusting, the idea of my fastidious father with no control over his leaking body. I preferred to believe Linda Ayah, who said the cotton was to keep Dadda's spirit in his heart. Remove the cotton and the spirit would stream out leaving Dadda in limbo, a *Trishanku* suspended between *swarga* and earth. The spirit needed to be released with the proper rituals, cleansed in the heat of a sandalwood pyre so that it would ascend into the air.

A warm draft puffed into the room from the open front door. People had been wandering in and out of the house all day long, occasionally stopping to straighten the edge of the sheet covering Dadda, light a few more sandalwood sticks, stare mournfully at his face or ask how Ma was doing. One of my uncles, after dressing Dadda in a clean *dhothi,* had daubed his face with Old Spice shaving lotion. Early this morning, the house had smelled like the flower shops on the road outside the colony where, all day long, women threaded flowers for weddings, funerals and temple ceremonies. But as the sun soared in the sky, relentlessly stripping the shadows from everything, the body decomposed, its juices vaporizing into the hot air mingling with the stale flowers, making the house smell like the Ralston Fish Mart.

Dadda's secretary had brought the monstrous tuberose garland threaded with wisps of silver which he, along with the other clerks and *peons* in the office, had chipped in to purchase. The secretary was sobbing and hiccuping and dabbing nervously at his swollen red nose when Ma said, in a sharp voice, that the garland was a waste of money.

"Are you a millionaire that you spend so much on flowers?"

"Oh Madam, he was a good sir. If we had thousand rupees we would have bought a bigger garland. What a tragedy!" he howled, offering a flurry of explanations.

I drifted through the still rooms, wondering if I should join Ganesh Peon and Linda Ayah as they kept a vigil over Dadda. He would lie there till Vijaya Aunty arrived the next morning. Every now and then Ganesh and Linda packed crushed ice against him. The white cloth wrapped about the body was wet and Ayah mopped up the melting ice, wringing the cloth into a bucket. She had to make sure it didn't flow out to the carpet rolled against the wall. It was an expensive carpet, forty counts per square inch, and Ma would throw a fit if it got damaged. Every time Dadda was promoted, Ma got something posh for the house—after all, a big officer had to have a house to match his status. When we had guests she got all tight-lipped and miserable if they didn't have the decency to take off their shoes before they walked on the carpet.

"Junglees!" she said after the offenders had left. "They are the sort who teach their children to draw on the walls, *junglees."*

I wondered what would happen to the heavy silk curtains with the Chinese pattern, the squishy-soft sofa set, the rosewood dining-room set. Without Dadda there could be no more promotions, no more office parties or memsahibs with chiffon saris to admire Ma's belongings. I glanced furtively at my father's body, almost expecting it to sit up. The ice must make him feel cold. Even in Calcutta, where it never went below twenty degrees, Dadda wore a balaclava cap to sleep. And now he was lying in a bed of ice with only a thin *dhothi* cloth covering him, not even a cap or socks. I shivered, the hair on my arms standing up in bumps of skin. Perhaps I should cover him with another sheet. One of the new

green-and-white ones Ma kept for guests, with the soft
perfume of Lux soap drifting out when you unfolded
them. Better than the stale stink of ice from the Railway Club. I could smell it, a thick stench of rotting ply-
wood same as the corner of the garage where the roof
dripped in the monsoons. A *dhobi*-fresh sheet all starchy
clean would take away that smell.

I peered into the room where Ma was lying with
Roopa curled up beside her. Both were fast asleep.
Roopa would sleep through a cyclone. I shivered, a
wave of anxiety washing over me, and wished that I had
agreed to sleep with them. But from that room I had a
good view of the drawing room where Dadda lay.

Ma had not wanted to sleep. "I have to start packing,"
she said, looking in annoyance at all the coffee tables
and chairs, cupboards and sideboards, cots and shelves
scattered about the house, a lifetime's treasures suddenly
a burden. She was already rearranging them to fit the
little apartment Dadda had built for their retirement,
already discarding the bulky pieces that might not even
squeeze through the low doors there. But Aunty Lalli
had forced her to swallow Calmpose tablets and Ma had
dozed off, snoring in the bed, her mouth open. Age had
stretched and altered her face, adding a padding of fat
here, taking away a sharp line there, so that I felt that my
mother looked like Plasticine moulded by a child. I tiptoed to the dark cupboard and drew out a sheet. I carried it to the drawing room where Dadda lay. The
ambulance men had placed him right in the middle of
the room. Roopa and I had watched silently from the

verandah, wincing together at the dull thud as the two men dropped our father's body carelessly on the floor. Then they stood, the dolts, talking quietly, waiting for Ma to sign the delivery papers. I wanted to slap them for their casual irreverence.

Linda Ayah looked up suddenly, startled by my silent entry into the room. She gave a little moan, "Oh-oh, amma-ma." Her glasses shone in the light from the streetlamp streaming into the room. Why she wore glasses nobody knew, she couldn't read a word, but she liked looking at all of our school-books.

"Ayah, shoo!" I whispered. "You'll disturb everybody."

"Yo-yo-yo," Ayah moaned again, a little angrily now. "It is you, child, why you scared me like that? What are you doing here you poor thing? Go, go, your Ma will get angry if she catches you here."

"Isn't he cold?" I asked.

Ganesh Peon giggled and remarked in a whisper, "In this pissing heat can anyone be cold?"

"Idiot, bite your loose tongue," said Linda Ayah, glaring at him. "No baby *chikkamma,* my pet, he isn't cold, see he is nicely covered with a cloth. You don't worry, Linda will take care of him. You go to sleep now."

I went slowly up the stairs to my bedroom and a minute later heard Ayah telling Ganesh, "Stop gaping, nitwit, and get more ice from the fridgi…tomorrow Sahib's sisters and all are coming, what will they think if Sahib doesn't look nice?"

⚜

Ten years ago, I had felt a simmering resentment against my
mother. I believed that she had wronged Dadda with her rigid
anger, her unkind words. I refused to acknowledge the years
that Ma had spent being a good wife, looking after her daughters, supervising the household, making sure that Dadda got
his meals exactly on schedule. How bored she must have been.
If she wasn't at home when Roopa and I came home from
school, we sulked, accused her of being indifferent.

"We were starving," we moaned. "Where were you?"

"There was food in the fridge, Ayah was at home," snapped
Ma, guilty at not having fulfilled the role that had been scripted
for her, annoyed at being coerced into playing it. Perhaps Dadda
was to blame for the person Ma had become. He shut her into
rooms from which there was not even a chink of an escape. He
himself had left again and again, and every time he came back,
he needed to be readmitted into lives altered daily during his
absence.

I reread the most recent of Ma's postcards. "The gulmohur
tree outside my flat will be in bloom in a few weeks," she had
written. "I should be home in time to catch the flowers as they
fall. Such a simple thing can give me so much pleasure. It has
taken me so long to see that happiness isn't hard to find. No?"

⚜

I remember little of the train ride that carried us away
from the Railway life, from Linda Ayah and Ganesh
Peon, of the last few weeks in the Guwahati house

surrounded by shapeless, looming masses of gunny-wrapped furniture. Our new apartment felt so tiny compared to the sprawling Railway houses. There were no echoes, no mysterious corners, dark hidy-holes. Our furniture looked gargantuan at first, but after a few weeks the tables and chairs, cupboards and desks seemed to shrink and shrug into their niches and stopped looking odd. For the next eight years, our lives were punctuated with nothing more remarkable than Ma's regular tiffs with a series of maids who arrived at four in the morning one day, two in the afternoon the next, and sometimes not at all. Once in a while Roopa or I missed our bus home from school or college, and Ma would sulk and scold and predict awful mishaps.

Then, the year Indira Gandhi was assassinated, Roopa announced that she was getting married and for weeks we had all our relatives streaming in.

"Who is this unknown fellow? Is he our caste? Are his parents good people? Does anybody in this city know them? Saroja, Saroja, you should have locked up this daughter of yours! Is she pregnant? Why this sudden marriage, no time to call anybody! What about the older one? How can Roopa get married when Kamini is still not hooked, hanh? Saroja, you are stupid."

"He is a good boy," snapped Ma. "My girls know how to pick their fruit."

Then after they had all left, she slapped her forehead and shouted at Roopa. "What will you do if he divorces you in USA? Maybe he has a white woman there already and you he is taking to be her maid. At least finish your studies, idiot girl, then you don't have to come back crying to your mother's house!"

"I am never coming back," said Roopa. "You don't have to take care of me any more, don't worry."

I stayed with Ma for a further two years after Roopa left and then decided to leave my job and try for a doctorate in chemical engineering. In a university as far away from Madras as possible.

"Calgary?" exclaimed Ma when I showed her the letter from the research centre that was willing to take me on. "Where is this place? Has anybody ever heard of it? What is so special there that you have to go, hanh?"

"Ma, it's in Canada. They grow wheat there, and cows. They have oil and natural gas," I told her, exasperated, feeling like someone from the Chamber of Commerce. Just like my mother to dramatize the whole affair, blow it up into a major thing.

"Canada, Canada, and where is *that* place? In the North Pole, that's where. Are you mad or what? Here itself when it rains you wear three-four sweaters, shawls, blankets and go hurru-hurru with cold!"

"But Ma…"

"And if you want to look at cows just glance out of the window, hundreds of cows you will see shitting on the roads."

"What a strange thing to say, Ma!"

"Strange? Your sister and you are strange, not me. She marries the first man she meets, and you so old and not a sign of wanting to get married. If only your father was alive!"

After Roopa's marriage, Ma had started beseeching Dadda to come back to life and look at the shambles he had left behind.

"See, I am stuck with two daughters who are busy doing god-knows-what!" she shouted in the general direction of the heavens. "While you are sitting up there relaxing with your pipe, no doubt. Always-always I am left with all the problems."

I locked myself in my room, cringing at the thought of all the neighbours listening in. They would troop by later to console Ma, glare accusingly at me, offer advice. Gangadhar Uncle, the retired judge in the apartment below, didn't even wait to come into the house, though. He preferred to join Ma in her histrionics from his balcony one floor down.

"I waste my youth showering love and affection on these children and what do I get in return? Nothing!" grumbled Ma, rattling pots and pans in the kitchen, fully aware that the little balcony outside was in direct line with Gangadhar Uncle's.

"That is a parent's fate," agreed Uncle. "Look at my own incompetent son. I told him do a management degree, forget about philosophy and all that. But he did not listen and now he organizes political rallies for that thief of a chief minister, while his wife earns the money in the house."

"My daughter wants to go to some place near the North Pole. I ask you, what is wrong with her life here? Do I ever stop her from doing anything? No. Did I say a word when she refused to look at that bone doctor from England? He wanted to marry her right away, no fancy engagements and all that. Right away. Such a good boy. And my other daughter, married to a meat-eater. Oh my heart breaks. All this I have tolerated. I have been a modern-times mother and these girls have taken advantage of me."

"Sister," consoled Uncle, "you have performed your duty. Now you sit back and watch 'Mahabharata' serial on TV. Don't worry-murry about ungrateful children. One day their mistakes will turn around and bite them in the face."

"All these years I have made sure she doesn't catch a tiny cold even. Her lungs are bad—she got that from her father's side—and now she wants to go and live in ice and snow."

"Let her go, let her go, I say," bellowed Uncle Gangadhar. "That's exactly what I said when the British left India."

There was a momentary lull while Ma tried to figure out what the British had to do with this discussion. Uncle had fought for India's independence and lost no opportunity to introduce the British into every conversation. I left the house, slamming the door behind me, cursing my mother for making it so hard to break away.

⁂

Ma had always been suspicious of the world around her. Everybody had a secret to hide, a motive to conceal.

Not a soul could be trusted, especially where Roopa and I were concerned. At the crowded, stale-smelling airport in Madras, as we waited for my flight to the North Pole, she hissed a warning, "You be careful who you talk to on the plane. Don't leave your bags here and there. Such stories I have heard of terrorists and whatnot planting bombs and drugs and all. Are you listening to me?"

"Yes, Ma."

"Don't eat or drink anything except fresh, uncut fruit and bottled water."

"Yes, Ma."

"And phone me as soon as you reach Calgary. Doesn't matter how late it is, I will be waiting."

"Yes, Ma."

"Can't you think of anything else to say?" demanded Ma. "Or you don't want me to talk? All right, not another word from me! Once you are gone, who will I have to talk to, anyway? Better get used to silence now itself."

"Ma, I'll phone every week, I'll write! Okay?"

Silence.

Saroja

I rest my forehead against the window grille and let cool morning air brush my skin. Beggars have touched these windows, spit from a thousand mouths has dried on them, they carry the germs of millions who have travelled before me. If Dadda was here, he would have rebuked me sharply, told me to wipe the bars with Dettol. Ah! Poor man, so worried about tinytiny details that he missed the big world around him. Butbut, now I travel alone, not even my daughters to watch me, wonder if my mind is decaying along with my body.

I will send them a postcard from Nagpur, my next stop. Perhaps I will rub an orange peel against the paper and write, "This is how Nagpur smells right now, of oranges ripening in the heat!"

As we approach a small station, I open the window wider. My mouth yearns for a khullar of sugary tea to scald the staleness of sleep off my tongue, clear my throat for a fresh round of stories. I have a captive audience in this rattling "Ladies

Only" compartment. In a moment, Latha the bank clerk's wife in the berth across will be awake. She is already twitching under her sheets, her toes curling. In the upper two berths are Hameeda Ali, the schoolteacher, and her sister Sohaila. Soon they will be down as well. There will be a rush for the bathrooms, which is why I like waking up before the sun has risen, and after we have all settled for the day's journey, Latha will lean forward and say, "So, Saroja bhabhi, then what happened?"

And I, depending on where my memories carry me, will tell them about my husband the builder of tracks, or Paul the Anglo mechanic, perhaps my widowed Aunt Chinna. We have a long way to go and I have so many stories for this compartment full of strangers who smile at me kindly, nodding as they listen to the reminiscences of an old woman. I am sure they look at me and think, "Ah, if it makes her happy to talk, why should we stop her? What else is there to do in a train anyway except spin yarns, eat and look out of the window?"

Now if I was my mother, or Delhi Aunt, or even Chinna, I would have no problem telling my story. I would only be drawing a line between two points, birth and the present moment. But what is one to do with a life like mine, scrawled all over the country, little trails here and there, moving, moving all the time, and never in one fixed direction? As if the seven circles I take around the marriage fire with Dadda dance out like the ripples from a stone dropped in water, carrying us on

wider journeys every time. That is the life of a Railway
memsahib. I pack our bags every three years, find new
schools for the children, settle in among strangers, learn
the local language so I can bargain with vendors in the
markets. People tell me that I should be proud of my
husband. After all, it is a privilege for an officer to get
a transfer, fresh responsibilities, a show of faith in his
capabilities. Like getting a pat on the back, being told
by the General Manager, "Mister, you are good enough
to handle anything in this country. You can take chal-
lenges like a Railway man." Only the useless fellows
remain in the same town, never getting a promotion,
rusty and creaking like condemned engines. And the
wives of the transferred officers, oh, we go from house
to house, for farewell dinners and lunches, smiling, smiling, and thinking inside, hope they have good schools
in that new place, hope we don't have to pay high-high
fees, hope the windows in the next house are the same
size as this old one, otherwise where to find money for
curtains that fit?

It is as if I live within a series of dreams. As long as a
dream holds I know where I am. I try to fix myself in
one place, a single context. Perhaps in my childhood
home, a long, narrow house on Mahathma Gandhi
Street, two blocks away from the Krishna temple. It is
a plain, ugly house with a flat terrace, none of the dripping eaves and red tiled roofs that some of the other
houses have. No shiny brass name-plate on the gate pillar, not even a house name, just "Number 21" in black
paint on the wall facing the road. A house needs a name

to suit its character, the people who live inside it. The only name that suits our stern house is "Dharma"— duty, the word by which we live. My father goes to work every morning because it is his duty as the man of the house to earn money for his family; my mother cooks and cleans and has children because she is his wife; and it is our duty as children to obey them, respect their every word. Even the neem tree in the front yard, with none of the knots, gnarls or hollows that give a tree character, obligingly blooms in March to provide the buds and flowers needed to make bitter-sweet *bevu-bella* for the Yugadhi feast. The house is whitewashed every five years by Balaji, the contractor who lives down the road.

"Why can't we paint it some other colour?" I ask.

"So long as you have a place to eat and sleep in, why do you care if a house is painted white or yellow?" My mother is content with the comforting boredom of our lives. She has a home that moves like clockwork and does not want any needless changes. A child is born every two years for ten years; Appa gets a promotion in his bank once every five years till he becomes a Manager; Amma finishes the housework at eleven sharp and comes out to the verandah with her tin of betel leaves, chalk and *supari* and sits there all afternoon contemplating the dusty street, the multicoloured billboard advertising the latest film across the road. My childhood is drawn within the walls of that house, the protective circle my parents form about me, the road taking me to school or to the market. I see the same faces every morning—Ambi Maami, who sweeps all the dirt from her front yard into ours, calling down a hail of curses from Chinna, and Srinivasa the music master, who wails out *raagas* in his garden at the crack of dawn while his wife stuffs cotton-wool in her ears.

"Baddi-maganey!" she grumbles to my mother, who sits serene as a Buddha in her whitewashed house. "He says his voice is a gift from God. What I want to know is, can we fill our bellies with song? Tell me?"

Professor Subhash Rao in Number 16, who has refused to speak to anyone on the road for ten years, stands as an Independent candidate during the elections and receives no votes, not even his wife's. He breaks his silence the day his wife disappears to ask if we know where she has gone. We wag our heads and say, "Ohho, how sad! No, we haven't seen her at all."

But later Chinna remarks, "Unh-unh. What an idiot! The cuckold is always the last to know. His wife has run away with the campaign manager for sure."

Our maid nods vigorously, slaps wet clothes against the washing stone and says, "When have men ever seen beyond their noses?"

"Who would live with an unstable like him?" Amma comments, her face pinched into lines of disapproval. She will not even acknowledge Professor Subhash Rao if they pass each other on the road, and he, aware of her dislike, never fails to greet her in a loud, mocking voice, "Good Morning, Madam, *namaskaara,* and how is your *perr-fect* family doing?"

After high school, my world stretches out to include

the Sriram College on the outskirts of town. How much I argue with Appa to study there. I beg my mother for support and receive nothing but a non-committal silence. Amma wards off decisions, unpleasant incidents that break through the smooth shell of her life, by erecting a fortress of silence. I have no way of knowing what her silence means, what feelings it cloaks in its mystery. Sometimes I imagine that a still tongue is a powerful weapon, and at others I believe that my mother is a coward, a fence-sitter, a politician, neither aye nor nay. Her nod means nothing, an empty gesture. It is as if she has swallowed all her wilder emotions along with the *paan* juice that stains her lips. When she finally speaks, it is to agree with my father.

"A woman can read and study all she pleases, her words mean nothing after all. So why you are wasting your youth and our money? Get married." Get married, she says. "A woman without a husband is like sand without the river. No man to protect you and every evil wind will blow over your body. Listen to your mother."

"No, I want to be a doctor," I argue.

"With a tongue like a knife, you aren't fit to be a doctor."

Where does she think I inherited my tongue?

I want to be an Ayurvedic doctor like Chitrangadhey, the Malayalee lady doctor on Old Parade Street, with her pure, bleached face, long hands that wave sickness away.

"Bad cough?" she asks. "Let me listen to your murmuring lungs." Bitter roots carry the warmth of the earth straight into your clotted bronchioles. "A fever shaking your body? Come, let me touch your pulse." A potion of herbs, *thulasi* to cool rushing blood.

Yesyes, I know, Chitrangadhey's tongue is mild as summer rain, but is there any rule that says an Ayurved has to be gentle-voiced? Hanh?

My mother is deaf to words that have no place in the calm pool of our home. I can argue all I please, but what use if my voice bounces off walls and falls unheard to the red stone floors?

"A woman's happiness lies in marriage," she says.

In a wedding photograph, Amma's face, now layered with folds of skin, is carved and delicate, the nose finely arched, eyes waiting for the happiness promised by the Sanskrit words mumbled across the marriage fire.

"Are you happy, Amma?" I ask her in the verandah one afternoon. Chinna mutters and moves in sleep on a mat at the far end, her body striped with shadows from the drawn bamboo blinds. At exactly three o'clock, she will awaken, leaping to her feet as if an invisible alarm has pealed inside her head, just in time to make the evening tea and snacks before father and my brothers come home. Amma glances towards Chinna to make sure she is asleep and not just pretending, and then turns to me.

"Why do you need to know such nonsense?" she demands. "Have you been seeing more of those stupid cinemas?"

"I need to know. Are you happy being Appa's wife? A mother?"

"What large thoughts for a small head!" Amma chews steadily on her *paan* and gives me an ironic look. This is her half hour of luxury—no work, no interruptions. She is in a good mood.

"You haven't answered me."

"I have a house over my body, there is food in the house. All I need now is to see my daughters married."

"Amma, Amma, why do you always dodge? I wasn't talking about us. I asked about you. Does Appa make you happy?"

My mother does not look at me. She concentrates on making up her triangles of betel leaf, occasionally glancing up to nod at an acquaintance passing our gate. The house has no lawn in front, just a narrow cement yard opening to the main road. There is more space at the back, where five coconut trees soar up into the sky, each one planted for a child's birth. Mine is already rich with fruit. There are guava, lime and mango trees, and in the slime near the well a profusion of fragrant mint. We eat mint chutney with steaming *idlis* every other day of the week. My mother, a thrifty woman, has lain out beds of green chilies and coriander, tomatoes and beans. A small square patch marked off with bricks has a single rose bush, a jasmine creeper, hibiscus and *maraga*. Amma does not believe in a garden grown for beauty alone. The flowers are for her daily prayers. Red hibiscus is the goddess Lakshmi's favourite, jasmine and roses strewn at the feet of Lord Krishna, creamy *champaka* from our neighbour's tree for Shiva the ascetic. Why waste money buying flowers when they can be grown in our own garden? Every evening Chinna strings yards of jasmine, her fingers looping and knotting the thread deftly over fragile green stems. The buds must be plucked at dusk, says Chinna, for, by then, they are bursting with all the gathered sweetness of the day. She wraps the fragrant strings in fresh-sliced plantain leaves and places them tenderly in Amma's silver flower basket.

"When you get married," says my mother, offering a bribe, "you shall have a basket more handsome than mine."

The buds unfold through the warm night and our dreams are threaded with their delicate scent. There is a string of jasmine for each of us three sisters and a special one with *maraga* leaves for my mother. We go to school, flowers tucked into oiled braids. I have long, thick hair that flicks off my back as I walk. Sometimes, in the early-morning darkness of my room, I wind my finger around loose strands and make a few curls.

"What are you doing?" calls Amma in a sharp voice. "Are you going to school or for a wedding party?"

One morning the two loafers on our street, famous for their never-ending uselessness, those rascals who loiter near the corner shop, whistle at me.

"*Haiyah,* my heart!" One of them thumps his chest. "Look at her walk, *chhammak-chhammak!* Ah! I will die with the ecstasy of watching her."

My middle sister tells Amma and she changes my hairstyle.

"Think you are a film star!" she mutters. I have to wake up a half hour before everybody else so that she can scrape a part in the centre of my scalp, drag the two halves into stern braids and fold the braids again in half before binding each hideous bunch of hair with black ribbon. She clamps her teeth on the end of a ribbon and jerks my head back as she knots the ribbon tight.

"You're hurting me!" I squeal. The flowers hang like a bridge from one braid to the other across the back of my head. The skin on my forehead is taut and uneasy, my eyebrows raised as if surprised.

My mother tells Appa, "She is as old as that coconut tree and the tree is already full of fruit."

This *raaga* she repeats with slight variations.

"At her age I already had a child at my breast."

"At her age I would not have dared to behave the way she does."

"Marriage is a crop that will last a thousand years."

Yet and yet, with all those years of wifedom behind her, she cannot, or will not, answer my question.

If she is unhappy why does she push me, her daughter, into the same jungle of sorrow? Why can't she allow me a chance to create my own shade instead of sheltering under somebody else's? Amma shuts her carved betel-nut tin, the tiny *choona* box stained pinkish-white with chalk, and finally looks at me.

"If I had remained at my parents' house, would I have been any happier? That is what I wonder when I look at myself in the mirror and see this." She jerks a hand at her body and then extends it for me to help her off the ground. "So, my girl, the next time you think we are ill-treating you, go take a look at some beggar near the Krishna temple gates and feel happy with your lot."

My mother has an argument for everything; she could have been a lawyer.

But all her arguments cannot keep my brother Gopal from going to England for higher studies. He is the first person in our family to cross the seas, and she is filled with superstitious dread. For once she does not agree with Appa, who feels that so long as the boy does not touch meat or drink alcohol he will be fine. Amma sits on his bed, occasionally tucking an item of clothing into the trunk, snapping at the rest of us for no reason at all. "What for you want to go to another country? What is wrong with this one? Do you have to go there to become a big-shot engineer?" she demands, as sulky as a child.

Gopal tosses a shirt at Chinna, our widowed relative. He wants to see the world. "Maybe you should all come with me, even Chinna, leave this narrow old house."

"Why should I want to go anywhere?" Chinna snaps the shirt in the air, smoothes it against her stomach and flips it deftly into a neat envelope of fabric. Nobody can fold clothes the way she does; it isn't even necessary to give them to the iron-man, who charges ten paise per shirt.

"Come on, Chinna! This house isn't the world, you know," teases Gopal. "Come with me, we'll visit the Queen of England."

"If the Queen wants to see me, she can come here to this house," declares Chinna. "This is *my* world."

"What I say is, get the boy married," suggests Amma. "A wife will keep him from bad habits and foreign girls."

"What *are* you thinking of?" My Grandfather Rayaru taps his cane on the floor, demanding attention. "Enough nonsense it is sending the boy to a foreign land, now you want to get him married before his older sister!" He points his cane at me. "Didn't I tell you to stop her studying? Get her a boy? Now see how it affects the whole family!"

Amma wants the family to make a trip to the Thirupathi temple to have Gopal's hair shaved off, for it is important to propitiate the gods before he leaves the country. "Just the family," she says. "It is cheaper than having a function at home."

But Appa will have none of it. "Are you saying I cannot afford it?" he demands. "We will have the ceremony at home for Gopal. I am still capable of spending for my son."

"Why not for us daughters, hanh?" I demand. "It's okay for you to spend money on your precious son. Just to shave his head in front of a big audience, why not go to a barber shop?"

"Who are you to decide what your father does with his money?" asks my mother, giving my hair a sharp tug.

"He makes such a big fuss about spending money for my college books, but he can waste it on rubbish like this."

"Mind your tongue Miss Too-smart," snaps Amma,

this time slapping the side of my head. My mother's hands do most of her talking for her. They fly through the air hard and sure, gesticulating, ordering, slapping, shouting, the symbols of her authority over us.

Old Putti, my grandmother, pats her cheeks rapidly. "Yo-yo-yo, what does that chit of a girl think of herself? Learns a little bit of English and see what happens, becomes as bold as a white woman!" She is a fine one to talk, I think. My grandmother has a vocabulary of words more foul than those used by a beggar denied alms. She follows none of the rules of womanly behaviour, so why should she set any for me?

Aunt Raji adds a little salt to the coals. "I believe there are lots of wild boys in her callij. God knows what her father is thinking of, sending an unmarried daughter to a place full of grown men."

"One of those wild boys is your son, Raji Atthey," I say sharply. "And believe me, if I told you the things he does, your hair would turn white."

Raji Atthey slaps her forehead and scowls, wagging her hand accusingly. "Too much of freedom, too cheeky, no shame! She is going to bring her parents grief, listen to me. It is time she had a husband, no doubt about it."

Actually, if not for Chinna, I might have married the first boy who had all his wits and limbs about him. That is Amma's favourite phrase. Whenever one of our relatives comes home with a prospective groom, she says, "First tell me does he have all his wits and all his limbs, then tell me his *kula-gothra*. What is the use of belonging to a high caste, being a descendant of the most illustrious sage, if the fellow himself is deficient in some way?"

My father was all for finding a boy for me when I turned sixteen. "She has finished high school, what use is any more English-Hindi-Arithmetic going to be for her? Now what she needs to learn is how to cook a good meal and make pickles for the rainy season," he says when I come home with my high school diploma. He barely glances at the parchment with its curly black lettering; only my brothers' diplomas are worthy of his attention. By that time Chinna has been with us long enough to ladle out advice with her strongly spiced *saaru* and curries and get away with it. She tells Appa that he is a clever bank manager but a stupid father.

"Look at me!" she points to her widow's garb, her bald head. "God forbid that such a fate should visit this dear child, jewel of my eye, but suppose something happens to her husband, what will she do without an education? If she has a college paper in her hands, you wouldn't have to worry. It will get her a good clever boy—see what a smart fellow Mangala Rao got for his B.A. daughter!"

Appa just laughs. "Our family adviser telling us what to do. So much she knows about life!" But a week later he picks up admission forms for Sriram College.

That does not stop my mother from sending out my horoscope to all our relatives—to Delhi Aunt, cousins in Calcutta, a brother in Indore, first cousins, second cousins, aunts twice removed.

"Find a groom for our oldest girl," she commands. "She is tall for a girl, wheat colour skin, almost seventeen. A well-educated boy would be preferable."

She takes me to Guhan, who has the only photography studio in Mandya. We go there every year to have a picture taken of the family. It is good to keep a record of the children. Who knows when death will arrive in the garb of sickness and carry one of us away? Unless you have the money to spend on a trip to William's Photo Palace in Bangalore, Guhan has to do. As he is also related to us by marriage, it would be a gross insult to him if we went elsewhere. My mother will not let me go to Guhan's studio alone. If you allow him to adjust your sari, he runs his hand caressingly over your breasts and shoulders, strokes your neck as he arranges your hair, and, according to some reports, kneads your waist, all the time murmuring, "Stomach in, stomach in, my dear, we don't want you slouching in your photo. Boys like brides who look upright and smart."

"Tchu-tchu-tchu," clucks Guhan the lecher as he bustles around, arranging a few potted palms behind me. "Last time missy was not looking pretty enough, eh? No boys were hooked, eh?" He dives beneath the black cloth draped over his camera. "This time, so beautiful I will make her, there will be a line as long as the Godavari River outside her gates. Now you want mountain background or park background?"

Guhan comes to our house carrying the photographs in a large green folder along with the negatives. Amma insists on the negatives.

"God knows what the dirty fellow will do with the girl's photo!" She drops a circle of dough into the sizzling oil, quickly rolling out another one while the first *puri* puffs golden brown. "I hear he attaches bodies to faces and whatnot, why take a risk with our child?"

Whenever Guhan visits us, he arrives in time for lunch or dinner, and talks right through the meal.

"How you like my haircut?" he asks, scattering rice particles across the table, his mouth flapping wet as he slurps his food. "New parlour I found in Bangalore, near Majestic Circle, haircut and massage parlour." He winks at Appa and grins. "Ohhh, what a massage, splendid-splendid, you should take a holiday from this family of yours and come with me, Sir! The massage, nono the masseurs, will make you ten years younger, guaranteed!"

Appa sits in silence, a stiff smile on his face, nodding now and again. "Unh-hunh, perhaps you can tell us all this another time."

Guhan licks food dribbling down his hand, his tongue a pink reptile darting against the large palm, lapping up liquid in quick strokes. He belches resoundingly, pats his belly and giggles. "May Lord Rama be praised, my belly is raised, five inches above the table!"

After he leaves, Amma fights with my father. "Are you listening?" She never addresses my father by name. "Why does that fool have to come to our house? Don't you have any kind of feeling for us, inviting him and allowing him to talk like that in front of the children?" She whips around the room picking up the dirty plates, slamming them together, rattling spoons to display her irritation. She knows that Appa cannot stand the clatter of steel against steel.

At first we get offers for my hand from parents of boys in Mysore and Chennapatna. They write long letters extolling the virtues of their sons, pointing out the kind of girl demanded by their horoscopes. Raghotthamachar, our priest, charges five rupees for each horoscope compared with mine and discarded.

"This one wants an oldest daughter whose father is dead," he comments, flicking a hand at one horoscope, his long, thin face crumpled in a frown as he squints at the birth charts and star positions. "And that one is Agasthya *gothra,* same ancestral family. He is like a brother, all wrong that will be."

"The fellow is making a fortune thanks to the fact that our daughter makes a fuss about every fellow willing to marry her," Amma complains. She thinks my father is far too indulgent with me. Easy for him! After all he spends only a quarter of the day at home. What would he know of her anxieties?

"Please Appa," I beg my father after each new letter arrives, "wait till I have finished college."

Amma grumbles a lot about these delays. "Why are you allowing her such a long rope? Don't forget, the other girls' futures depend on this one. We could have had a good match with that toy-maker's son in Channapatna."

"Oh, wonderful! Then we would get a cheap rate on toys for all our grandchildren," I tease my mother and get a sour look in return.

"Acting too smart, that's what, too-too smart," she snaps. "Thinks college-going makes her very great. All that has happened is that we have an eighteen-year-old dead-weight sitting in the house holding up a line of sisters and brothers."

"People think she is too clever for their sons," remarks Appa's sister Vani Atthey with malicious satisfaction. She has to poke her nose into all our affairs, she believes it is her duty to do so. "They say it is not good to have a wife who knows too much. Bad for her husband's pride."

"We don't really care what people think, Vani," says my mother, who bristles at any implied criticism of her children, especially from an interfering sister-in-law.

"You should have stopped when she finished high school and there were still good offers for her. Why, my own brother-in-law was keen. What's wrong with him, I ask you? But no, your daughter thinks she is the goddess of learning herself for all the college-vollege she is doing. What for is she doing a B. Sc. now, hanh? Where you will find an equally qualified groom? When you give a girl away, choose a slightly higher family, caste-wiseclasswise. When you bring a girl home for your son, pick one slightly inferior to you—that's what I say."

Amma snaps her fingers rudely in Vani's face. "There, that much I care for what you have to say!"

Vani also airs her opinions to my Grandfather Rayaru. With his thick, carefully combed white moustache, tall lean body and the gold-and-red *peta* that hides his snowy hair, Rayaru struts from one relative's house to another, dispensing advice and comment.

"Ho, so this is the girl who is creating trouble for the family." He pats my head and accepts a glass of mango *panaka* from Chinna. "What is this I hear about attaching all kinds of degrees to your sari *pallav* and not one marriage degree?"

"With all those degrees I don't need a marriage degree."

"Ohoho! Still have a strong tongue I see?" Rayaru frowns at me from under his bushy eyebrows. "Is this what they teach you in your college? To argue with your elders?"

"Tell her, Rayaru, tell her!" Amma's reputation for being a strict mother is at stake. It is immodest of me to be sitting in on a discussion about my own marriage. And I have actually dared to be insolent to my grandfather.

"Put some sense into this stupid girl's head," continues Amma. "And what a big head it has become! Look at the way she talks. Tomorrow she will get married and speak to her husband in this shameless way and he will kick her into the gutter!"

"Maybe we did a wrong thing sending her to college," says Rayaru.

"So that I can end up like all the other women in this family?" As soon as the words are out of my mouth I know that I am in trouble.

"Madam, will you please tell me what is wrong with

the 'other women' in the family?" When he uses formal words like "madam," he is really angry. But I can't
seem to stop saying what I think. This is a discussion
about *my* life.

"Saroja!" My mother jerks her head towards the door.
"I think you can leave the room now. Tell your father
that Rayaru is here and would like to talk to him."

"No, I want to know what is wrong with the women
in our house," insists Rayaru, tapping his stick on the
stone floor. "She can leave after she tells me."

"All right, I'll tell you." I toss my braid off my shoulder. "They are like cows. All they do is have children
and gossip. The only person who has any guts is Putti
Ajji, and I don't need to tell you why."

The room goes still, and I know that I have thrown
any chance of an appeal to study for a doctor's degree
far out of the window. Putti Ajji is Rayaru's wife, and
she is the only woman in our family who has dared to
show a spark of rebellion. For more than twenty years,
ever since Rayaru found himself a lower-caste mistress,
Putti Ajji has charged him a rupee for every meal he
eats at her house.

Rayaru reminds me of the foolish old man who had
two wives. The younger wife spent all afternoon pulling
out white hairs from her husband's head.

"My beloved," she said, pulling out each hair, *kichik*.
"When I have removed all your white hair, you will
look as young as me."

Every night, the older wife pulled out her husband's
black hair, *kichik-kichik*.

"My darling," she said, "when I am done, you will look as dignified as me."

When his two wives were finished, the old man had lost every single hair on his head.

Many years later, after her story has festered in my head, I ask Putti Ajji if she ever minded being the neglected wife.

"Come here." Putti pulls me into her room, drags her green tin trunk from under the bed. "I'll show you something." She selects a key from the big bunch that always jangles at her creased waist and opens the trunk. Inside are bags of rupee coins. From heavy silver to the newest stainless-steel ones, a fortune in coins. "Your grandfather is a hypocrite." Putti strokes the faded silk bags. "He didn't mind sharing the other one's bed, but he wouldn't eat from her low-caste kitchen. I was the fool who had to suffer the pain of mothering his children, I was the one he came back to for food." My grandmother is silent for a moment and then she chuckles maliciously. "But now the old whore is deaf and alone, and your grandfather lives on my charity."

I am certain that the whole town knows about this strange understanding between my grandparents. But by referring to it in Rayaru's presence, I have done the unpardonable—offended his dignity. Now even Amma will not be able to talk him out of his decision to get me married.

⚛

"Bhabhi-ji," *says Latha admiringly.* "How you could dare to talk to your elders like that? Baap-re! I would have been so scared."

Hameeda and Sohaila nod agreement.

"My father would have beaten me black and blue if I opened my mouth," *says Hameeda.*

"But you are a teacher, at least you were allowed to work," *I say.*

"That is because there were no sons to bring money into the house," *says Hameeda cynically.* "Someone had to earn it!"

I stand up, stretch my cramping back and peer into the tiny mirror. My face is dusky with soot from the engine, my eyes rimmed as if with kohl, even my nostrils have a fine, powdery lining of coal-dust. I go swaying down the corridor to the urine-splashed toilet, grabbing at window bars as the train takes a curve and catches me off balance.

Sohaila's voice follows me. "Come back quick-quick Aunty-ji, we are waiting to hear your story!"

⁂

My future husband writes to my father from Waltair, where he is posted for a few months. In his tiny, spidery script, he informs Appa that he does not have a horoscope to send us and anyway, horoscopes are the rubbishy imaginings of money-minded priests.

"But we believe in horoscopes," writes my father, equally adamant in his convictions. "Kindly send us your precise date and time of birth and we will ask our priest to cast your *jataka*."

"I don't know exactly which day and hour I was born. It was in a village where no one had watches," comes the eventual reply.

Does the fellow have a warped sense of humour or could this be the truth? My father isn't sure.

Amma is beginning to have misgivings. "What kind of irreverent fellow is this? It is true we want our girl married, but surely not to any crackpot who walks through our door." Suppose the crackpot decides to send me back home; the shame of it all! These things have been known to happen. Uncle Mohan's youngest was married to a foreign-educated lawyer and what happened? He sent her back to her father because she couldn't read any books.

"Educate her first," he commanded. "I have no use for a wife who cannot make conversation with me."

Uncle Mohan was so angry. "Is a wife for talking to? Or is she for bed and breakfast? If that fool wants a Goddess Saraswati for a wife, he can spend on her education himself. We are not responsible any more!"

Amma is doubtful about this strange man who cares nothing for horoscopes, but my father does not want to let the match slip away.

"Rubbish, he is a modern boy, nothing wrong with him. Is it his fault if his parents did not record his hour of birth?"

"True," says my mother doubtfully.

"If we let this one go, we might as well clap our hands, hold our heads and resign ourselves to a house full of spinster daughters!"

My father hurries to the priest, Raghot-thamachar, and lays out the matter before him. The priest plays a role in every major decision taken by my family. Should this child's name begin with an "A" or an "R"? What is a good time to buy a house? Should the windows of the new house face north or south? Then if things go wrong, no one can blame my father or the priest. Appa can shrug and say, "We tried our best, but the stars are unpredictable. Who knows which way they move?" And Raghottha-machar will roll his eyes piously and nod, his little knot of hair bouncing briskly, "Yes, Lord Vishnu throws the dice in Heaven and we are only the pawns in his mighty game."

Now, uncertain about this proposal sent by my future husband and eager to see me, a burden at twenty-three, married, Appa goes to Raghot-thamachar.

"Why you want to go after this fatherless-motherless person when there are hundreds of better boys available?" asks the priest.

"Never mind all that," says my father. "What I want to know is can anything be done about a horoscope?"

"Does he have any responsibilities? Like unmarried sisters, idiot brothers?"

"Two sisters. Only one of them is married," says my father uneasily. That detail has been bothering him as well. It is better to give your daughter to a house that has no unmarried girls. But I am too tall, too educated. So perhaps it is all right to compromise.

"Looks like you have found a gem so rare, his caste, his ancestry, nothing matters, eh?" murmurs the priest.

"Now let us see, do you at least know which month the boy was born?"

Raghotthamachar makes up his horoscope on the basis of an approximate date of birth. "Forty-forty match!" he exclaims to my mother, caressing the horoscopes smudged with turmeric around the edges. His matches mine point to point. "The boy was born under a mighty constellation. His star is so powerful it pushes away all the faults in your daughter's. It is a sheltering star, not to worry." Hunched over a sputtering sandalwood fire, his bare chest shining with sweat, he bribes heavenly beings with puffed rice and *ghee*. He waves his pudgy hands and creates an entire galaxy of stars to match with mine.

Amma is still doubtful. "He has too many sisters. With responsibilities like that, will he be able to look after my daughter?"

"Look," says the priest, holding up a pair of imaginary scales. "On this side education, looks, job, on that side big family. Are they going to live together? No. Maybe a few rupees every month will have to be sent; after all, the boy is the oldest son and has a duty to his family. And most important of all, the horoscope, where will you find such a beautiful horoscope?"

The *pujari* is so ecstatic over the compatibility that he has already told half the town.

"Invite the boy, let us have a viewing ceremony. I will pick a good date for you," he tells my father. Appa hesitates. He had not expected a ceremony, just a quiet get-together with the boy. "I will select a date at no extra charge," offers Raghotthamachar magnanimously, already planning to make up for that loss at the wedding, by asking for a silk *dhothi* with two lines of gold instead of one, perhaps. Naturally all our relatives arrive to view this auspicious creature with the marvellous horoscope. After all, if for some witless reason my family refuses this prince among grooms, there are other girls in our family in line for marriage.

This is how I like to imagine it all happened. The priest, lusting after a silk cloth, ten rupees, a bag of rice and a bottle of *ghee*—which is what my father paid him—fiddled with the positions of birth stars and forced our horoscopes to agree.

When I tell my mother this, she shrugs, irritated. "You are a disgruntled soul. From the moment you were born you could never be happy with what you had. You wanted everybody else's share as well."

"Not another husband," I retort, hurt by her lack of concern. "One is bad enough."

"I see the prospect of marriage hasn't smoothed that knife in your mouth. Is this how you will talk to your husband?" Amma never lets me forget that my tongue has got me into trouble more than once. There is a time for words and then another when it is better to keep quiet, she says, to sit and listen, to watch and wait. My mother has mastered the art of dropping her words into the right slots, and look how peaceful her life is! "Saroja, Saroja, why do you have to cause trouble all the time?" she continues. "Don't forget, you are a

woman now, with a life of your own, and you will have
to clean up the messes you create. I will not, and neither will your father."

My first meeting with the man I am to marry is
almost like looking at a photograph. I learn nothing
about him. And that sense of being in the presence of
a puzzle does not diminish all the years I spend with
him. He should have been a hermit, so distant is he from
the world we live in. But of course I don't know all that
when we first meet.

⁂

"Ah, Saroja, you are leaving us on a long journey," sighs
Chinna, her cataract-covered eyes milky with tears.

"Chinna, that sounds like I am going to die," I protest,
peering over my shoulder to look at my elaborate braid.
I know that as the day wears on, the clusters of flowers
threaded into a soft mat of new hay will become
uncomfortably heavy. But that, my Cousin Neela assures
me, is nothing compared to the waiting terrors of marriage. The flower-woman Jayamma made the *jadey* with
fresh jasmine buds, just beginning to open from the
warmth of my head, and thin orange *kanakambra* blossoms that match my wedding sari.

"Hanh, Chinna?" I tease. "Am I going to die, or
what?"

"*Ayyo-Rama-Rama,* don't say such wretched things
on this bright day," scolds Chinna, pushing my head to

one side so that she can screw the heavy gold drops into my ear lobe. "You are starting a new life, that's all, a beautiful new life, may all the gods bless you."

"How do *you* know it will be a beautiful life?"

Chinna's eyes fill with tears once again. "How cruel you are today, child." She wipes her eyes with the end of her sari. "But you are right, what would I know of the wonders of married life, unfortunate one that I am?"

I immediately regret my words. Today I have promised myself that I will be good and sweet as the almond *burfi* that the cooks have prepared for the wedding feast. How can I forget that Chinna is a child-widow? Appa's second cousin, she has been with our family for more than two decades. Her husband died when she was barely ten years old and her father, unable to bear the shame of a widowed daughter, packed her off to relatives.

"She is no use to me," he said mournfully to my grandfather. "Perhaps she will help in your home."

Chinna moves from house to house, cooking, looking after expectant mothers, bathing newborn babies, soothing quarrelsome children with sugar cubes and stories. My father's sister, Vani Atthey, tells me that a widow is worth less than a servant. "Why your mother is spoiling that chicken-headed one, God only understands! Waste of money, that's what I say!"

For a few years, Chinna lives with Vani Atthey, who has just delivered her first child. One day after lunch, Atthey disappears into her bedroom to feed the baby, and my mother sits in the curving verandah making herself *paan*. I sit close beside her playing with a hand-ful of cowrie shells, watching as she deftly spreads white chalk on the *paan* leaves. Chinna appears silently from the cool dark of the inside rooms and settles down near Amma's feet.

"I can't live here," she says abruptly, twisting the end of her sari. "You have to take me away. I will die if you don't."

"Why, what is wrong?" Amma carefully folds a leaf around a small pile of betel-nut shavings and coconut and places it in her mouth. She purses her lips with pleasure and her heavy chin breaks into little creases and dimples.

"I feel ashamed to tell you," hedges Chinna, giving me a sidelong glance. I ignore the look, which clearly says "Go away, child."

"If you don't tell me, how do I know what you want to say?" says Amma, applying *chuna* to yet another leaf. After lunch, regardless of whose house we are in, she settles in the verandah with a silver tin full of tiny con-tainers of the white paste, betel-nut and coconut shav-ings, small red sugar balls, *kesari,* cloves and fresh *paan* leaves. She allows herself all of thirty minutes to make up the tiny triangles and another half an hour to chew five of them, slowly, one after another, her eyes nar-rowed with pleasure. She isn't very happy about having her reverie interrupted.

"Well, what is wrong?" Tiny flecks of crimson betel juice trickle out of the corner of her mouth. She wipes it delicately with the edge of her sari. All of Amma's saris have red stains at exactly the same spot on the *pallav,* even her good silk ones. With time, the stains fade from bright red to brown, and when she pats one of the saris and says, "You can have this when you are married," I have to force myself to smile and act excited. I do not want any of those saris marked by my mother's life; they disgust me.

"It's Vani's brother-in-law, that loafer Juggi, he isn't decent." Chinna lowers her voice so that I have to strain to hear what she is saying. I want to lean forward but am afraid that the movement will attract their attention and Amma will ask me to leave. I can sit through most adult conversations by keeping absolutely quiet, pretending to be absorbed in my games.

Amma's mouth, like a cow's, is chewing, chewing steadily. I know that she doesn't like Juggi very much. When Vani Atthey asks her to look for a bride for him, Amma tells her straight away that she cannot commit any poor innocent to Juggi's hands.

"I even talked to Vani," Chinna sniffs, wiping her nose with her sari *pallav.* "But she can see no wrong in the wretched idler. She told me I was imagining things, I thought I was a great beauty and was hungry for a man's glance. *Chee-chee!* I was so upset, I didn't know what to do. Please take me away from here."

My mother, as usual, is silent. She does not trust herself to make any decisions without getting my father's "Uh-hunh" of approval. I can hear her telling Appa, "Are you listening? We need Chinna again."

And Appa, smoothing a long hand over his dark, oiled hair, "Ohho?"

A few weeks after we return home, Amma tells Vani
Atthey that once again it is her turn to keep Chinna,
for now she is expecting my brother, and soon she will
be too heavy to bend and lift and cook and clean. For
many years after that, I believe that Amma has five children just to keep Chinna as long as possible.

My father spares no expense for my wedding. A lavish
display will, hopefully, draw grooms for my sisters like
flies to honey. Our guests will go home and tell their
friends, "Raghava's daughter's wedding? What a pity
you weren't invited. The food, cooked by Vishnu Bhatta
himself, was fit for the gods. Such delicate *pheni* I have
never tasted. Aha! you should have seen the arrange-
ments they made for the boy's party. Soap in silver cases
for each person, two-sided *zari* saris for all the women,
all, mind you, even the unimportant ones!"

After the main ceremony, comes a series of smaller
ones, for prosperity, for progeny, for health and long life.
My cousins and aunts surround me with advice and
information.

"Do whatever he asks, he is your husband," whispers
Vani Atthey, coy and overdressed. She has forgiven me
for refusing her brother-in-law.

"Do not be as sweet as sugar, your in-laws will over-
whelm you with work," says a distant cousin known for
the quality of her almond *burfi,* "nor as sour as tamarind
or they will spit you out."

"Keep your jewellery in your own locker," advises another aunt. "Such stories I have heard of men taking away the jewellery and giving to their own sisters and all! A woman's *bangaara* is her safeguard against future calamity."

"Why do you have to say such unlucky words?" snaps my mother.

The crowd stays with me for what seems to be the entire night, till somebody remembers that I am supposed to be in my husband's room. I am escorted there with a lot of whispering and giggling, nudging and pinching. The room is on the second floor of the wedding house. Someone has strung yards of jasmine from ceiling fan to walls and it dribbles down the mosquito net poles, against the curtained windows. Brilliantly coloured pictures of gods and goddesses adorn the white walls. On a small table next to the bed is a jug of milk with crushed almonds.

"Don't forget to give him a BIG glass of it," whispers a cousin. "I give my husband a glass every night and oh my, he turns into a stallion."

I let all the comments wash over my demurely bent head, allow them to shepherd me into the room. The day-long festivities have left me too exhausted to think, too numb to be nervous. My husband is already asleep. The relatives leave, disappointed, and I settle down in the easy chair for the night. How can I sleep in the same bed as a man I met only once? I am now Mrs. Vishwa Moorthy. I married this man in the presence of *agni, varuna, vayu*—fire, water and wind. To be certain, I am awed by the rituals that have bound us together: my sari *pallav* knotted to the end of his shawl, his fingers inserting rings on my toes, filling the part in my hair with blood-red *kumkum*. But, I ask myself as I sit in the darkened room, what is the significance of this blood and gold and silver? The priest has all the meanings wrapped up in Sanskrit, hidden from me.

We leave for the station early next morning to catch the train that will carry my husband and me across the country to Ratnapura. The smell of our wedding still clings to me, a fading aroma of jasmine and sandal paste. Fresh vermilion singes a fiery mark on my forehead. My bangles tinkle every time I move and my toe-rings rub against my skin, raising thin blisters. I let them chafe against my toes, reluctant to take them off lest I draw ill upon myself.

My family fills the compartment, smiling, awkward. They are here to say goodbye, for it is rude to parcel off daughter and new son-in-law without any ceremony. My brothers, shy with my husband, arrange my new trunks beneath the berths, and then crowd the entrance, smiling uneasily at nothing in particular. The entire compartment is reserved for us, and my mother cannot hide her awe.

She nudges Chinna, who is weeping, rubbing her nose repeatedly in her sari *pallav*. "Did you see? What a fine boy we have got for our girl, eh? A whole compartment! Oh, her stars were auspicious!"

My mother has lost her stoic expression, her usual lack of interest in everything. Perhaps it is just relief that

I am finally out of her hair. My sisters shift from foot to foot; their eyes slide to my silent husband and drop almost immediately to stare at their feet. Appa disappears to return with a brown paper bag full of Cadbury's chocolates, oranges and some magazines. I am taken aback by this sudden indulgence. When we were children, chocolates were an unusual treat in our home. After all, they were foreign, and anything British was suspect. My father notices my surprise and shrugs. Then he glances at my husband, the silent man standing a little away from my family with his hands clasped behind his back, and says, "A small something for the journey. To while your time away. As they say, time-pass, heh? Now we will have to leave, station-master just gave a green light." He pats my head and looks significantly at Amma. "Let us go," the look says, "we cannot waste the whole day here."

My mother touches my cheek and says, "Be good, be happy. Write us a postcard."

I nod silently, pushing away the urge to grab her hand and plead to go home with her and Appa. I don't know this man, I want to say, how can you send me away with a stranger?

Chinna hugs me fiercely, her nose wet and sticky against my neck. "A hundred years of happiness waits for you," she mumbles. "Come back soon with an armful of good news."

At last we are alone in the compartment. The train starts moving and the station, ebbing gently away, is an undulating blur of colour and smell. Yellow bananas on the fruit-seller's cart, the flash of white robes as we pass a group of Jain mendicants, the A.H. Wheeler book-store, Lambani women in mirror-work skirts like pea-cocks, army *jawans,* all khakhi green, sitting on their trunks. Odours of stale milk and rotting fruit, sweat and smoke, cigarettes and drains, sometimes rising above and at others buried under the sweet aroma of camphor sticks, jasmine and sandalwood. I perch nervously on the edge of my seat, stare out the window. A vast cloud of smoke belches from the funnel of the engine ahead, darkening the sky. There is a smell of burning bone. My new husband slides the door shut, sits across from me and shakes a newspaper open. All in all, we have spo-ken five words since our wedding the previous day.

"Do you mind if I smoke?" The man taps a pipe against the edge of the compartment window.

He does not wait for me to say anything. Just takes out a pipe—a pipe! Does he think he is an *angrezi* sahib or what? And a tin of Three Nuns tobacco.

"I think smoke affects my lungs."

"You *think?*"

"I hate the smell of smoke," I reply.

My mother would have been horrified. I disagree with my husband only a few hours after marrying him!

"You will have to get used to it."

I open the window violently and feel the air rush-ing into my face. Hold the bars tight and glare out at the ripe sugar-cane fields flashing past. What will my mother say if I knock the pipe from his mouth and fling it out into the cane? What will my husband do?

Be indulgent about the capriciousness of a bride? Or compress those thin lips and invoke his status as a Railway officer to order the train to stop? Perhaps he will make me crawl among the sugar-dripping canes to search for it.

"You might catch some disease," my husband tells me. He has a pleasant voice, a Mukesh playback-singer voice. Maybe he is musical.

"What?" I ask, puzzled.

"Beggars have been holding those same bars." He wrinkles his nose fastidiously, as if he can smell rotting flesh. "We should have brought some antiseptic solution to wipe down the windows."

The *thak-thaka-thak-thak* of gravel hitting the wheels fills the compartment with noise. There is a thin whistle of air through the slats in the metal window shutters. My husband has pulled them down so that people on the platform looking for an empty compartment will not know that there is space available. We can hear thumps on our door all night, people wheedling to be let in, cursing our silence.

"Excuse please," a peremptory voice. "I have six children needing place to sit for night only."

"Excuse please, don't be selfish. Share and share alike, my children can sleep under the berths no problem."

"Excuse please, God will punish you for your lack of concern for fellow citizens." The unseen man kicks the door hard. "Bloody high-class selfish no manners no kindness!" he rants. There is a brief silence punctuated by the scrape of a trunk against the corridor

floor, a child's cough. Then the voice again. "Ay Chun-
noo, Munnoo, go to the toilet *phata-phat*. You piss here
at night and I will twist your ears off. Tunnoo, put
those pillows here." A slap is followed by a howl of
pain and a sharp reproach. "Witless like your mother,
I said here, HERE!"

We sit silent as breath, my husband still buried in his
newspaper and me fighting the urge to open the door
and let that swarm in. I would have welcomed the chattering warmth of other people in the compartment.
Perhaps he is a shy person, I think. Tense as a clothes-
line, I wait for a tentative sound, a touch. Isn't that why
he has booked a whole compartment for us, a honey-
moon on wheels? Will I seem forward if I make the
first move? I want to ask my new husband a hundred
questions—after all, our lives are now linked. What is
your job like? Do you travel a lot? Will you take me
with you? What are your favourite foods? I hate bitter-
gourd *gojju,* how about you? I will tell him how I long
to be a doctor. I'll warn him of my sharp tongue, assure
him that it wags a lot but rarely causes any harm. I want
him to know that my favourite flower is champa with
its gentle perfume. My father buys my Amma flowers
every Sunday from the temple. He does it even though
she tells him that it is a complete waste of good money.
But she tucks the long strand of jasmine into her oiled
bun, a pleased smile teasing her lips. Will my husband
perform these little courtesies, I wonder? Soon I can
hear his even breathing over the clatter of the window
shutters, the slap of gravel against the wheels. The

narrow space between the berths is striped with light from passing stations. I lie awake for a long time, missing my room in my father's house with its tiny barred window set high in the wall, and the rustle of wind in the coconut palms outside.

The next morning I find speech blooming in my mouth. If he does not speak, I will. He is my husband, after all, even if he is fifteen years my senior. My mother isn't around, hovering over my shoulder telling me how to behave, how to address a husband.

"It is wrong to address him as 'you,'" she would remark, her mouth pursed with disapproval. "Be respectful, say 'thou.' Don't give him the impression that we haven't done our duty as parents and brought you up properly." All her advice is given to me during the long Sunday baths when she rubs and slaps warm mustard oil into my skin. Those are her private sessions with each child, when she has the time to pass on wisdom handed to her by her elders, or to scold misdeeds. With me she always-always starts with, "How many times have I told you and still you don't listen…" Her hard hands knead the muscles of my back, and I sit in a daze of steam from the copper pot, the acrid stink of oil, and the muscles in my body slowly unwind. But this man is my husband, I have a right to talk to him.

"I wonder when we will reach Ratnapura?" I ask.

My husband mumbles a response, his lips clamping and unclamping like some strange fish on the stem of his pipe. It occurs to me that he is almost as old as my own father, a difference of only six years between them.

The realization shocks me into silence. Why did my parents have to get me married to this old man? I could have finished my studies, found a job and supported myself. Of course Appa objects to the women in his family working. It demeans him somehow.

"I haven't reached the stage where I need to send my daughters out to earn money," he roars when I suggest that I can get a job in the local college. "Only harlots work for a living."

"But Appa, all my teachers are women."

"They are all harlots!" says Appa, ending the argument.

I sit in the dusty compartment and brood. I do not use the right tactics. My own mouth is my worst enemy. Look at my younger sister Lalitha, so docile, her eyes pleading as a cow's going to slaughter, never a word, but gets her way every time. She is two years younger and knows all the tricks. She even tells me that all I need to do is make Appa feel as if he is dispensing a great favour.

"Why do you fight with him?" she asks. "Cry a little, beg, wheedle. How does it hurt you? Appa feels that he has the power to refuse and you get what you want. All men are like that. Why you have to say this and that and make everybody angry?"

"What your sister said is true," nods Sohaila, the afternoon sun catching her nose-pin and making it glitter fiercely. "You can get more done if you keep your mouth shut and your eyes and ears open."

"Rubbish," says her sister, "if you don't like something, let the whole world know, that's what I say."

The train slows down and stops in the middle of pale-green fields of dal. There is a smelly pond just outside our window, and a few huts in the distance.

"Chain-puller," says Latha wisely. "Some fellow lives in those huts there, too far from the station, so he must have pulled the chain. Thinks this train is his personal tonga to stop wherever he wants!"

"Latha-ji, do you think it is wise for a woman to keep her thoughts to herself, or shout her anger to the whole world?"

I look curiously at the sweet-faced woman, with her inexhaustible supply of food. She has a large red bindhi on her forehead, like Shiva's third eye, and pendulous gold earrings.

She shrugs. "There is a time for this and a time for that. When I am very angry, I cook so badly that it sticks in the throat. Then my husband and the children all look up from their busy lives and say, ah, something is wrong, she is upset."

"But your man, what does he do?"

"What can he do? Am I neglecting my duties? Oh no! If he gets angry, my cooking becomes even worse." She beams contentedly at us, and goes back to cracking her endless supply of peanuts.

⚬≈⚬

When I talk too much or say something nasty, my mother remarks, "Both your tongues are wagging today." Or, "You create too much noise, must be the little tongue."

The little tongue is completely silent in some people. In others it adds drops of honey to their conversation. The little tongue can also make you choke and die if it drips poison. That is what happens to Seethu Akka who lives down by the Thousand Lights Temple.

Seethu Akka cannot stand her sister's husband, Prakash. People say that it is because she wanted him to marry her and he turned to her younger sister.

Seethu Akka sits on her doorstep, doing small household chores like shelling a basin of peas or scraping coconuts. Now and again, she spits in the direction of her sister's house and curses her brother-in-law. "Bastard birth, bastard brain. Bastard keeps my sister's belly heavy so she has no energy to see what he is up to."

Seethu does not move from the doorstep except when her bed-ridden mother yells for her from within. Then she spits once more towards her sister's house and hurries into the bedroom where her mother lies, shrivelled and noisy, against brilliant pink-and-green-and-yellow Chennur sheets.

"I called and called," she yells in a voice piercing enough for people out on the road to hear. "What sins I must have committed in my last birth to deserve this. Hold my shit till this *maharani* daughter, whose bottom I spent my youth wiping, decides to appear!"

After taking care of her mother, Seethu reappears to spew yet more venom from the front doorstep. She dies, one day, cursing her brother-in-law, her rage exploding through the blood-vessels in her head as she hurries in to tend to her screaming mother.

When my Amma gets angry with me she says that Seethu's evil voice has flown straight into my throat. On those days she furiously chops up pale-green bitter-gourd, fresh from our back garden, and boils it in a soup of tamarind and *jaggery,* red chilies and coriander. It is a delicacy for the rest of the family, but I hate the taste. For me, it is a punishment which I swallow, gagging miserably at every mouthful, my mother's eyes mean on me.

"If you vomit," she threatens, "I will make you eat it off the floor."

Amma no longer has the right to punish me for the things I say, for now that I am married, that right has been transferred to my husband.

In the rattling compartment, I turn to him. "Why did you wait so long to marry?"

He is surprised, I can sense that, and he has to reply. He cannot brush this question away with an "Unh-hunh."

"I had responsibilities, things to take care of before I thought of marriage."

"What responsibilities?"

In the background, I hear my mother's voice. "A good wife does not go *bada-bada* at her husband asking him this and that." Amma, I think, I am no longer a daughter of your house. Remember? You gave me away to this old man with a handful of puffed rice and some Sanskrit words that even you could not understand.

"One brother and a sister, they were my responsibilities," says my husband.

"I thought you had two sisters."

"Yes, Vijaya is her husband's headache." He smiles slightly and I can almost hear him thinking, "Like you are now my headache."

My little tongue, the one my mother tries to soften with bitter-gourd, rushes in to say, "How do you know your sister is the headache? Could be the other way around."

He shrugs. "Perhaps. My second sister is still our responsibility."

"We have to find a boy for her?" I wonder at the sudden shift of responsibility from "mine" to "our." Married only two days and already I am expected to share his burdens?

"She will stay with us for a few months every year," he says.

"Why? What does she do the rest of the year?"

"She is sick. She stays in a nursing home. She will spend the summer with us."

Not only have my parents tied me to a man so old and silent I feel I am enclosed in the quiet of a funeral-ground, but he also has a sick sister for whom I must care. I am their sacrifice to the fire god so that my sisters might get fine young men. I turn away from my husband, and the scene outside the window blurs as my eyes fill with tears. The train is slowing down, probably at a station, a large one going by the number of tracks criss-crossing away in all directions. I glance at my husband from the corner of my eye. He has a severe face, which in later years dissolves into plumpness, hair straight back on his skull, a small moustache, large ears. He isn't bald yet, thank goodness. Just a touch of grey in the sideburns. His fingers are long and knobbly but not wrinkled. I have heard that age shows first in the knees. He stands up abruptly, hauling all our bags down from the upper berth.

"We've arrived," he says. "There will be somebody to meet us."

The train grinds to a halt, a final scream of wheels against the tracks, the moaning hiss of steam echoing against the arched tin roof of Ratnapura Junction. My husband slides the door of the compartment open. There is a brief pause, and suddenly it seems as if the entire station is in our compartment. A cacophony of voices.

"Salaam, Sir, congratulations on your marriage."

"*Shubh kamnaye,* Saar!"

"Good afternoon, Sir, and the new Medem."

The trunks and bags are unloaded and whisked off to a waiting station-wagon. A woman in a crisp green cotton sari presses my hand and says, "Congratulations Mrs. Moorthy, and welcome to Ratnapura."

Mrs. Moorthy. The name tastes strange.

In the town of my childhood, there is a sugar factory that marks the middle of everything. It is always there. If you are lost, you stop a moment, look for the tall chimney and say, "Oh yes, oh yes, now I have to go

left," or right, or straight ahead. And if you have lost
the use of your eyes, your nose and ears will tell you
where you are. The early morning wind carries the
sickly odour of boiling *jaggery* to the east of the factory, and towards the west, you can hear the strong rustle of sugar cane in the fields. But when I become a
Railway wife, I lose my bearings. One year I might be
in Guwahati, the next in Calcutta. Lucknow I remember for its sweet-sweet watermelons which swelled on
the banks of the Gomti River. In Guwahati, I become
familiar with the roads, the trees, pineapple blades in
every garden, smell of oranges ripening in the heat, the
grumble of traffic outside the colony walls. On that
side of the sullen Brahmaputra, which might flood or
not, depending on the moods of the goddess and the
monsoon, is Phookat Bazaar, where I go to get my new
sari for the Diwali festival. On this side of the river is
Colby School, where Behari Lal the farmer keeps his
cows—only after class, you understand, and he always
cleans up the hay and the droppings before school
opens the next morning. Behari's father donated all the
ceiling fans for the school and so the principal cannot
really refuse him. In Calcutta there is the Hooghly
River, steaming, ugly, flowing filth. During the day it
sucks air away from the colony, leaving a hole of heat,
and in the evening it puffs warm stinking breezes back.
The botanical gardens across the river are a green
apparition, inviting only from a distance. Cunningham
Road frothing bedlam just outside the colony gates, the
pavements alive with people, dogs, cows, vendors,

fortune-tellers, madmen, lawyers saving on office rentals, tailors, barbers, butchers, quacks and palmists. The ragged old woman in a palace of gunny sacks, Dalda tins, tires and plastic cans. She says she is the ex-queen of Dholpur, waiting for the government to return her riches to her.

"Remember, remember, the twelfth of December, when the bastards stole my home," she howls, slamming a long-handled pan on an overturned metal bin that was once full of Parlé biscuits.

Beside her, just where Cunningham Road swerves to meet Elphinston Lane, a thin young man has set up shop. On the pavement in front of him, like mountain ranges, are rows and rows of brassieres. Red, white and black, the colours of Durga, the goddess of illusion.

"For Rekha-actress figure, sister!" shouts the man, thrusting his fist to fill the cup and pulling it out again to show how the fabric maintains its shape, "34 A, B, C, 36, 38, even extra large available. Sister, sister, even when nothing is there, it will give you a Rekha-actress figure."

The illusion-monger holds a red bra over his own chest, bare brown, a thin coating of skin stretched over his ribs. "Best quality, lowest price," he says, mincing up and down the pavement. "Export quality, sister, suspension like the Howrah Bridge, strong everlasting."

And in Ratnapura Junction, we live in a whitewashed bungalow with a red tiled roof and a wide *bajri* drive-way. Hyenas giggle and scream in the hills behind the house, snakes slip under the garden leaves, and a curl-

ing wrought-iron stairway winds up from the verandah
to the terrace where I sometimes dry my hair.

*There is a shift in the rhythm of the train as it picks up speed,
whipping through warm-hued landscape rising out of the dust.
Arundhathi, the evening star, is already a pale gleam in the
sky, and far across the slow curve of mustard fields you can see
the lights of a town like gathering fireflies. Double-stringed electric wires hum and sway, punctuated by rows of sleek, coat-
tailed swallows.*

"So Aunty-ji, you married the man with no horoscope?"
asks Latha. *She snaps a peanut open and pops it into her tiny
mouth. She has been diving into her baskets of food at regular intervals, fishing out burfis, pakodis, kachoris, mixture,
om-pudi. She likes munching when she travels, it helps time
move faster.*

"Aunty-ji, so much you travelled, so lucky!" *remarks*
Sohaila. *"I never go anywhere except to my mother's house for
this."* She pats her pregnant belly. This is her fourth child.
*"Whattodo but, that mother-in-law of mine says have sons,
many many sons, they will be your arms and legs, your eyes
and ears when you grow old. I would have liked to see the
world a little before my children tied me down."*

"Yesbut," *I assure her,* "it was no fun packing-shacking
every two-three years. You just start making friends with your
neighbour, talk about children and ayahs, and then husband
comes home with transfer orders—go to Chittaranjan, Khurda
Road, Kachrapara. So again you have to start all over...."

⁂

The Ratnapura bungalow. In that rambling building with its bare windows like hungry eyes, its verandahs wide as roads and creaking fans rotating dust in lost ceilings, the first thing I notice is the thunder of passing trains. At first I think that my long journey has left the sound of the Madras Mail in my ears. I have just spent sixty hours in the slow chuffing train with my new husband. Two and a half days of solitude in spite of the fact that there were two of us. The trains fill my first night in the house with muffled sounds. Distant vibrations shake the window panes in our bedroom, the room where finally my husband touches me, his hand a dim creature faintly visible in the light filtering through the plain white curtains. Pure star-shine, for the house is separated from the roads by a vast garden, too far away for streetlights to reach. That first night neither I nor my husband has the courage to turn on any lamp, each afraid of the imperfections it might reveal. His warm hand drifts questingly across my face, the hollow guarded by two bones in the base of my throat, my breasts. I hold my breath, lying stiff and silent as the hand moves delicately, pushes my sari away, fumbles with the hooks on my blouse. I wish that he would say something. His breathing fills the room and I shut my eyes from the shame of being seen naked by a strange man.

My mother is the only other person who has seen my body unclothed. Every Sunday, I wait for Amma in the smoky warmth of the bathing room, an old petticoat tied below my armpits. In one corner, where the slime needs to be scraped away daily, a huge copper pot simmers over the cement oven. Burning coconut fibre, set alight by Chinna, blazes up crackling hot. By the time I have my bath, the water is scalding. But till Amma arrives, I have to wait.

"Amma, I am cold, hurry up."

"A little cold won't kill you."

"Amma, the fire is dying, send Chinna in with more gari."

In that house, where every word is heard in every room, Chinna grumbles, "Did you hear that? She thinks she is the Queen of England ordering everybody about!"

Amma likes making me wait. It will teach me patience, the art of sitting within my own thoughts. So I shiver sullenly, glare at the fire spitting out tiny sparks, the dry leaf-stems and coconut husk smouldering red. I cannot sit any closer to the oven for it snaps out burning embers that sizzle angrily on the wet bathroom floor. The knots in the husk crackle and explode. Nothing in the house is wasted. Every part of the coconut tree is thoroughly used, the leaves along with coconut shells dried for fuel, the extra sold to the grocery shop around the corner where two hags silently peel long veins from the leaves and bunch them together to sell as brooms. Amma arrives finally, bringing a sharp draft of air into the bathroom.

"It's slippery near the fire," I warn.

Deep within my heart is the fear that one day something will happen to her. She is too fleshy, her heart might stop beating. She chews too much *paan,* cancer will eat her away. She hurries too much, she might fall and break her hip. But we do not demonstrate our affections in that house, so I hide my fears beneath a bruising tongue and an argument for everything she says.

"Take off your petticoat," orders Amma, her fingers scooping up a hot drip of mustard oil from the brass bowl on the stove. I shiver with the anticipation of my mother's strong fingers working the oil into my flesh.

Does Vishwa Moorthy notice how soft my skin is from all those weekly oil baths? He says nothing that first night. Instead, he fumbles with the knot on my petticoat, the sari a pool of purple and green about my body. He speaks finally, his voice cracking with impatience, "Open this." I am glad to have something to do with my trembling hands. His body descends on mine, warm and heavy. What am I supposed to do? If I part my legs will he think that I have done this before? Stupid, I tell myself, he knows I am not ignorant. I am not an illiterate poorthing like Mariamma the tailor's daughter who thought that a demon was hiding in her body when she swelled with child. Who did not know she had been raped.

Somewhere in the distance, probably from the servants' quarters, floats the tinny bleat of a Hindi film song.

O-o-o your eyes intoxicate,
makes my heart palpitate.

The silk of your skin
makes my blood rush wild.
O-o-o your eyes like wine.

His breath puffs rapidly into my ear, his legs coarse
with hair rub against mine. Then he rolls off, slowly col-
lapsing on the bed, his head turned away from mine. I
lie still on my back, stare unblinking at the ceiling fan
rotating *kiti-kit, kiti-kit.* A rusty ball-bearing protests
periodically, interfering with the sound of my husband's
rapid breath. I wait for him to stroke my face, tell me
that I am beautiful. He stirs and stretches without a
word, his breathing slows, eases into the soft snuffle of
sleep. Moonlight from the window picks out the curve
of his spine, shadows his buttocks.

⊰⊱

*"Oh bhabhi-ji," giggles Latha, her face smeared like a baby's
with mango pulp. "What naughty things you are telling us.
You are making it all up, no?"*

*Hameeda looks at me, a bit shocked, I think. Her full mouth
is pursed censoriously and she wags her head as if to say, "This
old woman, so shameless!"*

*Her sister Sohaila has no such inhibitions. She waggles her
eyebrows mischievously at me and says, "Arrey, just because
she is old means that she must be like a sadhu? Go on,
bhabhi-ji, tell us more of your xxx, censored stories. This is
like sitting in a cinema house."*

Hameeda looks at her and giggles. "Good thing this is a

ladies only compartment, otherwise bhabhi-ji *would be click-ing her prayer beads in the corner."*

"Somehow I can't imagine her with prayer beads," says Latha, her sharp eyes gleaming amusement. For all her glut-tony and seeming lassitude, she is an observant woman.

❦

A strong odour wakes me from the thankful dark of sleep. That, and the warm band of sun lying across the bed, streaming in from the open windows. I blink and for a few minutes watch the specks of dust perform-ing an energetic dance down the slide of light. I remember the soundless love-making of the night and wonder that my body neither thrills nor cringes at the memory. Perhaps this is because all that I can recall of the experience is my fear and my husband's merciless quiet, his hands moving over me without any tender-ness. I glance towards the windows, wide open, the curtains drawn apart. There are trees outside, the one closest to the window appears to be a mango. I can hear the insistent cawing of a crow and a whole cacophony of other bird sounds. Mynahs, perhaps. Another sound intrudes, one that I can't identify immediately—*khchak, khchak, chak-chak*—rhythmic, with small pauses in between.

I drape my sari across my shoulders like a shawl and gently draw the curtains. They are still warm with the sun. Outside, the grass stretches for several acres till it is stopped by a dense hedge. Two lines of crotons march

down from the portico to the front gate. The road seems
so far away from the house, so different from my childhood home where the entire town, it seemed, enacted
a daily drama at our doorstep. The rhythmic sound, I
discover, is the gardener scything grass in the front lawn.
His thin, muscled arm swings in arcs, sending showers
of green every time it descends.

The wire mesh on the window adds a blurry edge
to everything, making me feel that I am looking
through a haze of dust. I gather my trailing clothes and
head for the bathroom. What do I do? Should I make
the bed, wash the sheets? Or leave it for the maid to do?
Disgusting! How could I allow a maid to touch the
marks and stains from my body and that man's? I stand
there in a debris of doubts and confused thoughts, not
at all comforted by the river of sound that flows outside the room. A bath first, I remind myself, before I
open those towering doors and go out to meet the
household that is already awake and buzzing.

My room opens out to a long corridor with screened
windows, which in turn look out onto a courtyard. Two
of the servants I remember seeing last night are squatting beneath the custard-apple tree in the centre. The
door squeaks sharp and high when I open it, and both
of them leap to their feet. The woman rushes to the
edge of the courtyard and yells to somebody I cannot
see, "Yay! Come quick-quick! Memsahib is awake!"
Then she turns to me and beams, revealing two rows
of brownish teeth. "I am Linda Ayah," she declares, jab-
bing herself in the chest. "He is Ganesh Peon." She

points to each of the other people, "*Dhobhi, jamedaar,* ironing-man, maid."

They smile and nod, "*Namastey,* Mem, *namastey!*" I feel panic sweeping through me. I am supposed to supervise all these people by myself?

"Hanh! Now Memsahib has seen all your faces. Why you are all standing here catching flies with your open mouths?" demands Linda's shrill, energetic voice. "Go, go finish your work."

That is Linda Ayah, bossy, irrepressible, wrinkled as an old leaf, ridiculous glasses perched on a sharp ridge of nose. She has a dusty silver nose-stud, absurdly out of place with the thick glasses.

"Who do you think you are? Giving orders like a memsahib! First find out if she wants you to stay or not," says the *peon,* Ganesh, his dignified face creased with annoyance. He has been hired by the Railways, he explains, but Linda is just a nobody who lives in the servants' quarters. She was the previous mem's *ayah* and just stayed on after they were transferred. "You can get a different woman, Memsahib," says Ganesh smugly, "a young and smart one."

"Young, hah!" Linda Ayah waves her thin arms furiously at him. "So you can wear out your randy eyes looking-looking?" She turns to me and adds reassuringly, "Memsahib, I know everything. You don't worry notatall. This old grumble-pot Ganesh is okay at cooking and looking after Sahib, but who will look after you, tell me? And when the babas and babies are born, Linda will teach them a-b-c and jingle-bells and all. Mem-sahib, I will take care of you, not to worry."

Faced with this declaration of loyalty, I surrender, for a while at least, command of the house.

"What is that smell?" I ask, sniffing at the remnants of the odour that woke me up.

"See-see, what did I tell you?" explodes Linda Ayah, her voice ricocheting off the bare walls. She glares at Ganesh Peon. "Before you know anything about our new Memsahib you start cooking up a stink of egg-*bhujiya*. Memsahib, I told this fellow, make plain *uppuma,* but he thinks he is too smart!"

"No, no, it is okay," I say, catching sight of Ganesh's worried face.

"Sahib likes egg and toast every morning," he says defensively. "What can I do if Sahib wakes up and asks me for egg and toast?" He shoots a filthy look at Linda Ayah.

Reminded of the fact that I now have a husband, I glance around quickly, expecting to see him appear from one of the doors. Linda Ayah reads my thoughts and says, "Sahib has gone to office, he will be back at five o'clock. Then he will go to the club. You will have to wear a nice sari to go with him."

"Sahib told *me* to tell Memsahib that." Ganesh Peon snaps a tea towel in the air to show his annoyance.

"Yes, but did you remember till I opened my mouth?" demands Linda.

"Your mouth is always open, *baka-baka-baka.* Nobody

has a chance to say anything," retorts Ganesh, and he stalks away to the kitchen, a wounded rooster.

Such a tenuous thread, this relationship forged in a single day, at 7:30 in the morning on the sixth of September. Priest Raghotthamachar said it was the perfect moment for the union of my star with V. Moorthy's. My father had an unshakeable faith in the priest, who, he believed, carried the wisdom of ancient sciences in his head. The priest knew all about the stars laid out on yellowing sheets of paper, the movements of those distant points of light and how their wanderings affect the lives of us mortals. When I was still in my mother's womb, warm in the waters of her body, the priest was summoned for the *Sreemantha* ceremony. He would carry my parents' messages to God. "I am only a postman," he was fond of saying, his tiny eyes gleaming benevolence. "I take your prayers to the Almighty: sometimes they are heard, sometimes not. Nothing else I can do."

"Eat, eat well," said various female relatives to my mother as she sat there in a green silk sari with gold zari all over the cloth. The first day of the eighth month of her pregnancy she was spoilt with an abundance of food, clothes, gifts and jewellery. For who knew what might happen when the pains finally started? She might die, the baby might be a deaf-mute or an idiot. So many uncertainties. The women squeezed glass bangles onto my mother's swollen hands, pressed vermilion on her forehead and asked Raghotthamachar to murmur prayers for her well-being. I was the first child and it was good for godly words to wash over my mother. Was it not true that the unfolding child heard everything the mother did? Was it not true that my mother heard only honey words and music, laughter and praise?

Afterwards, nobody could explain where my bitter tongue came from.

Eighteen months after my wedding, I am heavy with child. When I inform my mother, she writes to me, "It is the custom for you to be here three months before birth. That is, if your husband thinks it is all right."

She addresses the letter to my husband, for she knows that I will lie, say, "No, my husband wants me to have the child here in my own house." Not that he cares where the child is born. Of course I do not tell my parents this.

I can imagine my mother discussing it with my sister. "He is a good man. It is her, my own daughter, her fault. She never learned to say the right things. Hasn't learned to hold her tongue."

I have held my tongue but the silence filling the house drives me insane. There is so much quiet that I can hear the spiders crawling across the ceiling, their spinnerets whirring. The immense silence is broken only in the summer when my sisters-in-law arrive.

Meera, with her bags of knotted, fraying wool, and Vijaya, unwinding long threads of story about her family, both of them irritating me with their helplessness, their need to depend on my husband, their brother.

My father gets all prickly when I complain. "He is a worthy man, your husband, we did the best we could for you."

And Amma, his echo, tells me that I should learn to shoulder my responsibilities. "I have four sisters-in-law to cope with, all in the same town. Have I ever complained?"

So I write pleasant letters assuring them that I am happy, managing my life well, a memsahib.

"Dear Amma, how are you? We are fine here. I know you want me to have the baby in Mandya, but I can manage here by myself. Really."

My mother is offended. She says I hurt her by showing such reluctance to have their first grandchild in their house, I am too proud for my own good, always have been, and one day I will trip over this awful pride.

"Dear Amma, I am sorry you feel that I don't want to come to Mandya. No, I am not behaving like a great memsahib. Neither do I think your house is too small. I will have the child there, if that is what you wish. My husband will not be able to accompany me. He has lots of tours to make in the next few months. They are building new lines in the North-East sector where the monsoons held up the work. Now they are trying to finish before the winter sets in, and my husband has to be on site. He might be able to bring me and the baby back home if nothing important comes up. The weather has cooled down considerably, for which I am grateful, as I will not find it so hard to travel down to Mandya in my condition."

My parents are rigid about conventions, which is why they insist on my having the child there. They worry about what people might say if I don't go.

"What a paisa-pinching miser of a father," they might say. "Cannot even spend for their oldest daughter's first delivery. *Tchhu-tchhu-tchhu!*"

It fills the hollow spaces of my body, this child conceived in silence, it squeezes against my lungs, makes me breathless, sends sour belches searing up my throat. Chinna is kept busy making snacks and sweets for my aunts and cousins who come and go, my pregnancy giving them a reason to visit. They pat my back, exclaim over my looks, offer to press my swollen feet, give advice, make predictions.

"It will be a girl, look at the shape of Saroja's belly, a perfect cone. A daughter for sure!"

"Nono, look at her hips, definitely she is carrying a boy, a male child needs all that space."

"There's a glow on her face. It is a girl, a daughter gives her mother beauty."

I feel like a buffalo, awkward and waddling, wearing my mother's blouses, which are as large as *shamianas*.

"Do I have to eat this?" I demand petulantly when Amma serves up spinach or a mashed mess of boiled bottle-gourd. My mother has a gourd for every problem.

"Yes, it will bring out the milk," she replies.

I resent being in my mother's house for the birth of my child, feel like a little girl all over again, forced to follow rules.

"I don't think it fair that women have to go through all this fuss-mess," I complain, patting my stomach. I find it difficult to sit, sleep or even walk comfortably.

"That's what women said long, long ago to Brahma the Creator, and look at what happened," says Chinna.

"What women? What happened?"

"Listen and I will tell you. Once a group of women decided to go to Lord Brahma with a complaint.

"'O Lord,' they grumbled. 'It really isn't fair the way you have divided things between men and women. Not only do women have to carry babies for nine long months, looking all fat and ugly, they also have to undergo labour pain.'

"'Un-hunh, you have a point,' said Brahma, nodding all his heads. 'What do you think I should do?'

"'I have an idea,' said one of the supplicants. 'The woman will carry the child in her belly, but the man who fathered the child must suffer the pains.'

"'So be it,' said Brahma, raising the lower of his two right hands in blessing.

"Many months later, one of the women was ready to give birth to her child. But as she lay in bed, to the astonishment of the entire street, her neighbour's husband started howling in labour. And so women decided that they would rather bear the pain and keep their secrets."

I glance sharply at Chinna.

"Well, did you like the story or not?"

"Un-hunh," I say, but she has turned away.

Soon, soon, my child will be born and I will have to go back to my own home. Will my husband be a better father than a husband? It occurs to me that by the time the child is ten, my husband will be fifty.

❀

The engine flings a long whistle to the rushing wind, mango trees hurry backwards into a darkening landscape. A teenager, Vicki, has got on at the previous station. She is travelling only for a couple of hours.

"But he was a kind man, no?" asks Hameeda. "He gave you a good life!"

"True. But I was young and didn't think of kindness and all. I wanted him to talk to me, tell me my hair was like silk, my voice a sitar song."

"I would have walked out if I didn't like my husband!" remarks the teenager, full of scorn. "Why you stayed?"

"Arrey baba!" Latha claps her hand to her mouth. "How you young people talk! Can she just walk away from her home? What do you say, bhabhi-ji?*"*

"Walking away is hard," I reply. "It is easier to grit your teeth and stay."

"No-no, you have got it wrong," protests Latha. "Going away is the easiest thing in the world. It is like dying. So simple it is to die. Living is hard, to make this small amount of time loaned to you by the gods worthwhile is hard. The

real test is life itself, whether you are strong enough to stay and fight."

⚜

A man stands at the bottom of the steps leading to the verandah, staring at me, smiling.

"Mr. Moorthy asked me to have a look at his car."

"He is having his breakfast," I say. "Wait here till he is done."

"Ten minutes. I cannot wait longer."

Who is he to decide how long he should wait? He can stay there as long as it takes Dadda to finish his breakfast, which might be ten minutes, it might be an hour. But when I go inside to tell Dadda that a mechanic fellow is waiting for him, he pushes his plate aside. "Good, good! He can take a look at the spark-plugs."

"Why don't you finish your breakfast, he can wait," I say, as if it is going to have any effect at all.

In between cleaning the car, wiping the spark-plugs, tuning the ancient engine, Paul da Costa sits in our verandah sipping hot cups of tea. He asks me for the tea, not Ganesh Peon. As if I am his servant, what cheek!

"Go around the back to the kitchen and ask the *peon*," I say.

"Your *peon* is ver-r-ry high and mighty," says Paul, grinning. "He might not want to make tea for a caste-less Anglo."

Nevertheless, he saunters off to the kitchen door and

returns in ten minutes with a tumbler of tea. Ganesh Peon has served Paul da Costa in the tumbler reserved for the toilet-cleaner, and I imagine him handing it to this swaggering fellow with a condescending look.

The mechanic settles on the steps leading into the verandah and sighs. "Good *chai*," he remarks. "My granny used to make tea like this."

"Is she dead?" I ask, looking up from my sewing. I feel obliged to make some comment.

"Why you want to kill my poor granny, Memsahib? Nono, she is in Australia with my Uncle Albert."

I don't know how to respond to this half-breed man who sits in my verandah and tells me about the latest films, about his cousins in Australia, about everything and everything. I smile timidly, afraid of what the servants will think if I join in his full-bodied laughter. I am, after all, a memsahib, and there is a distance to be maintained between us.

After Paul da Costa leaves, I tell Dadda, "Why don't you ask that mechanic man to come every Sunday to start up the car and keep it okay? Not good for a car to park there for days and days without running."

Linda Ayah looks disapprovingly at me. She squats in the verandah like an ancient crow, her knobbled fingers sorting through piles of tamarind fruit. She mumbles under her breath as she collects the pods scattered under the delicate branches at the far end of the verandah. The ground is littered with them, each thickly coated with red ants. The tree is very old, its thin green leaves throw a matted shadow, it scatters yellow flowers every-where. You can eat the leaves and flowers and pods, make them into chutneys and sauces, so sour that you have to twist your face, screw up your eyes and squeeze your gut muscles to take the acid juice. Smack your tongue against your mouth and take another nibble, that's the way to eat tamarind, a tiny bit at a time. Feel the sour sliding against your teeth edges like fingernails down a blackboard. Linda Ayah has been begging me to cut the tree down, she is fed up with keeping the children from eating the pods. My daughter Kamini, especially, for the more you tell her not to do some-thing, the more likely she is to do it. Roopa is too young to disobey. But Linda has other objections, too. It is a spiteful tree, she says. If you sit under it too long it will gather all your secrets and then its feathery little leaves will whisper them out to the world. If you sleep under it at night, the tree spirits will fill your ears with non-sense and turn you into a lunatic.

"Memsahib, tell me, if you sit in a mortar can you avoid being hit by the pestle?" she asks suddenly, her hands full of tamarind.

Linda Ayah rarely spills a word that is useless. She might wander about spouting proverbs and fables, but always, always there is a message for me. I pretend deaf-ness and continue picking stones from the *soopa* of rice grains. Linda squats across from me in the sunny veran-dah, carefully removing seeds from the pulpy brown tamarind. In between us, on a sheet of newspaper, is a growing pile of stones, glass bits, rat shit. I make a mental

note to talk to Theli Ram the grocery store owner
about the quality of the rice. He told me that his stock
was guaranteed good.

"Personal eye I keep, Memsahib," he said, placing a
hand on his heart, his eyes honest. "On my mother's
body I swear that each grain in this humble shop is personally checked by myself."

"The rascal's mother will writhe in *jahannum!*" I hold
up an orange bead. "Out of ten kilos of rice, two kilos
are stones."

"What I mean is," says Linda Ayah, ignoring my comment as completely as I ignored hers, "what it is I want
to say is, if you put your hand under the wheels of a
running cart it will surely get crushed, no?"

She looks at me, waiting for me to unwind her string
of thought. I stare back, unable to see her eyes behind
her glasses. She is facing the sun and the light turns the
lenses into two radiant orbs.

"Hanh, answer me, will you or won't you crush your
hand?" she demands.

"Linda, you want to say something, then say it quick-
quick and get back to work," I say, trying to retrieve my
authority.

And that spectacle-face, as stubborn as the *dhobi's*
mule, asks again, "Will the pestle hit you?"

"Yes *baba* yes! My head will be paste and my hand
will be smashed by the wheel. Happy?"

"No, I am not happy, that is why I dare to open my
mouth." Linda flexes her fingers stained with sticky
tamarind. "You think, who is she to tell me what to-do

not-to-do? You will even think kick her out, get another *ayah*. But my heart will not let me hold my tongue."

"Linda, if you don't stop wandering around the world to reach your neighbour's house, I will have to find another *ayah*." What *is* she getting at?

"Why you look *tukur-tukur* at that three-fourth person?" asks Linda finally.

"Who are you talking about? And what do you mean three-fourth?" Does Linda know about Paul? Has she told anybody? Servants are like drains, they carry all the muck round and round from house to house.

"Three parts low caste and one part pink-face."

"He is just like you, then, Linda."

"Memsahib, what you are getting by insulting me, henh? See this skin?" Linda pulls a wrinkled flap of skin off her forearm. "This skin is tough, so many years it has fried in the sun. My parents were good people, no half-caste business for us. Respectable people. They owned five acres of land. My grandmother, she had ten *tholas* of gold. But I was a fool and married a no-good drunk. My fault. I had no brains, only wet loins. That is why I am telling you, this Linda Ayah has now collected brains after many-many years. What you see in that Paul person that your own mister doesn't have, henh?"

I find no words to reply, and in the silence all other sounds are magnified. The crow on the electric wire over the road is going *kaan-kaan-kaan*. Maybe it has spotted a dead mouse in the ditch below. Thick earth is being dug and loosened by the gardener next door, and the sound reminds me that it is time to start preparing beds for the nasturtiums and poppies. The peanut-vendor approaches our road, "*Garam-thaaja,* hottest-fresh *chana choor!*" He gives the last word a questioning lilt, a blandishment.

Should I tell Linda that my husband likes me to screw up my hair in a bun like an old Anglo aunty because he cannot stand its loose abundance? He says I look like a slut when I wear the long emerald earrings my grandmother gave me for a wedding gift—green for a full womb, she said. He sleeps with me on Wednesday night at 21:40 sharp and Sunday same time if his train is in town. My feet tangle in his pyjamas for he doesn't like undressing completely. How can I explain to her the yawning monotony of my life with this man? How do I translate the dislike that rages through me when his voice touches my ears, or his hands brush mine?

Linda interrupts my silence. "Does your mister drink? No. Does the poorgood man smell of some other woman? Nono. Does he beat you? No."

"How do you know?"

"I told you," she says. "This Linda was born Jesu knows when, but I got a brain in my skull now, after all these years. I can see things."

"Oh, a *chudail* in my house! Tell me, o four-eyed one, what else can you see?" I ask.

"Make fun, what do I care? You want to know what I see? Lots of tears for you, that's what. And for those poor babies of yours. No fault of theirs either."

Suddenly I have had enough of this conversation. "I am glad your brains have multiplied since your birth,

Ayah," I snap. "But I can see your tongue has also grown longer than it should. You want to give advice, give it to your own daughter. I hear she is called scissor-legs by all the *goondas* in town. Grab her arms, they say, and she will spread her legs."

Linda glares at me. "I opened my mouth because you are like my daughter. To me no difference." She has to have the last word.

She smacks the tray of rice down and huffs away into the house. What a nuisance she is getting to be! Did I escape from my mother's home to listen to her voice coming from this soda-glasses witch?

⚜

"But Aunty-ji," says Sohaila. "So many servants and all you had, how you didn't get caught?"

"She didn't do anything, to get caught." Latha turns her round, trusting face and looks at me. "Did you bhabhi-ji, did you?" And when I smile faintly at her, she is shocked. "Bhabhi-ji, you really left your husband-children-home to go behind an Anglo? Hai-Ram! I don't understand why. You are truly crazy!"

I push my face against the bars in the open window and catch the wind with my mouth. It is dark now, and I can only guess at the names of huddled trees. Puddles and ponds stream by, silver in the passing light of our windows.

⚜

"A woman is her husband's shadow," says my mother. "She follows him wherever he goes."

She says this so many times it runs as the blood in my veins. Only after Paul da Costa interferes with my placid life do I take her words apart, piece by piece, examining them for all their faults, if only to give myself an excuse to disregard them. A shadow follows its body around, yes. But I am an individual who makes my own shadow. Sometimes this shadow stretches out longer than my body; sometimes it pools like ink about my feet. It changes, dances along behind the body, beneath its feet, in front and beside it, eccentric, erratic, moved by light. My mother sees herself only as an extension of Appa, refuses to be anyone other than his wife. She does not want to lose him like Putti Ajji lost Rayaru.

"She did not lose him," I say. "He was the one who was dissatisfied with one woman. He was greedy."

"No," insists Amma. "Your grandmother talked too much for a woman. She had too many opinions, she drove him away."

My grandmother Putti might have lost her husband to another woman, but she held on to her pride, and to my grandfather's property. Small and spiteful, tart as a raw *amda* fruit, she reigned queen of the vast ancestral house, thankfully ceded to her by her husband, my grandfather, who preferred to give her all she asked rather than be attacked by her scorn. So what if he escaped to his mistress's house, a tiny whitewashed structure at the other end of town?

"Think, think," said Putti Ajji. "Who is the winner here? I have my self-respect, my children have a house and a father's name. The slut your grandfather visits has nothing."

I admire Putti for exactly the reasons Amma does not. My mother wanted to get as far away as possible from her mother, and so she followed every rule Putti Ajji broke.

"I didn't want you children to grow up with shame," Amma tells me.

"But Putti Ajji did not care about shame and things like that," I argue. "The shame belonged to Rayaru's mistress."

"You don't understand anything," says Amma. "What is the use of having a palace of a house, boxes full of jewellery, when your man is busy admiring another woman's charms? And have you ever thought how we, their children, felt? Those pitying looks from all our relatives. Poor children, they seemed to say, paying for their parents' sins. Nobody blamed Rayaru, you know, the fault was entirely Putti's."

At least my grandmother fought for all that she could get from that hollow marriage, I think to myself. She didn't leave any doubt about what she thought of her husband.

"*Baddi-suley maganey*, son of a whore in debt, fucking an untouchable piece of flesh. Even a pariah dog will not sniff that woman and my fine husband goes to her!" Ajji screamed to her neighbours from the terrace of her house, where she spent whole mornings supervising the servants as they laid out sheets of *appala* and *shandigey* to dry in the silver heat of the sun.

My mother refused to fight for anything. But who am I to say that her life with Appa was unhappy? She framed her conditions for contentment and found them within marriage. My father gave her security, a home, the freedom to do what she pleased inside that home. His affection for her was as solid as a pillar, and my mother's life grew rich and bountiful twining about that pillar.

I, on the other hand, am married to a man who has no feelings to spare for a wife. A dried-out lemon peel whose energies have already been squeezed out caring for a sick mother, worrying about his sisters, inheriting his dead father's unfinished duties. It ate up his youth. With my tamarind tongue, never yielding a moment, I use my grandmother's strategy of words to ward off the pain of rejection. His aloof, merciless cool, my defensive anger. I will not beg for the affection that is due to me, his wife. Why, even a cat demands a caress, a gentle word. Deprive it of attention and it will wander to another home.

The Ratnapura house is strangely designed. All the rooms open onto one verandah or another, even the bathrooms. Probably built in a more trusting period. No, that can't be true. The house was made by the British for the British, and they didn't trust anyone.

They could not, for they were foreigners in a hostile land. The mutiny—for us it was a battle for freedom—of 1857 erased the fragile peace between the rulers and the ruled. Perhaps this open house, which can be entered from twelve different doors, was created by a madman. Or a fatalist. Perhaps the person who made this house thought the worst that could happen would be that the people who lived here would be killed. The best was that there would be cool air and the scent of jasmine wandering about the house all day and through the night.

My parents, on the other hand, live in a place that is strictly Hindu. A corridor flies from the front door right out the back. A single straight line, so that if an evil spirit enters, it will be carried out on a draft of air. The rooms open out off the corridor like neat rows of teeth. One tiny set of barred windows in each room. The walls in between the rooms are thick, but it is possible to hear sounds.

My brother murmuring his lessons aloud, "Ten two-za twenty, ten three-za thirty."

Chinna pressing her swollen feet and moaning softly with the painful joy of blood rushing through her numb veins.

The rhythmic creak-creak of the wooden slats on my parents' bed.

As a child the creaking comforts me, assures me of their presence when most of the world is dead asleep. As a teenager it fills me with curiosity and then disgust. They are doing what the dogs in the alley behind our house do. As I grow older, the bed creaks less frequently. My parents are getting old, perhaps the warmth of my father's back against my mother's is enough.

I am the first daughter, and it is time for them to discuss my marriage: perform it well and the offers will come rushing in for my sisters. In my room, I imagine my future husband. He will be gentle and caring, discuss his work with me, talk to me often. My imaginary husband has no face, just a body that drifts tentatively over me. I am too frightened, even in my dreams, to let that hovering body touch me, for a girl from a good family does not think such shameful thoughts. My mother's voice is there, always, always. As are the stories Chinna brings back from various relatives.

"Did you hear, Radhu's youngest has brought shame upon the whole family! Pretended to go to her friend's place and what was she doing instead? Having coffee with a boy, not any boy that too, but a Muslim from Rajan Road."

And, "Have you seen where Leelavati Gururaj ties her sari? Down here." Chinna runs her palms indignantly along her hips. "No wonder every useless *goonda* in town follows her with his tongue hanging out. A sari tied that low is an invitation for youknowwhat!" Chinna rolls her eyes meaningfully. "If something happens to her it will be her own fault."

And my mother, "Decent girls don't go to the movies alone or with boys. Decent girls spend their time at home learning to cook."

We are decent people living in that long, secretive

house with its furtive night noises. And then I marry and move to a Railway house with such soaring ceilings that I have to tie two long bamboo poles to the broom so the servants can brush out cobwebs. Its windows conceal nothing, gaping spaces that I cover with yards of heavy fabric.

I glance at Kamini and Roopa sprawled out on the ground. We are in the spare bedroom, the one that opens without any preliminaries onto the lawn. When Dadda goes on line, I spend the evenings in this room. The large bed has a bright Rajasthani cover. In the corner, a heavy chair with ochre cushions. Kamini calls it the waiting-room *kursi* because it has arms that grow out into footrests just like the ones in the ladies' waiting room at the station. It is a hideous chair, but large enough to cross your legs when you sit. Dadda bought it from an old Anglo couple near the Medical Clinic. Massey, that's the name, Jack and Valerie Massey. They are leaving India for Australia, to live with their daughter. Jack is a fitter in the Railway workshop and has known Dadda since he was a probationary officer. Dadda takes me and the children to visit the Masseys on their fiftieth wedding anniversary. I, in my turquoise silk sari with a gold border of mangoes, sit upright on the edge of a huge curving sofa, a starched smile stretching my lips. I am the only one in a sari. The other women are in frocks, mostly sleeveless, mostly with low necklines.

"Couldn't you have made some kind of conversation?" says Dadda later, furious.

"Couldn't you take your eyes off those *bazaari* bosoms?"

The older women wear wide floral dresses, their varicosed legs lumpy like bags full of marbles. They flock around the room, talking in hearty voices, uncomfortable with a Hindu officer and his prim-mouthed wife in their midst.

"Hey, Johnny boy, whatcha drinking, man?"

"Annie darling, you made that frock yourself or what?"

"Ooh look at these cutie-pie girlies. Whatch your name, sweetie?"

I resist the impulse to snatch my daughters close to me, watching to make sure nobody gives them any of that cake, it has brandy in it for sure. I hate this house crowded with ponderous furniture from another era, the aged Royal Doulton china with its pattern of pink and yellow flowers, the rows of wine glasses and whisky tumblers. Mrs. Massey is telling someone that they are genuine Waterford crystal. She rings a spoon against one of the glasses and the clear bell note stops the chitter of voices for a few seconds. The desperate gaiety of these people, the few that remain in the country, frightens me. They are all slipping out, moving to Canada, Australia, Britain. They will pass there with their fair skins. Nobody will notice their knees. Mrs. Simoes tells me that you can spot an Anglo by the knees. "Knock-knees, every one of them. You can make out straight away. White skin, light eyes, coloured hair, just like an *angrezi*. But look at their knees and you will know, *chhata-chhat*, mixed breed."

Paul da Costa is the exception. He is dark. Darker even than Ganesh Peon. He does not have knock-knees. When he comes to tinker with Dadda's car on Sunday mornings, he wears a pair of khaki pants, cut off mid-thigh. His legs are long and hairless and the knees join the thighs to the calves smoothly, with no hint of bony protruberances. Only his eyes, bright green, give him away. The servants call him *kaala billee,* the black cat, right to his face. He might be a skilled mechanic, but on the social scale he is at the same level as the servants, lower maybe, because he is without caste.

I stand at the window in the girls' room, shielded by the light bamboo *chik,* safe in the knowledge that I cannot be seen from outside, and watch him bend over the car, the muscles high on his back bunching and relaxing as his arms move. If Linda Ayah comes in I grab a frock, a panty, a petticoat from a pile on the chair near the window, and pretend to fold it.

"Nice day, hanh, Memsahib?" she says nastily, picking up the pile of clothes. "Why you are sitting inside and spoiling your health? Go, go out and get some clean air. Bad for you to hide inside here and do nothing."

It is useless for me to protest, to say, "Linda, I am folding the clothes, I want to fold the clothes today. You never fold them right. *You* go and do something outside, watch the gardener."

Linda is a witch who can smell out secrets. She glares at me, her eyes stern behind the soda-glasses she insists on wearing. "Why you always want to argue with me?

I am only thinking of your own good. Your eyes will go bad staring out of this window."

As a girl, I wanted to wear a sleeveless dress.

My mother said, "No, decent girls don't show their bodies to every passer-by."

"That is so silly, only my arms will be seen."

"I don't care," replied my mother. "You can do what you want when you are married and belong to someone else. Then dance naked for all I care."

But after marriage there are new rules to follow, fresh boundaries. There is always someone in the house, the *peon,* the gardener, the maid, the *dhobhi,* and Linda Ayah with her terrible glasses. They watch me, discuss this new memsahib, make sure I do not stray from the correct lines of behaviour. They keep an eye on me for their sahib, for Dadda, the man to whom my parents hand me like a parcel wrapped in silk and gold. He is at home maybe one week out of four. As I stand near the window, grasping the edge of the sill to still my trembling hands, I can feel my mother's disapproving glare in the middle of my back.

"Devaru nodtharey ninnana," she will say—the gods will fix you!

Evenings such as this one, with Dadda away, the house empty except for Linda Ayah snoring in the kitchen where she spreads her *chatai,* such evenings I love the most. I leave the windows open and gusts of air puff at the curtains, set the light bulb swinging wildly. Shadows fly around the room, dancing patterns created by the bamboo lampshade. Kamini is immersed in a colouring book, pastels scattered around her. Roopa has her doll across her legs.

"Oolulu-oolulu," she sings patting the doll, imitating Linda Ayah. If you ask her what she wants to be when she grows up, she says, "An *ayah*."

She moves her leg up and down in a rocking motion, her face absorbed. Parts of a stainless-steel kitchen set lie on the floor, catching the light here and there. Dadda bought her the set on one of his line-duty tours. He is an affectionate father, imaginative, too. More imaginative than he is as a husband. If he goes somewhere he cannot find books or toys, he nevertheless brings an interesting gift, always with a story attached. A jar of translucent honey smelling of oranges with bits of waxy honeycomb trapped in its viscous depths.

"This is the honey Rama and Sita and Lakshmana ate," he tells the girls, placing the jar on the dining table. His train has returned from deep within the Dandakaranya forests. For a month he wanders through dense jungle, moist, humming with mosquitoes. He taps and measures, guesses and gauges, filling his notebook with information about the land. He draws stories from this timeless landscape, which will soon be altered, and brings them home for his daughters.

Every month I check to see if I have put all that Dadda needs into his line-box. A large Horlicks bottle of sugar. Dadda does not add sugar to his coffee, but the *peon* on line duty has a sweet tooth. Salt in a Bournvita tin. I must remind Ganesh Peon not to throw away the empty ones. Even if I don't use them all, I can sell them

to the *kabaadi-wallah* or exchange them for stainless-
steel utensils. Mrs. Baagchi in Number 16 bungalow
shows me three stainless-steel bowls she got in exchange
for old newspapers and tins.

"But of course those *kabaadi-wallahs* make a profit,"
she says. "Are they simple-heads to just give away good
steel? Arrey, I have heard they are millionaires! Yes, they
take our *raddhi* to big factories. The factory-wallahs turn
the *raddhi* into fancy boxes and whatnot and sell them
back to us. But am I going to look for those factories
with my garbage on my back? No *baba* no. Let the
kabaadi-wallah do that. I am happy with my steel *dibbas*."

The *kabaadi-wallah* also buys old bottles, especially
the ones with wide necks—Complan, Nestlé coffee,
Parlé jam. I prefer to keep these bottles. They fit neatly
into the line-box and the *peon* can straight away see
through the glass what is inside. Did I pack two bottles
of *dal* or three? Two should be more than enough. I can
never stop worrying, though, because no matter how
often I check, there is something I forget, and then I
never hear the end of it. One month it is salt.

"I had food without salt for three days," says Dadda
when he comes back. "Three days of *dal* without salt,
do you know what that feels like? Or *bhindi* absolutely
tasteless? Even the chilies don't taste of anything without salt."

Dadda, normally silent as the Delhi Iron Pillar, is pas-
sionate when it comes to food.

I want to say, "So what if you haven't eaten salt for
three days of your life, is it such a big tragedy?"

But of course I don't. I have been married seven years and the lessons my mother drilled into my head hang like a sheet between Dadda and me.

"Your husband is your god. Always obey him, it is your duty. Never refer to him by name, it is a disrespect. And for god's sake don't let your too-smart tongue wag-wag more than necessary."

If I allow my tongue to wag, the good strong sound of words might blow the sheet aside. But I do not, and the sheet grows stronger and more opaque. Dadda remains far on the other side, a dim figure, the father of my children, but that is all. When the most intimate space in a home has no words in it, what then of the rest of the house? I try to fill the other rooms with my voice.

"How was your trip?"

"Good. Next time don't forget to pack a suit. I needed it this trip."

"For what?"

"Meeting."

All his words are reserved for his children.

Our train makes a tea-stop at another station, a small one. Two ragged boys push into the compartment. "Shoe polish, shoe polish, clean and dust dirty floor?" they sing hopefully.

"Go away," says Latha, frowning at them. "They are big thieves, you know, they sit under the berths polishing shoes and steal from our bags."

❄

We never travel with Dadda except when we are transferred. I am not allowed into his private world of journeys, long spaces, trees that touch the sky, sky that meets
the sea. Before the children are born, I cannot even call
him by his name, and he never uses mine. Never
"Saroja," jewel, flower, gem, nothing. Just "Ay." After
Kamini arrives I find a name that I can utter without
feeling discomfort—"Dadda." But in the caverns of the
children's bodies are particles of his being. He is in the
blood pumping through their hearts, their flesh and
their bones. The currents running through their brains
find some of their impulses in his. I feel a twinge of
jealousy when I see the way he is with his daughters.
He shows an interest in everything they do, an affection he never shows me.

Kamini is absorbed in drawing a boat, displaying it
proudly to her Dadda. Enclosing her small fist in his,
he guides the crayon over the paper, corrects mistakes,
redoes proportions, murmurs instructions.

"See, this sail is too big. Your boat will drift away into
the sky and then you will have to tell everybody that
you have drawn an aeroplane."

He likes to make them laugh, cannot bear their
sorrow.

"Let them be," he says if he hears me scolding either
of them. "They are children. They will learn."

The indulgence in his voice. Roopa and Kamini
think he is Baba Cheeni, the kind old sugar-man in

Linda Ayah's stories. They probably believe that I am the witch, the *daayin* who says, "Do your homework; don't pick your nose; sit properly, the whole world can see your knickers. Why did you get this sum wrong? Did you say good-morning to teacher-miss?"

I buy them bloomers, petticoats, school notebooks, water-bottles, toothbrushes. Dadda comes home like a magician bearing strange gifts, tales of wonderful things and places. He returns from the hills of Aarlong with two silkworm cocoons. One of them is sliced open and the silken interior glows like a moonlit cavern. The girls caress the rough, dull-brown outside of the cocoon and beg him to reveal its mysteries.

"These cocoons came from a farm where the cater-pillar isn't boiled to yield up its trove of silk," says Dadda, spinning his yarns, his gift to his daughters. While I, his wife, the other half of his body, I have only silences and the vast distances his travel creates between us.

"The caterpillar is shaken out of its nest of sleep onto fresh mulberry leaves and the silk is drawn out of the cocoon," Dadda explains, bringing out two small pouches made of pale golden silk. Then from the bot-tom of the suitcase, which is still full of sweat-smelling shirts and underwear, he shyly draws out a sari, the same soft, golden silk, but with a flash of turquoise for the border.

"Give this to your mother," he says, nudging Roopa.

This is his first gift to me, and I am not sure how to accept gifts from my husband the traveller. There are so many things I want to say, but my clumsy tongue takes

over and the words fall before I can hold them back.
"Yes, but this is too dull for my skin."

The thread that Dadda spins towards me snaps, and
his silence once again covers his tentative smile. I could
so easily have said, "This is beautiful," and meant the
gesture rather than the gift. But now I must stumble to
cover up the disappointment that hovers between us.

"It is beautiful, though," I try. "I think if I wear it with
a turquoise blouse, it will look perfect."

Too late; Dadda moves out of the room to the verandah and sits nursing his pipe and the newspaper. Kamini
scowls at me, tears threatening to rush out of her eyes.
She calls me a mean-mean witch, says she hates me.

I have nothing to discuss with this stranger who takes
me from one town to another, showing me a whole
country. He sits with his daughters about him, telling
his tales, while I hover in the penumbra of their shared
happiness.

"There was only one line in Kantabhanji," he tells
them. "But a troublesome one. Nobody wanted to work
there for the villagers were sure it was haunted. The
train arrived every evening at nineteen hours."

"Seven o'clock," chorus the girls.

"Yes, it was dark by then and a porter had to walk
down the tracks, about three furlongs or so, to change the
signal. Those days the signals were not automatic. The station-master reminded the porter of the time by hitting
a gong, so loud that it could be heard by the villagers
for miles around. Everything worked fine for a while,
and then suddenly the porters started disappearing.

Sometimes their lanterns were found near the signal, sometimes not. The train drivers would get no signal and go right past the station. That's when I was sent in to see what was going on."

Dadda lives by rules. Just as he makes sure that nothing, not a syllable, in the *Handbook for Railway Officers* is ever violated, so does he follow an unwritten book on the duties of a Brahmin father. He is determined to avoid all the mistakes his own father made. But he is a good son, respecting his father no matter what he did, and so he never tells me what those mistakes were. Only once he says, "He neglected us. My father forgot his duty by us." When he died he left Dadda, the oldest, to gather up all the pieces. I marry a man who is already old, who fulfils his obligation to society by acquiring a wife. I am merely a symbol of that duty completed.

Sometimes, Dadda orders a basket of apples from Simla, where his inspection carriage is stationed. Golden apples. Some men buy underwear for their wives, my husband is more down-to-earth. He is doing his duty by his wife and family, providing the nourishment a body needs. Sometimes, looking at a bridge over a tiny, ferocious river, checking for weaknesses in the enormous rock-and-iron pillars, Dadda remembers to send Banganapalli mangoes from Tenali. A sack of Basmati rice from Dehradoon, nuts from Delhi, lichees from Patna, oranges from Nagpur. They arrive without any message and Dadda never asks afterwards if we enjoyed these unannounced gifts. It is almost as if he remembers us till a certain point and then, by sending a basket

of fruit, exorcises us. We are not to wander out of that
little space he draws for us, as if we are his designs, those
precise lines with which he fills drafting sheets, the
minute scribbles that designate those drawings into
their slots, taking into account every possible landslide,
waterfall, monsoon storm, flood or wild animal that
the earth could throw up. He studies the land, knows
every pit and tumour on its surface before pinning on
it endless tracks of steel and teak. But of us, his family,
he knows nothing.

When Dadda leaves on line and Paul da Costa creeps
onto the shadowy verandah of the Ratnapura house
like a thief, I tell him that I cannot destroy my life for
a half-breed man, a caste-less soul. I want to reach out
and touch his warm skin, watch his clear smile. But
words like duty and loyalty clamour in my ears. I think
of Roopa and Kamini, their soft skins smelling of milk,
their heads so vulnerable. They hold me with their
helplessness, they twine about me as tenacious as
bougainvillaea. I tell Paul that I will not leave my children. I don't want to cut myself off, become a pariah,
have other children who will be bastards. I let my evil
tongue reduce him to a pile of nothing dust. Perhaps
then he will stop asking me to go with him to England, to Australia, to Canada.

"This fool has two types blood in his body and your
high-caste Brahmin mind cannot handle that? Can't

do anything about this, Memsahib, it is part of me, will go to my grave. Whattodo?" Paul rubs his skin. "I will kill myself," he says. "You wait and see, you will be responsible."

I smile at such melodrama. Has a man ever lost his life over a woman? His mind maybe, but his life? As my Amma would have said, such tragedies belong to the cinema screen. Only a Majnu would die for his Laila, a Ranjha for his Heer. And they exist between the lines of a bard's song.

I need to straighten the cyclone of thoughts filling my mind, so I let Linda take responsibility for the children, the house, me, everything. Linda Ayah teaches my children all sorts of rubbish. But it keeps them occupied so who am I to say this or that? She tells them not to clip their nails at night. A *daayin* might collect the clippings and cast a spell on them. When she takes the girls to the club to play in the evening she makes them fix their gaze on the road.

"Watch out," she says, frightening them out of their wits. "Watch out for evil things. If you see a pile of cut hair or a lemon tied with turmeric-stained thread, make sure you don't step on it! You will be caught in a witch's web for sure."

Linda Ayah teaches Kamini and Roopa good Christian songs. She doesn't like leaving anything to chance, feels that my careless Hindu ways are a bad influence on my girls.

Jesu Christo super star
Twinkling in the hea-vens
Jesu Christo son of Mary
Shining bright and haa-ppy!

she sings, clapping her hands and urging the girls to repeat.

She tells them long, rambling stories and nursery rhymes:

Baa-baa black ship,
Have you any oon?
Yessir, yessir theen bags phull.

The sound of the Ranigunj Mail rushing past the house at exactly 21:56 hours deafens me so that I miss the first scraping, hesitant knock on the verandah door. The door is normally locked because the room is for guests, hardly used except in summer when my sisters-in-law arrive. It leads through the verandah onto a vast, unkempt gathering of trees and bushes which I toy with eliminating, perhaps making a park for the children to play in. The gardener is enthusiastic but finds an excuse every time I ask him to start work.

"For that kind of jungle you need big clippers. I have to requisition from the main office, Memsahib," he says, squatting in the shade of the rain tree separating our compound from the neighbours.'

His passion is the front garden, where he has managed to coax a riot of flowers out of hard soil. Lazy bugger, I think, but keep the thought to myself. I don't want a full-scale union fight on my hands. The union is exceptionally powerful—strikes occur at the drop of a hat, *gheraos,* stop-the-train movements. For example, a train is delayed for two hours. Nobody is at fault, but passengers at the station shout at the engine-driver, who yells back and is slapped on his face.

"No more work," says the engine-driver, his linesman, the guard, the signalman. "We won't work. No engines will run, no trains will move. We demand compensation for this insult. Are we dogs to be kicked by this person and that?"

In the colonies, *jamedaars* put down their pails and brooms, let garbage pile up on the roads; gardeners refuse to water the lawns, just sit in the shade of the tamarind trees chewing *khaini.* Even Paul da Costa joins in the *thamaasha.* Such stories I hear about how he leads a gang of workers in the loco-shop to down their tools, to paint posters in red and white—"No Pay No Work, Are We Animals Or Human?" Later, after the strike has blown over like a spent storm, Paul smiles at me. "Scared your officer sahibs, didn't we?"

Kamini is singing *"Baa-baa black ship"* the night Paul knocks on the door of the guest bedroom one last time. The Raniganj Express rattles the windows of the house so loudly that I think that the first knock is just a shutter banging. Only after the entire train has passed, in the sudden stillness as the house settles back to listen to the night, only then do I hear the second knock. And pretend that I do not.

❧

"Mrs. Moorthy!" I hear Ruma Ahluwalia calling me from her side of the hedge between our houses, but I do not reply. This is the first moment in the day that I have had to sit down to a cup of hot tea. All by myself. When Dadda is home he has his breakfast at eight o'clock sharp—a minute later makes him furious and a minute earlier means that a fresh batch of crisp *dosai* or toast has to be made. Food cannot be kept waiting for him and he refuses to wait for it, either. In this house things run like trains, by the clock. The girls leave for school at eight-fifteen, the *dhobhi* comes at eight-thirty, the vegetable-man at eight-forty-five and the ironing-boy at nine. My neighbour's voice reaches me from across the hedge as soon as I settle into the easy chair. She can't see me sitting in the verandah through the thick wall of morning-glory but she knows that I am here.

"Mrs. Moorthy, did you hear the news?"

Since I came to Ratnapura, Ruma has caught me every morning as soon as I come out into the verandah, inviting herself for a cup of tea and staying to lunch as well. It is because of her that I plant my morning-glory wall, now a thick, crawling forest of tendrils, leaves and pale-purple flowers. Black ants march crisply up and down the stems, dropping on my shoulder if I sit too close. A wasp has been trying to make a nest in the corner where the morning-glory meets the verandah pillar. I scrape the still damp mud off every day, refusing to let her lay the eggs hanging within her body. It is a small act of cruelty worked into the pattern of my daily life. Maybe for that I will be reborn as a pregnant wasp. Every morning a sun–bird shimmers over open blossoms, inserting its long beak delicately into the violet interior. Its wings vibrate frantically, holding the bird up till it drains the flower.

Today, Ruma wants to discuss something unbearably interesting with me. She has not seen me leave the house, the front door is wide open, and my maidservant is washing the dishes in the courtyard outside, all of which are signs that I am around. I toy with the idea of slipping into the house and out through the verandah on the far side, but Ruma is already at my gate. She spots me on the verandah, waves and huffs up the driveway.

"Why you didn't answer me?" she demands sulkily. "I called you and called you, what you were doing?"

"I must have been in the bath, with the water running, you cannot hear anything you know."

"Such shocking news, *baap-re-baap!* I need some hot tea, so upside-down my system is from the shock," says Ruma, clutching her left breast which forms a plump nest for her heart. She pulls a chair into the sun and settles down with a sigh.

"Ganesh!" I call, resigned to a day full of gossip. "Bring two *chais,* super hot. Boil the milk, don't forget."

"*Hanh,* Memsahib," replies Ganesh from inside the house.

I already know what Ruma's news is. I have known it since eight o'clock yesterday evening.

"They found a mechanic in the billiards room," says Mrs. Ahluwalia.

I know that Paul da Costa hanged himself.

"Istupid idiot, why defile our billiards room tell me? No manners or respect for other people's feelings."

I broke his heart. As if a heart is made of glass!

"Why you are so quiet? You know the fellow?" Ruma gives me an inquisitive look.

How could he live without a heart?

"Paul de Souza or something, he did repairy work on cars and all. Didn't I see him with his head inside your car also?"

"Paul da Costa, his name was da Costa," I say.

"Something, the *bechaara* is with his Christ, *baba,* how it is mattering what his name is?" says Mrs. Ahluwalia.

"When you die, would you like it if people call you something else?" I snap, and Ruma gapes at me.

"You want *me* to die?"

I shrug. "Why should I care whether you live or die?"

Ruma stands up and glares. "*Baap-re-baap!* What a wicked tongue you have, Madam! Tell your *peon* not to bother with tea and all."

I know that she will rush around the colony later today complaining to the other ladies about me. "That woman is such a *chunt*," she will tell them. "Too-too moody, I tell you. I knew, first time I met her, not a nice type."

Did I truly tear out the mechanic's heart like the *daayin* in the stories Linda Ayah tells my girls? What if, like Paul, I had forgotten that I was a memsahib?

❀❀❀

"Come, come," says Latha kindly, offering me a slice of mango. "Don't feel sad, behen-ji, it was time for the man to leave this world, so he left. Whattodo?"

"What did you do then?" asks Sohaila.

"Did your hubby ever find out?" Even the teenager Vicki is snared by my tale.

I shrug. I don't know. He never said anything.

Hameeda shakes her head. "You shouldn't have done all that," she says. "It wasn't right."

"Why not?" demands Vicki. "She was unhappy with her life, no?"

"And what's wrong with sharing some words with the poor man?" asks Latha, whose kind eyes allowed her to see only more kindness.

❀❀❀

Before my marriage, the world seems a smooth, round place. My father is a true patriarch. As long as Appa is in charge, we don't have to worry about anything. We live in one little town from birth to marriage or death and thereafter. That makes a difference, you see, living in one place. You know everybody as if they belong to your own family. If you have a problem, there are at least ten shoulders to help you carry your pain. Your happiness lights up the whole place. And in a small town, which gets its livelihood from sugar refining, nothing ever changes. Postman Subanna could wander

blindfold about the place and still deliver the mail cor-
rectly. Then when I turn twenty-three, that same Subanna brings a letter from our Delhi Aunty. "There is a
good boy, son of a family friend," she writes. "Good
steady job." How could she use the word "steady"?
Nothing is steady after my marriage. I have no friend
to talk to without feeling that I am revealing my inad-
equacies as a wife. Friendship is like a tree, it needs time
to mature, and we never stay in one place long enough
for that! And my husband is a gypsy who I see for a short
while every month.

The first time Dadda tells me he is going on line
duty, I stare at him, baffled.

"What does that mean?"

"I am going out on tour to check the railway lines."

"I want to come too," I say firmly, certain of my
power as a bride.

"Women don't go on line."

"But I want to know what you do there," I tell him.

"That's where I work," says Dadda with a smile. "Like
you work in the home."

Who could think that those beautiful Railway
colonies that I have often admired from the outside
would be like jars crowded with mosquitoes, full of
bored women waiting for their sahibs to get back? In
the colonies, there is nothing to do but spend your time
going from house to house, sip a hundred cups of tea
and exchange stories. Most of the time I sit in our bungalow, the lonely house at the north end of the colony,
listening to the trains rattling by. I even write up my

own timetable—1:30 a.m., Howrah-Bongaigaon Express; 2:30 a.m., Shillong-Dehradun passenger; 3:00 a.m., Delhi Mail. Another list to add to my growing collection; it will go nicely in the spot next to the Godrej cupboard in my bedroom. I draw red lines to show arrivals and blue ones for the departures and begin to be quite pleased with the effect I create on the walls. A room twelve feet by thirteen feet is now papered with long lists. The one with the green and yellow lines is an inventory of vegetables I buy from the *haat* every Wednesday. I have to make that list to remind myself of the things Dadda dislikes. Cabbage and cauliflower give him gas pains in the lower left hand corner of his stomach, radish and capsicum smell too strong, tomato is a non-Brahmin vegetable, and *jhinga* is a low-caste person's supper. That doesn't leave too many vegetables. So I have to look all the time for different-different recipes for potato and peas. The recipes are a growing collection which I use to cover the empty wall to the left of the window. I decorate the edges with a clever collage of mouths clipped from the magazines to which we subscribe—some open, some pursed up like Dadda's when he is full of gas on the left side of his stomach—so many different sizes. The plain blue sheet of paper near the mirror is a list of the clothes I pack for his duty tours—the going-on-line list. Two white pyjamas, two white *kurtas,* two white underpants and two sleeveless *banians.* Dadda also purses up his lips if I pack the *banians* with sleeves. Those are for nylon shirts which make him sweat in the underarms.

This particular section of the railway lines is very, very hot. I hope and hope that my husband will soon take me with him on line to Darjeeling so that I can get away from the heat, from the silence of this house broken only by the sound of trains. I wait a long-long time but he never takes me. And then Dadda is transferred to Calcutta, where everything is different, except for the heat. Here the trains are far away, but their movement stays with me, for the river runs by the house, restless, eager for the sea. When the monsoons thunder across from the Bay of Bengal, the river swells and floods into the colony. Lawns turn to vast dirty lakes. There is no way of knowing where the drains end and the roads begin. If you are brave enough to step out of your house, you walk by guesswork. A step in the wrong direction and it is possible for you to drown in a river of sewage. A person looking down from the air might think that we are a population floating on water. Eventually the river recedes, leaving behind a mush of salty mud which it churns up from the sea, bones and corpses of dead dogs and pigs, and a stink that takes months for the sun to boil away.

Across the river is the Botanical Garden, which is really an enormous myth. The main attraction is an ancient banyan tree, a growing umbrella of shimmering leaves. Other than that, there is nothing, not a flower, and no birds but the crows. It is important, though, to have this green-green place across the ugly river, an enchanted forest away from our dull-brown monotony. At one time or another, every family in our colony makes a pilgrimage to that tree armed with baskets of *puri* and *aloo subzi,* lemon rice and curd rice, *laddoos* and banana cake.

In the Calcutta house you can hear the neighbours all about you. The building is an old bungalow, grandly named Godfrey Mansions, its wooden walls pockmarked with windows. The house originally belonged to some big-shot British sahib, and after the British leave, it is sectioned off into five apartments. Sounds sail in and out of rooms with no regard for privacy. Next door, the Saigani twins quarrel noisily, and in the second-floor flat, Ranjini Abraham pedals on her ancient Singer machine, turning out perfectly tailored clothes for her children.

I find myself recovering slowly in this building full of cheerful, everyday noises. Our flat has a fireplace which the servants tell us is actually a secret passage leading to Allahabad. If you stick your head up a little way into the chimney, you can hear Mrs. Anderson singing. When the British Empire ebbs away from Indian shores, it leaves a few shells behind, like the Andersons, Mr. and Mrs., who are too deeply embedded even to think of leaving. They live on the first floor, and while other families either transfer out of Calcutta or are promoted to Arundel House or Type Six bungalows, the Andersons stay. At half past eight in the morning Mr. Anderson leaves for work. Just as he emerges from under the portico of the building, Mrs. Anderson leans out of her window like a faded Juliet and calls in a high singsong voice, "Bye, Dorling, see you at six o'clock!"

At ten o'clock she starts playing the piano. You can hear it *tink-tink-tinkle-tonk, tonk, tonk, tonkle-tink*, right through the day. It crawls through the old cement walls into the flat next door, drips down the cracks in the wooden floors to the flats downstairs. The servants in their quarters behind Godfrey Mansions time their work by Mrs. Anderson's piano. At one o'clock she stops for lunch and picks up again at two. She never speaks to any of us. One day, moved by her isolation, I try to make friends with her. Mrs. Anderson opens the door a crack, the safety-chain still on. She is in a cotton dressing gown, her hair piled in a bun on top of her head.

"Yes, can I do something for you?" she snaps.

"Just thought I'd drop by to say hello."

"I'm fine, thank you," Mrs. Anderson replies, and shuts the door. A few minutes later I can hear the piano. I never visit her again.

"She thinks she is the Queen of England," I remark to Linda Ayah.

At four in the afternoon Mrs. Anderson starts singing along with the *tink-tonk* of the piano. That is when when the children of Godfrey Mansions, back from school, play in the porch and on the lawn outside.

"*Lavender Blooo,*" sings Mrs. Anderson.

"*Ooo-ooo-oooo,*" chorus the children downstairs.

"*I loove yoooo,*" Mrs. Anderson continues.

"*Ooo-ooo-oooo,*" yell the children in a perfect frenzy of mirth.

Kamini informs me that when I am not at home, Roopa and her friends make obscene noises up the chimney in tune with Mrs. Anderson's music. They burp and make farting sounds by pressing their mouths against their palms and blowing hard. Kamini is becoming a sanctimonious little nuisance. Perhaps Dadda is right, I shouldn't have sent her to the nunny-*amma* school. She refuses to wear skirts above her knees, or sleeveless frocks.

"I don't want lustful eyes to fall upon me," she says when I ask her what her problem is.

"Whose lustful eyes?" I demand.

"Anybody's," says Kamini the saint.

She spends her pocket-money on issues of "Soldiers of God," which the nuns sell at school. Roopa steals them from her room and reads them aloud at the dinner table, making up sentences as she goes along. "God's message to all young people: Wear not the sleeveless dress. Tattle against thy relatives."

Dadda glares at me. These girls he loved as babies are now as puzzling as I am. That closeness they shared has begun to fade.

"See the trash they learn at your convent school?" he snaps.

"It's just a phase she is going through," I say.

Dadda does not reply. In the early years of our marriage, the argument would have been continued later, in whispers, in privacy. It wasn't decent to quarrel before the children. Those days he was worried about losing the argument in front of them. Even later, in the bedroom, he was pleased if I gave in.

"It's all right, everyone makes mistakes," he would

tell me, allowing himself a small smile and then sleeping soundly through the night. If I refused to let him win, he withdrew into a frozen silence for days, acting as if I did not exist.

Now Dadda's silence, punctuated by hard coughs, is that of a man who is losing a painful battle against illness and so does not care about small victories any more. He scrapes his chair away from the table and moves slowly out into the verandah. My daughters continue their squabbling, their voices filling the momentary silence he leaves behind.

"She wants to become a nun, Ma," says Roopa, waving the "Soldiers of God" at her sister. "If she becomes a nun, who will make cow-eyes at Frankie Wood?"

"*Chughal-kore,* tattle-tale. I'll never tell you any secrets," screams Kamini, her eyes filling with tears.

"I told you not to go near that Anglo fellow," I say, glaring at Kamini. "Do you ever listen to anything I say?"

"I do nothing but listen to you," she shouts. Where on earth did she learn to be so mouthy? "And you are a fine one to tell me not to mix with *Anglos!*"

Roopa glances wide-eyed at us. Kamini stares defiantly at me, slightly frightened by her own temerity. She is almost as tall as I am, I think with a shock. I wonder whether I ought to slap her for her insolence. No use, the only person who feels the pain is me, my palm hurting as it bounces off her hard, bony legs. "Do what you please," I say finally. "And don't come running to me if you are in trouble afterwards."

Kamini bursts into tears. "You never care about a thing I do. You never did. And now *he* doesn't either." She points towards the verandah where Dadda sits, staring out at the sunny garden, and then rushes out of the room. All these dramatic exits! Are we in a play or what?

❦

"My oldest is at that age," remarks Latha. "Do this and he wants that, say that and he thinks this. Every day a fight with his father. God knows what happens to them suddenly, henh?"

Linda Ayah used to tell me that a child is like a little god till the age of five, is human till it turns twelve, and after that it becomes a donkey. Perhaps the sudden descent from divinity is too much to bear! I stare out the window at barren sweeps of land, not even a bush to make shadows with the sun.

Vicki, the teenager, laughs suddenly. "And I, Aunty-ji," she says to Latha, "I am taking a holiday from my mother. God knows what happens to parents when their children grow up!"

❦

With the arrogance of youth I had believed that health, wealth, wisdom and happiness were all mine for the asking. I would have a house larger than the one my parents lived in, for I meant to become a doctor and set up a bustling practice. My husband would be a Hindi film star, all song and sacrifice, heroism and romance. But the strong dreams of youth can waver before the harsh mirror of reality. Dadda was not the husband I wanted him to be. He could not be, for he was a living, breathing man, not a cardboard film character. The realization came too late. His body had yielded to an invasion of sickness and his mind was busy warding off the savage onslaught of pain. Too late, too late for me to say let us begin again, I have eaten my anger, swallowed my conceits. Too late to say come back.

A person grows on you like an ingrown nail. You keep cutting and filing and pulling it out, but the nail just grows back. Then you get used to the wretched thing, you learn to ignore and even become fond of it. Same with Dadda. His quiet became a part of my noise. If he had not been so silent would I have babbled on? Can you clap with one hand? Which means that I cannot put the entire blame for our life on him. I can, but my daughters tell me I am being unfair. But that is an old story, enough to say that I learned to live with the man I married. As my mother might say, it is the lottery ticket I picked, and I could do nothing about it. Marriage is a game of give and take, sometimes one has to give a little more than the other, and so the balance is maintained.

"Nobody in the world is entirely happy," Amma says, her voice creaky with age. The years have run by, both my sisters have married, my brothers are ponderous old men with a puffed-up air of importance about them. Amma's hair has ribbons of grey, her skin is crushed into pouches and lines, her hands shake slightly as she folds her *paan* leaves. She no longer snaps at Chinna for making mistakes. Chinna's bald head, which has been barber-shaved every month since she was widowed more than fifty years ago, is like a grey brush now. She forgets things, leaves half-eaten food in various parts of the house and then curses the servants for being lazy.

"So careless they are," she grumbles to Amma. "I have to follow them cleaning up like a scavenger!"

My mother nods and nods. She clings to Chinna these days, frightened of her sharp-tongued older daughter-in-law who has assumed the position of mistress of the house since my father's death.

"I don't want any bad blood between us," she has told my mother firmly. "I won't poke my nose into your kitchen and you keep yours out of mine. You know the old saying, 'A man can have two women in his bedroom, but more than one in his kitchen is murder.'"

So Amma keeps her mouth shut. Sometimes it is wiser to be quiet. And anyway, she has completed her responsibilities as a wife and a mother, now she can retreat into silence.

I, on the other hand, have a long way to walk before I can settle quietly in a corner. After Dadda dies I still have my daughters to bring up. It is hard for me to believe he isn't here. I find myself saying things into thin air. I smell cigarette smoke where there is none and resist the impulse to tell Dadda that he is killing himself inhaling all that tobacco. Kamini and Roopa prefer to think of their father as they last saw him, his face calm in death, untouched by the cankers that swarmed through his body, eating steadily through the flesh and marrow, turning wholesome red blood pale and sickly. They do not want to acknowledge the slow death that moved through his body, or remember the bottles leaking fluids into him, the tubes draining piti-ful wastes away. Such indignity for a man who could not bear the smell of his own sweat.

My crazy sister-in-law Meera sends me two mangoes in a box a week after Dadda dies. "For my brother's chil-dren and his widow, a small gift from my orchards to relieve your sorrow."

What orchards? She is in an asylum for the mentally ill.

Meera always surprises me. For a person who doesn't know who she is or why or where, her handwriting is remarkably lucid. Beautifully formed, neatly rounded, every "t" precisely crossed. She even used to write let-ters to me sitting on my own verandah.

"Respected lady, I would appreciate it very much if you put three spoons of sugar in my evening coffee instead of only two."

"Madam, I have noticed two young girls entering the house. When I asked them who they were and if they required anything in particular, they made discourteous faces at me. I am offended by this behaviour and would request you to take immediate action."

Polite, meticulously neat letters. And then suddenly a wild burst of anger, pure lunacy like a raging summer storm. The girls stayed out of sight and worried about whether the neighbours could hear the awful raving. I locked her into her room and prayed that she would, in the grip of the nightmares that possessed her, kill herself. But why think about her? It is time now to shed the past, to begin yet another phase of life. We are no longer a part of the Railways, this house is ours only till the end of next month.

I start selling all our things. The car goes to a motor-parts dealer. It was never anything more than a collection of nuts and bolts and wires anyway. The carved rosewood chair with the scratch down its front leg made by Meera's knitting needle, the teak coffee table carved by Girdhari the carpenter, both are sold. The *niwaar* beds, the big mango-wood cots—how much the children jumped on them and still they are as good as new—the sideboard, the meat-safe, toy cupboard, Dadda's father's mahogany office chair with the broken wicker back, all gone. I am beginning to feel weightless. With each piece of furniture that leaves our house, a sliver of memory escapes, forever lost. Kamini says that is impossible, you can never lose memories. She is sixteen and dangerously sensitive about every little thing, from the way she looks to the way I behave in front of her friends. Roopa is too young to feel anything other than bewilderment at the loss of her father, but Kamini imagines that we are somehow discarding our past along with the furniture.

"Do you have to sell my grandfather's chair?" asks Kamini. Why is she making such a fuss over that chair? Kamini never even knew her father's father!

"It is an ugly thing," I argue. "And the only memory I have of it is of Dolly Aranha sitting on it, telling me about her husband."

"Don't, don't! I refuse to hear another of your stories."

"It's not a story," I protest. "It's true."

Dolly's husband had returned from a trip to France with a suitcase full of lacy undergarments for his wife.

"I asked him for an umbrella," Dolly complained, tears running down her curved cheeks. Everything about Dolly was sweetly round—her face, her little nose, her eyes, even her hair, which she wore in two coils on either side of her head. "See what dirty things he got for me. He told me that they were naughty things for a naughty girl. I am a good girl, my Mamma brought me up to be nice and respectful. Where this man got such dirty ideas from you tell me?"

"They are pretty," I remarked.

"Pretty? Pretty? What is here to call pretty?" Dolly gasped as she held up a tiny pink panty. "Low-caste rascal, says to me, 'Dolly, this is for you and me.' Shame-shame things he says."

I wanted to tell her, Dolly, you are so lucky. My husband never bought me anything to decorate myself. My husband hardly even saw me.

"My Mamma was right, she said men have unnatural needs," continued Dolly. "But it is my duty to close my eyes and do what he wants."

"Ma!" interrupts Kamini. "Why are you selling my desk? I might need it. I still have to finish my studies, you know."

"Do you remember when Dolly Aranha saw the first ghost?" I ask.

And Kamini, my first-born, full of virtue, says, "Why don't you leave poor Dolly alone, Ma?"

"Do you remember or don't you?"

"I don't."

"She made Mr. Aranha into a ghost. She even sprinkled holy water on him when he came home from work, remember? Dolly would not sleep with him because he was a ghost."

"He was a creep," says Kamini. "He stared at all the girls. Ma, you aren't selling my grandfather's chair! It's an heirloom."

Between her and Roopa, we end up with a lot more baggage than I intended to take with us to our apartment in Madras. But at last, we are ready to leave. The furniture, wrapped in old newspaper, faded bedsheets and yards of gunny sacking, waits like oddly shaped mummies in the spare bedroom before being loaded on to one of those goods bogies that meander across the country dropping off rice or wheat, coal or wood. Ganesh Peon and Linda have washed the floors of the house with Phenyle so that the place smells like a hospital ward. They stand awkwardly near the front door while we wait for the car that will take us to the station. All of a sudden they look like strangers to me, these two old people who I have known for eighteen years and might never meet again.

⊰⊱

Five minutes more and the train will move away. The station bubbles with people haggling with the coolies and making sure that children, relatives and baggage are all safe. The tea-boys rush up and down the plat-form, shouting in high, nasal voices, *"Chaichaichaichai-chaaaii!"* The tea they sell is scalding, the skin on your tongue peels off and you tell yourself that the muddy numbness is the delicate taste of brew in an earthen tumbler. A woman in a green sari is thrusting a hand-ful of rupee notes to a boy peering out the window in the compartment next to ours. Have you wiped the bars with some tissue dipped in Dettol? I feel like ask-ing him. Beggars put their faces festering with sores against those bars; spittle dried there not five minutes ago! The woman in the green sari is crying now, shak-ing with large sobs. She wipes her nose with the end of her sari; the boy at the window looks embarrassed. He draws away from the window, but the woman shoots out a hand, the red glass bangles tinkling, and holds on to his shirt. She is his mother? Lover? Sister? No one ever weeps for me at a station, not even when I leave my mother's house for my husband's. Isn't that when your female relatives burst into tears? Back away ululating their sorrow at having given away a daugh-ter, not knowing if her life will be scattered with grief or filled with joy? Only Chinna cries a little for me, Chinna, who cries for everything from third-rate movies to the announcement of a stranger's death in the newspapers.

"Did either of you count the cases before we left

home?" I ask Roopa and Kamini. If Dadda were here I would not have to worry about our luggage.

Roopa sits with her legs sprawled out, flicking through a comic book. Kamini perches nervously on the berth next to me, alternately staring out the window and biting her nails. I have booked all four seats. I tell Kamini to make sure the safety-catch on the door is closed. That way no last-minute passenger can barge in to occupy a seat with bags, *potlis* and water-bottles. I have paid for the luxury of extra space and I don't mean to let anyone else have it. Perhaps I should shut the windows on the station side. The windows on the corridor side of the compartment are already shut, so no one can peep in and see that there are only three people in here. All they will have to do then is bribe the conductor and that will be the end of our privacy.

"Four *sleeping* berths, Madam," the conductor will argue. "Daytime it is six seating. Railway rules, Madam. I am helpless."

I am familiar with all the rules. I have lived with them for eighteen years. After all those years, I am entitled to break a rule or two. So until the train starts up and is well outside the station, past the stinks of Guwahati and into the clear air of the country, the doors and windows on that side remain shut. Never mind the terrible heat that envelops us, sweat springing out and filling the compartment with sourness. A low, booming horn is sounded, a diesel engine, the old steam engines are disappearing off the tracks and are lying unused in a workshop somewhere. The platform begins to slide away; the faces outside the windows look like distorting clay as we gather speed.

"Hold your noses, the stinks are starting," says Roopa.

We are all familiar with this geography of smells. The platform first, with its odours of cigarettes, *beedis,* over-ripe fruit, urine and frying fish. Then the drains sluggish with faeces and engine oil. The slum with the monotonous grey pall of poverty and the slimy green pond. There is no way to define the stench from that noxious pond. A leather factory vomiting out smoke. And then, just when you feel that you will explode from holding your breath, the paddy begins and the air is clean.

"I wonder if we will ever come back here," says Kamini.

And Roopa, in a nasal voice, "I'll die if we do."

꣸

It is pitch dark outside, not even the flicker of a kerosene lamp from a passing village.

Hameeda yawns and cracks her knuckles. "I am going to sleep, Aunty-ji, tomorrow I will listen to your story."

I smile at her, knowing that she doesn't entirely approve of me. Irritation, sometimes shock, flickered across her face as she listened to me. Was I telling the truth or making up everything? Why should I care what she thinks? I will be getting off this train early tomorrow morning and she will never see me again.

Her sister Sohaila is more sympathetic, nodding every time my words strike a chord in her. "Sometimes I feel like running away too," she says, her soft thin face filled with guilt at her own declaration.

Latha stands up and yawns, scattering biscuit crumbs. She has finished a whole packet of Marie biscuits in the past two hours. She spreads a sheet on the berth and slaps her pillow a couple of times. "You don't mind, no bhabhi-ji, if I sleep also? You too must be tired, so much talking-talking."

Sohaila checks to see if the door is securely locked and turns off the lights. I stretch out in my berth and allow memories to cover me like a blanket.

Into the compact space of the new apartment I move our steel trunks which carry scars from practically every corner of India, so much they have travelled. On the faded green sides are remnants of destination stickers—Ratnapur, Bhusaval, Lucknow, Calcutta—a summary of my incarnation as a Railway wife.

For a few months the trunks crowd up the flat, making it look smaller than it is. Eventually the girls and I arrange our belongings in the cupboards, and the place looks more like home and less like a loading yard. I drape our old curtains on all the windows, snipping off more than half the length, so that I will not have to look at the road running behind the flat. Nobody is very sure of the name—my maid thinks that it might be Ammattan Palai, but Uncle Gangadhar, the old man downstairs, has a different story. A hundred years ago, the British sahibs arrived here, couldn't get their short

foreign tongues around the name of the road. Maybe a
Hamilton sahib peed here, and so they called it Hamilton Bridge Road. Who knows why things are named
what they are named? Then the people in the town
rolled this new name round and round in their mouths
till the edges wore smooth. When they spat it out like
a well-chewed *paan,* it had become Ammattan Paalai.
But the British couldn't say "Ammattan," so they put
on their solar-hats and thought, "Hmm, what does
Ammattan mean?" And someone, a *peon* or a clerk-*babu,*
said, "Saar, saar, it means barber, *ammattan* most surely
means barber."

Until that time, the shops around the bridge sold
Canjeevaram silk saris. It is said that when the sun hit
the inside of the shops where the saris were piled high
the whole bridge glowed like a valley of jewels. But
when the name became Barber's Bridge, all the barbers
in town thought, "Hunh, why not open a shop there in
that place which already has our name?"

And so the road truly became a barber's strip. Today
if you go in there you can hear the scissors going *kitiki-
kitik,* the air a fine mist of hair and a smell of Dettol can-
celling the pig-shit stink of the drains. And while it is
true that these barbers give you the best haircuts in all
of the city, they also leave a louse or two in your head.

There is also a fruit vendor whose apples and bananas
and mangoes and oranges need to be washed several
times to remove the fuzz of hair that has settled on them
from the barber shops. One-armed Muruga is a permanent fixture beside the bus-stand. He sells pornographic

books inside innocuous covers like *Gone With The Wind*, and *Palgrave's Golden Treasury*. His books are displayed on a large bedsheet, and when he sees a policeman strolling by, he quickly gathers up the ends of the sheet, slings the makeshift sack over his shoulder and disappears into one of the many back-alleys leading off the road. A fortune-teller, who, my maid tells me, is richer than Kubera the god of wealth himself, has staked a claim to the spot beneath a pathetic neem tree with barely any leaves or branches. The fortune-teller's eyeballs move in their sockets completely out of control, engaged in a weird dance against the walls of his eyes. He claims that although he cannot see the people before him, he can see their future lying in wait all around their helpless bodies. My daughters are fascinated with him and waste their money sneaking out to have their fortunes read.

"You will travel far and away," he tells Kamini. "Baba Blinding Light sees what ordinary eyes cannot."

"Why you want to listen to that old bandicoot?" I ask her. "Study well, and work hard, you carve your own fortune. Look at me, if I had had the courage to take my future in my own two hands instead of listening to a pot-bellied priest, I might have been a doctor!"

Perhaps if I charge my girls fifty paise for each bit of advice I give them, they might listen to me.

My apartment is small, with several windows and balconies. A gulmohur tree dapples the corner of the front balcony with its shade. When my daughters and I move in here ten years ago, we have to look down from the balcony to catch a glimpse of the tree. I barely notice how it has grown till Roopa and Kamini leave the house.

These days, to fill the hours that tick by so gradually, I catch sight of the tiniest changes, hear every whisper. In the morning I sit in the front balcony, watch the sun swim out of the darkness and listen to the grey, fluffy birds—called the seven sisters, I think—quarrelling over worms. The gulmohur tree creaks in the wind, and a few of its brilliant red flowers drift reluctantly onto my balcony. They are whole and unbruised and I pick them up to float in a shallow bowl of water. All of this summer, the tree was covered in blossoms, fiery with colour sucked from the sun. Now I can sense the approaching shift of season. The flowers are fewer, faint green leaves, multi-pinnate, feathery, are beginning to dust the branches once again. A sign that moisture gathers, the monsoons blow over the Ghats. With so much time on my hands, I seem to smell these little shifts. Feel them as well, if the growing ache in my right knee is any indication. Yes, I can almost hear the clouds, swollen-bellied, rolling in from the sea. The winds are cool and soft, the rain touches the earth tenderly. This is a gentle city to live in.

A year ago they changed the name of the road outside my house, yet again, to Vallabhai Patel Marg. The new minister is full of nationalistic fervour. He is the fellow who wears dark glasses all the time, because, his party men whisper, he doesn't want to dazzle people with the brilliance of his eyes. The other party says that he is blind from syphillis caught from the whores of the city.

"Remove every sign of the blood-sucking British," the minister said to justify renaming the road. I don't know why it should matter, the Brits are gone forty years! But these ministers are like that, when they run out of ideas to collect votes, they attack the past. What is the use of that, I ask you? The past changes in the context of the present. But who am I to comment?

By the time I came to terms with my new address, another donkey, who I confess I voted for, decided that what we needed was a woman's name for our road. So it is Indira Gandhi Marg now. Why our road, I ask you? Out of sixteen thousand roads they choose ours. These constant interruptions in what I had hoped would be a smooth stretch of existence are beginning to get on my nerves. Just as my feet settle into the soil, the ground itself starts shifting. When my daughters phone, I tell them about the way the earth moves beneath my quiet feet, and they go into a silence that stretches uncomfortably long. They think I am senile or maybe even crazy. They think that the earth can move only when there is a quake. How wrong they are, but they are young. It is only when you reach my age that you notice the slight tremors, the nervous shifts that the earth makes beneath your tired feet. Or perhaps, like a sailor, I still feel the rocking of the trains on firm land.

The apartment is on the same street as the Chief Minister's bungalow, which has its advantages. I never have a shortage of water, for the very same pipes that carry water to his bungalow also carry it to my flat. Heads will roll if the important gentleman does not have water to wash his bottom in the morning. Politics touch all our lives one way or another. Thanks to the chief Minister, our road is swept clean, the trees are lush and well tended, none of those ragged limbs shorn of leaves by wandering cows, branches torn off by urchins in search of firewood. Someone with imagination—a poetic imagination—planted those trees. In the boiling heat of summer, the sky is a delicate mist of lavender jacaranda. The steaming tarmac of the road is sheeted with purple flowers, and the minute you enter the road, you are in a tunnel of fragrance.

Every morning at five o'clock I am awakened by the milk van. Not so much the van as Manja, the fellow who owns the dealership. The pavement in front of my apartment building is his distribution centre. He parks there noisily and straight away begins a quarrel with the delivery boys—young fellows with bicycles who stream in like a circus parade, bells jangling, chains rattling, cracking obscene jokes. They pile plastic bags bulging with milk in baskets attached to the handlebars and the backs of their bicycles and wobble precariously away. Manja likes to heckle them, shouting about accounts and balances, lack of speed, lack of orders, anything to start an argument. The boys shout back, defying Manja's authority as he struts around his van gesticulating furiously, his face screwed up inside the green muffler he wears through every season. I hurry down to collect my packet of milk. Although I am a regular customer, Manja resents the fact that I don't pay a delivery charge. Why should I waste five rupees every month when all I need to do is step outside my own gate?

"No milk left," Manja says, a mean glint in his eyes, if I get there just as the last boy cycles off on his rounds. "I told you, get it delivered, otherwise you have a problem."

That is my cue to wheedle. "Come, come, I am an old customer, forever I have been getting from you only. If I wanted I could have asked Dhanraj Groceries to bring milk for me. But I thought, why should I go to someone I hardly ever see?"

It usually works. Manja looks at the sky for a few minutes, taps his foot and says, "I will have to see if I have any extra quota left. These days my business is growing all the time, and it is difficult to provide milk to everyone who asks. Only this time though, I will give you. Can't say what will happen tomorrow."

It is a game with him, makes his day worthwhile. He has power over someone in this world. I don't grudge him that tiny satisfaction, I am only interested in getting milk. But when the Diwali festival rolls around I give nothing more than a five-rupee note as *bakhsheesh*.

"What Ma," he says disappointedly, "no sweets for my children? What is Diwali without sweets?"

And I retort with satisfaction, "I have to take so much trouble to get two litres of milk, where do I have the energy to make sweets to distribute, Manja?"

He understands what I mean, and for a few months after, I get milk without grovelling for it.

Now I rush up the stairs, leave the packet in the fridge, get into my walking shoes and set off down the road for a brisk stroll. In the morning, every minute counts. I have to be back at six sharp, or five minutes before if possible. Any later, and my maid Puttamma will have arrived, banged perfunctorily on the door and left in a huff. Another one of the games I play with the people in my daily life. These little tantrums and shows of temper never interrupted my routine as a Railway wife. Linda Ayah showed up every morning, the *peons* never fell ill, the *dhobhi* arrived on Tuesday to collect the laundry. That was another existence altogether. When I left that life I felt naked and vulnerable, the rough-and-tumble of the ordinary world scraping against my skin. Only after you lose something do you realize how valuable it was. Then you get used to the loss, dust the memories off your body and begin anew.

When I ask Puttamma why she doesn't bother to wait she tells me that she thought I had gone abroad to visit my daughters.

"You saw me only yesterday, wouldn't I have told you if I was going away?" I demand.

"People forget," shrugs Puttamma.

She knows that I cannot afford to lose my temper with her. It is difficult to find honest maidservants, and if she feels offended in any way, she will demand her wages and leave. So I control my tongue, although I long to comment on the way she sweeps the rooms in my apartment, the broom flicking across the floor, barely touching it, or the way she leaves a trail of damp after slapping a wet mop around, not even bothering to squeeze out the extra water. My helplessness infuriates Roopa and Kamini.

"Why don't you get rid of the rotten woman?" shouts Kamini across the phone line.

"Because the next one I find might be worse."

"How much worse can they get?"

"Well, I could end up with a thief or a murderer," I say. "These days anything is possible. Gone is the era of the devoted *peon,* the doting *ayah.*"

"Ma, why do you do this to us?"

"What?"

"Scare us out of our wits? You know we worry about you."

"I worried over you and your sister for more than twenty years each. Now it's your turn," I retort. "And anyway, what's the point worrying about me from the North Pole?"

"Are you still going for a walk at the crack of dawn?" Kamini changes the subject.

"Yes."

"All alone?"

"No, arm in arm with the Chief Minister and his *bibi-ji,*" I say.

"Well if something happens to you, walking around all alone, don't blame me," says my daughter, sounding almost as illogical as I am.

As a matter of fact, I have never even seen the Chief Minister's face. He wears large goggles and a furry cap, both of which hide his face almost entirely. Maybe the stories about him are true. The minister has suffered a stroke and is an imbecile. A double has taken his place to help prevent political turmoil. Doubles are very popular these days. In at least two Hindi films and one Tamil film the hero plays multiple roles. Twin brothers are separated in childhood; triplets lose each other; identical sisters marry twin brothers—endless variations. Doubles create all sorts of interesting problems. They fall in love with the same girl, or they fool their alarmingly stupid mother who doesn't seem to remember that her body produced two children on the same wave of pain. In any case, this Chief Minister, or his double, is very popular. He has been re-elected to office at least thrice. He used to be a film star long ago, and the residue of that life is evident in the way he conducts his manoeuvres. The state is his kingdom, he the benevolent *rajah*. The man makes flamboyant speeches, soliloquies almost, wears glittering clothes and addresses all women as "mother" or "sister." He gets most of his votes from the women—that's what the polls say. The older ones dream of cradling the Chief Minister's stubby body against their breasts. He is the son who made it to the top, the one who will take care of them in their old age. Younger women, like my maid Puttamma, adore him for his swaggering walk, his succulent lips, the eyes enigmatically hidden behind the dark glasses.

"The man I marry has to be like Him," says Puttamma, pointing to a picture of the Chief Minister in the newspaper. She is in a rare good mood. "Full of vigour, you know." She tosses her head naughtily and giggles.

I am tempted to say that the man is a pot-bellied old buffalo with a piece of straw for a penis. She will most definitely leave me then, and I will have to explain to my daughters long-distance. What will I tell them? My maid quit because I jeered at the Chief Minister's organ?

My daughters aren't happy about my decision to live here alone. They believe that I should move in with them, a few months with Kamini, the rest of the year with Roopa.

"I don't want to go anywhere, I need to rest my tired feet," I say firmly.

"Come here and rest your feet," says Kamini. "We can't come to India every year, Ma."

"Nobody is asking you to come to India every year," I retort with some of my old asperity. It makes me feel glad to hear that tone in my voice; at least I have not changed as much as the world around me. In my younger days, when I was a Railway wife, the servants called me Tamarind Mem for my acid tongue. And they thought I didn't know! Stupid idiots, with old Linda Ayah at my side I saw and heard and smelled every-thing in and out of the house. She looked after me, that one. But…but…there I go wandering off into new sto-ries without finishing the old.

Kamini continues to whine long-distance. "But we need to see you," she protests.

"Why?" I ask, beginning to get bored with the con-versation.

"Ma, stop being silly, we want to see you because we get worried about you," says Kamini sharply.

"Nothing to worry about, I am fine. I eat and drink and sleep all without any problem, so what do you have to worry about?"

"Roopa heard from someone that you were not well, why didn't you tell us? What happened?"

"Tell that air-headed sister of yours not to listen to gossip. I scratch my behind and people tell you I have piles, sneeze once and they think I am dying of consumption. When I am sick I will personally inform you and Roopa and you can catch the next flight home, okay?"

"Ma, you are really crude. And mean! We are your daughters, after all, and if we don't worry about you, who will?" Kamini's voice wavers with tears. That is Kamini, a fountain stationed right behind her eyelids, ready to spurt any time.

"Okay, okay, I am sorry," I say. "Look, I told you I am fine. I just don't want to go anywhere this year. I need to stay in one place for a while—in my own place."

It is necessary to add that last bit. I know my daughter's arguments far too well. "You can rest in my house," she will say. "What's wrong with my house, don't I do everything for you?"

I also know that this conversation will be repeated verbatim to the younger one, who will call later when she thinks that I have cooled down.

Her tactics are different. "Ma, I need you," she starts, with a slight insistence on "need." In the past, even last year, I might have panicked at that word and gone racing to be with my emotional Roopa. But not any more. They are grown women now, with worlds of their own, and decisions they alone can make. Do I interfere in their lives? Ask Roopa why she ran away like a thief to get married to a perfectly acceptable man? Perhaps the melodrama of the whole thing appealed to her, she was always so fond of cheap films. Do I ask Kamini why she never marries, why she had to go to Canada to study? As if there aren't any colleges in this country! No, I leave them alone, but they cling to me like leeches, sucking up my energy with their constant nagging.

They call in the middle of the night.

"Ma, it's just me, Roopa, to see if you are okay."

"Do you know what time it is?" I demand.

"Sorry Ma, it's cheaper to make transatlantic calls now."

Cheaper! It nearly costs me my life, my heart startled out of its sleep-rhythm as the scream of the telephone echoes around my empty flat.

"Ma, Ma, are you still there? Say something, this is a waste of money if I have to do all the talking."

"Who asked you to call?"

"What do you do there all alone?" asks Kamini.

"I have a busy social life," I reply. "Yesterday I had coffee with the Chief Minister, today the Minister of Industry and Development is visiting, I think he needs to consult with me."

My replies annoy her. But she is even more worried when I tell her that I spend most of the time sitting in the balcony enjoying life, remembering my past, telling myself stories—something I never had time to do as a memsahib.

"Do you *talk* to yourself? What things do you remember?" she asks, suspicious, as if I am about to embark on a life of crime. Why is she always so worried about everything? Even as a child she sat silently, nibbling at her fingernails, spitting out the little arcs of calcinated skin. The incessant uselessness of that activity drove me crazy, and every time I caught her, I slapped the hand away from her mouth. Why tell her what I remember? My memories are private realms, rooms that I wander into, sometimes sharply focused, sometimes puffy and undefined. When Dadda was transferred to Guwahati, we travelled in an inspection car, an oval glass bubble, which stopped every fifteen minutes on its slow route up green hills that became higher and higher and finally grew into distant Himalayan ranges. We entered thick banks of fog, the only humans in this soundless blanket, and I began to feel that we were afloat. Roaming through my memories feels like that trip in the bubble, breaking from soft welling banks of cloud into landscapes so clearly defined they seem almost unnatural.

But these are *my* memories, I want to remind Kamini. Why should you worry about them? Why do you allow my history to affect yours? Why should it matter to you if your father made me happy or an Anglo mechanic? They are dead and gone.

Yesyes, our stories touch and twine, but they are threads of different hues. Mine is almost at an end, but yours is still unwinding. Go, you silly girl, build your own memories.

Nowadays, I make long exploratory trips on the top of a double-decker bus around the city. As a child, living just a small distance away in Mandya, a visit to this city was like going to a foreign place. It is a city of fragrant trees, of cinema theatres and women dressed in fashionable clothes. Down on Commercial Street is the tailor where the Bell sisters, Clarabell, Isabell and Anabell, came to get shamefully tight blouses stitched. Once, soon after we had moved into this apartment, I wandered down Commercial Street and found it crowded and utterly devoid of the glamour I remembered from my childhood. Farrah Tailors was a shoddy little place, bits of thread and cloth littering the floor, the air cloudy with fluff and dust and the smell of cut fabric, the tailors hunched over their humming Singer machines. My daughters refused to go in.

"The master tailor is a creep," commented Roopa.

"What do you mean 'creep'? He's supposed to be a really good tailor."

"He fingers you," she said airily. "You know, gives you a good feel-up. Pokes his measuring tape up and down and in between, you know?"

"Yech, he's a lech," added Kamini.

"He won't do anything if I am there, will he?" I said, wondering how my daughters collected these snippets of information about a tailor, that too, one of hundreds in this city.

"Ma, he's a dirty old man," explained Kamini as if I

were a slow child. "He'll feel you up, too. Why do you want us to go in there anyways?"

"Well, he does good *katora*-cup *cholis*," I said lamely. No use telling them about the Bell sisters, they would wrinkle their noses and say, "Oh, Ma! Another of your old-old stories."

"Ma, I don't want my boobies sticking out like little come-grab-me beacons," said Kamini. Roopa giggled and nodded, "*Katora*-cup! What if you are built BIG? Will your Farrah Tailor make bucket-cup *cholis?*"

Disgusting brats, I think to myself, and they expect me to be decent and strait-laced. Double-standards, that's what! That's how my daughters are. Do one thing themselves and expect me to do something else—fit in with their image of the good mother, one who stays at home, waits for their phone calls, piously visits the temple to listen to religious lectures. How depressing, this future my flesh and blood have drafted out for me. They probably imagine that I have nothing else to do, no energy left.

The first few years after they both left India, I admit that I felt like a husk of rice, empty of energy, thought and feeling. I spent hours sitting in my darkened room trying to hold on to fading pictures of Dadda, of Railway friends, my daughters as babies. I couldn't recollect why I was so unhappy those first years of marriage. Why I had liked a car mechanic so much. Was it because by wanting him I was defying the rules of conduct that defined me as a memsahib, a good Brahmin wife? I cannot even remember.

But now I have rested enough, my feet are beginning to grow wheels. Yesyes, it is time for me to pack up and go. Once I travelled because my husband did. Now it is time for me to wander because *I* wish to, and this little apartment with the gulmohur flowers will be here for me to return to when I am tired of being a gypsy. My daughters are surprised and not a little annoyed at this decision. So many years I refuse to visit them, and now, all of a sudden, I chart out a pilgrimage around the country, a *jatra*.

"Go where, Ma?" ask Kamini and Roopa together on one of those ridiculous conference calls where everybody yells together, pauses for a breath at the same time and then *gaba-gaba-gaba* like a flock of ducks. Stupid idea, waste of money.

"Anywhere," I say and cut off the call. Then I pull the phone cord out. Hunh! They hop from plane to plane, go here and there, and I am supposed to sit at home and wait for them. What is that phrase the boy in the flat downstairs uses? No way, honeybun! I do not belong to anyone now. I have cut loose and love only from a distance. My daughters can fulfil their own destinies. In days of yore, aged parents left their worldly lives to retreat into the forest, where they shrugged off the manacles that bound them to their responsibilities and duties, and spent the days contemplating their histories. They shuffled their memories like a pack of cards, smiled at the joyous ones, shed a tear or two at others. They shook their heads over youthful follies and thought quietly about the journey, yet unknown, that stretched before their callused feet. I too have reached that stage in my life where I only turn the pages of a book already written, I do not write.

Dawn seeps into the compartment like pale grey milk. I roll up my bedding and buckle it tight, shake out my old Pashmeena shawl, fold it and place it in my suitcase. It won't be needed in Nagpur. Lock the suitcase, slide open the door gently so as not to disturb Latha, and Sohaila, and Hameeda the teacher, and sway down the corridor to the washroom. Soon-soon Nagpur will arrive in a warm, steaming puff of noise and colour. If my companions are awake, I will smile farewell. Otherwise, I shall slip away, leaving them with memories of an old story-teller, a weaver of myths.